BOBBY'S EYE LANDED ON ONE PARTICULAR WOMAN AND STOPPED

She was one handsome woman, all right. Short black hair that framed her face, softening what, on another woman, would be a too-hard jawline; flawless makeup that didn't try to hide her age, but enhanced her beauty; a crisp white shirt with French cuffs, even; black-and-gold cufflinks that matched the necklace and earrings she wore; and black tailored pants that covered long legs, made even longer by patent leather high heels. Her clear blue eyes were scanning the crowd, and Bobby had just enough time to envy whomever she was looking for before her eyes met his. The corners of her mouth twitched in a small smile before Bobby looked away, back to the crowd.

With a shake of the head, he realized he'd been staring like a hormonal teenager. And worse, he'd been caught. Still, a woman like that had to be used to it, he rationalized. He supposed he could forgive himself for being human. Hell, might even allow himself another look before . . .

"Sheriff?" A voice to his right made him turn . . . and look straight into those crystal blue eyes of hers.

BOOK YOUR PLACE ON OUR WEBSITE AND MAKE THE READING CONNECTION!

We've created a customized website just for our very special readers, where you can get the inside scoop on everything that's going on with Zebra, Pinnacle and Kensington books.

When you come online, you'll have the exciting opportunity to:

- View covers of upcoming books
- Read sample chapters
- Learn about our future publishing schedule (listed by publication month *and author*)
- Find out when your favorite authors will be visiting a city near you
- Search for and order backlist books from our online catalog
- Check out author bios and background information
- Send e-mail to your favorite authors
- Meet the Kensington staff online
- Join us in weekly chats with authors, readers and other guests
- Get writing guidelines
- AND MUCH MORE!

**Visit our website at
http://www.kensingtonbooks.com**

Fall Into Me

PAULINE TRENT

ZEBRA BOOKS
KENSINGTON PUBLISHING CORP.
http://www.kensingtonbooks.com

ZEBRA BOOKS are published by

Kensington Publishing Corp.
119 West 40th Street
New York, NY 10018

All Kensington titles, imprints, and distributed lines are available
at special quantity discounts for bulk purchases for sales promo-
tion, premiums, fund-raising, educational, or institutional use.

Special book excerpts or customized printings can also be created to fit specific needs. For details, write or phone the office
of the Kensington Special Sales Manager: Attn. Special Sales
Department. Kensington Publishing Corp., 119 West 40th
Street, New York, NY 10018. Phone: 1-800-221-2647.

Zebra and the Z logo Reg. U.S. Pat. & TM Off.

ISBN-13: 978-0-8217-8142-5
ISBN-10: 0-8217-8142-1

First Printing: March 2010
10 9 8 7 6 5 4 3 2 1

Printed in the United States of America

For Joshua, Hunter, Ethan, and Akira,
the next generation of men.

May you be strong enough to accept love,
wherever you find it.

ACKNOWLEDGMENTS

First and foremost, thanks to everyone who bid on the "Win a Character" prize for the Teri Pittman Foundation, but special thanks to Justin Erixon, who placed the winning bid. I hope you like what I did with your character. To Teri, Tim, Lori, and the rest of the family, too.

To Dennis R. Upkins and Delilah Marvelle, two amazing authors and even better people, who have been cheering section and sounding board; Michelle Supelana-Mix, for being indispensable; Dan McConnell, who helped me understand Southern gentlemen; and Megan Records, for stepping up and stepping in when I needed her.

As always, this book wouldn't have happened without the usual cast of characters: Christine and Scott, Mitchell and Ed, Shanna, Betty Witt, and Dr. C. Rex Mix. And, of course, my dear David, who always believes.

Prologue

She couldn't be dying. Doc Montgomery had to be wrong. The man was a good doctor for colds and flus and babies and even broken bones. Hell, that's all this was, anyway. A broken rib. Bobby was even willing to face some kind of investigation from the boss. After all, it didn't look good when the deputy's wife shows up with a broken bone the deputy admits to giving her. He understood that. He'd face that. Because Abby couldn't be dying. Doc Montgomery had to be wrong.

He wandered over to the pay phone on the wall of the waiting room in order to call and check in on the girls. The girls . . . they were so little. Carter Anne was already losing her memory of her parents. How could she lose her aunt now, too? And Angie. So serious, so worried about taking care of her sister, even of him and Abby. Nope. She couldn't be dying. Dropping a quarter into the pay phone, he waited for the phone to be picked up on the other end.

"Hello?" The woman on the other end was laughing about something.

"It's Bobby," he said. Without being able to see them,

there was no way to tell the difference between the Jones sisters just by their voices, even for him, and he'd known them all his life.

"Oh, Bobby, it's Mary." The woman lowered her voice. He could all but see her, moving as far away from the girls as the phone cord would allow. "How are things there?"

"Still waiting," Bobby sighed. "I haven't seen a doctor since she went in. How are things there?" Bobby could hear children's laughter in the background. It was a beautiful sound and too rare these days. He closed his eyes and put his forehead against the wall.

"We're fine, Bobby," Mary assured him. "Margaret's got them rehearsing a show for you when the two of you get home. You'll be quite impressed."

Bobby choked out a laugh. "I'm sure we will be."

"We're having macaroni and cheese with hotdogs for lunch. I know it's not all that healthy, but I figure they could use a treat. And we've promised them ice cream if they clean their plates. Is that all right?" she asked.

"Of course it is, Mary," Bobby sighed. "I'll pay you when we get back to town."

"You'll do no such thing, Bobby Granger," Mary's voice soothed. "After ice cream, we may go to the park for a little while, run off the energy, before taking naps."

"You'll need it after an afternoon with those girls." Bobby managed a smile. "Abby says she can't . . ." His voice broke. Clearing his throat hard, he continued. "Can't wait for Angie to start school in the fall. But I don't think Carter Anne will be much less of a handful for her without her sister."

Mary laughed. "Well, for now Margaret and I have everything under control here, Bobby." She paused. "You focus on Abby."

"Mary—" Bobby started, then stopped. He wasn't good with words. Words were Abby's strength. She always knew what to say. He thumped the wall with the flat of his hand. "I don't know how to thank the two of you . . ."

"Now stop, Bobby." Her voice was low, gentle. "She's gonna be fine. And you've got lots of people who are willing to step up. While her ribs heal."

"Thank you, Mary."

"Do you want to talk to the girls?" she asked, voice low. More laughter came down the line behind her.

"No." Bobby shook his head. "Better not. They sound like they're having fun. How much do you think they know?"

"Carter Anne doesn't know anything other than Abby's hurt and going to the doctor. Really, that's all Angie knows, too. But you know that girl."

Bobby did. "Yeah. Suspects."

"Well, she doesn't like it when y'all are out of town anymore," Mary stated.

"Understandable, considering the car accident. All she knew was that her parents were going out of town for the night."

"So, she'll feel better once the two of you are home safe," Mary concluded.

Bobby snorted. "Won't we all."

"You go on, Bobby," Mary assured him. "We're fine here."

"Thank you, Mary. I'll call when we're on our way home." Bobby hung up the phone, standing against the wall for a moment longer. He dragged himself back to his chair and waited.

"Mr. Granger?" The nurse came into the waiting area.

"Yes." Bobby was on his feet in a flash.

"You can come on back now," she said with a small

smile. Surely she wouldn't be smiling if the Doc was right. "The doctor wants to talk to you with your wife."

Bobby followed her through the door, into an office. Abby was sitting on the table, dressed and pale. She smiled and reached for him as he came through the door. He couldn't reach her soon enough. Standing next to her, Bobby put his arms around her, but Abby gasped in pain.

Bobby jumped away from her. "Abby, sweetheart, I'm sorry."

"Don't let me go, Bobby." She looked up at him. "It doesn't hurt that much."

Bobby draped an arm around her shoulders but didn't hold on too tightly. The doctor came in the office and sat down.

"Mr. Granger, Mrs. Granger, I'm afraid I don't have very good news for you." The man's voice was professionally polite. "The tests have shown something called osteosarcoma. It's a bone cancer. Not common in a woman of your age, but not unheard of, either."

Bobby's knees wanted to buckle. The doctor saw something in Bobby's eyes and moved a chair over to him. Lifting his arm from her shoulder but still holding her hand, Bobby lowered himself into it.

Abby found her voice first. "What does this mean?"

"It's spread, Mrs. Granger," the doctor sighed. "It's in your ribs—which is how we found it—your pelvis, and your scapula."

"What's that?" Bobby asked. Why did he care what a scapula was?

"That's her shoulder blade, Mr. Granger," the doctor explained. "With this much of the disease present, we can assume there's more and that it's spreading quickly."

"So what do we do?" Abby asked. What little color she'd had, she'd lost.

"There are treatments. Chemotherapy is often effective," the doctor said.

"So we fight it," Abby said.

"Attitude can go a long way," the doctor said. "I know this is difficult news to hear." He stood up. "Take a few minutes, then we can discuss options." The door closed silently behind him.

Bobby turned to Abby. It was only a broken rib. A little arthritis in the mornings. Sometimes in the middle of the day, if the girls had been really active. She took his face in her hands.

"Did you hear him, Bobby?" she asked firmly. All he could do was nod. "There are treatments." She stressed every word. "Attitude matters. Chemotherapy works. Did you hear him, Bobby?"

"I did, Abby."

There were tears in her eyes. There were tears in his.

"I love you, Bobby."

"I love you, too, Abby. I love you so much."

"Then we fight. With everything we've got." Abby's voice was hard. "We fight."

Chapter 1

Almost twenty years later, it was still sometimes hard to believe she was dead. The days of coming home and expecting to find her waiting for him—or worse, the nights of rolling over and not remembering why she wasn't next to him—were long past. Still, on days like today, when the rest of the world was still festive between Christmas and New Year's, it struck him as surreal that he was standing at his wife's grave holding flowers instead of standing somewhere else holding her hand.

Bobby Granger looked over at his nieces, Angie and Carter Anne Kane. They were good girls—good women, now, he corrected himself. He'd give himself a bit of credit for that. Raising them alone hadn't been easy, but, seeing them there, he had to admit he'd done something right, even if it had been simple dumb luck most of the time.

Carter Anne was working full-time as the receptionist at the elementary school and attending community college part-time. Considering her grades, Bobby figured one more year and she'd finally be off and away, the way she'd always wanted.

Angie, on the other hand, was blossoming right here in Lambert Falls with a confidence born of a successful business and the love of a good man. That man, Chris Montgomery, had moved to town, put that rock on Angie's finger and, Bobby was proud to admit, become the son he and Abby had never had the chance to have. Right now, Chris was waiting in the car. Not out of indifference, Bobby knew, but out of respect. To give the three of them a moment with Abby on her birthday, but still show his support.

He knelt down and pulled some grass away from the edges of the stone before placing the flowers across her name, between the two bouquets from the girls. "We're all doing well, Abby," Bobby said. "I know you're proud of them." Automatically, he knocked his thumb toward his nieces, then laughed gently at himself for doing so. Awkwardly, he lowered his hands to his knees. "More importantly, they know you're proud of them. Angie was just saying the other day how much she wished you and her mama could be here for all the wedding stuff. Of course"—he laughed again—"that might say more about my skills as a wedding consultant than anything else, but you get the idea."

A breeze rustled his hair. Bobby lifted his face and let it blow across his skin. Yeah, she got the idea. He stayed in that position, the sun shining through his closed eyes, until the breeze moved on. Once it had, he stood up, with only a slight complaint from his knees.

Angie crossed to him first, slipping her hand into his. "Those are awful pretty." She indicated the riot of colors created by the three bouquets. Carter Anne had stepped up on Bobby's other side. He wrapped his arm around her.

"Not as pretty as my girls."

"Oh, Bobby." Carter Anne rested her head on his shoulder.

Bobby kissed the top of her head and squeezed Angie's hand. "Come on, then. Life doesn't stop, even for birthdays." He turned and the three of them headed back to the cars.

"Y'all still coming for dinner tonight?" Carter Anne confirmed with Angie.

"Oh yeah," Angie agreed. "Chris says I'm getting better with cooking, but I don't taste it yet. We'll be there. Bobby, what time do you . . ." Angie's voice died away as she looked up at her uncle. She figured no one else but Carter Anne would've noticed the shift in him. It was something in his chin, the set of his jaw. Her uncle had been replaced by the sheriff of Lambert Falls. Angie followed his gaze.

Chris was sitting in the driver's seat of the squad car, door open, one leg dangling casually—and speaking into the radio. Someone at the station had called looking for Bobby. Today.

"Say about five-thirty, Ang." Bobby answered her unasked question without looking at her. "I'll have the burgers off the grill by six."

Carter Anne's eyes narrowed at the car. The whole damn town had damn well better be on fire or under alien attack, hand to God. The man took one afternoon off a year and they were calling him. "The potato salad is already chilling in the fridge," she said.

"Now, Carter Anne." Bobby glanced at her. "Don't be that way."

"Be what way?" Carter Anne asked. But she knew.

"Thinking ugly thoughts. I'm sure Jimmy's got good reason to be on the other end of the squawk."

Angie laughed, but Carter Anne just made a face. "It's all in your tone, honey," Bobby explained with a smile.

Angie kept laughing and finally Carter Anne joined in. "All right, all right," she conceded. "I'll stop bein' ugly, but I still say it had better be good."

They stepped up to the car to hear Chris speaking. "He's here now, Jimmy. Wait one. Over." With a shrug, he handed the radio to Bobby and stepped out of the car so Bobby could slide in.

"What do you have for me, Jimmy?" Bobby asked into the hand piece.

"Hey, boss. The mayor's here and he's in a right state. I told him you had the afternoon off, but he's . . ." Bobby listened as Jimmy struggled to find a diplomatic word. The mayor must have been in hearing range or Jimmy wouldn't have bothered. "Insistent," he finally offered.

"And what's got him riled up?"

"He won't tell me, boss. Says it's gotta be you and it's gotta be now."

Bobby closed his eyes. Jimmy was solid, the best right hand a sheriff could want. If he hadn't been able to talk the man down, the man couldn't be talked down. With a loud sigh, Bobby hit the talk button. "Tell him I've got an ETA of fifteen minutes."

"Will do," Jimmy answered. "And, boss?" Jimmy's voice was low, just sounding over the usual radio static.

"Yeah, Jimmy?"

"I'm sorry about the timing."

Bobby sighed again, this time touched by the sincerity in the other man's voice. "It's not on you, Jim. See you in fifteen. Mobile out."

"Base out."

Bobby rolled his eyes at his family. "Y'all heard?"

Angie nodded and Carter Anne made another face.

"Now can I be ugly?" she asked, eyes twinkling in spite of her expression.

"We'll run Carter Anne home," Chris assured his friend.

"You get anything from him?" Bobby asked.

"Not much more than what you just got. Jimmy's good." Chris nodded at the radio. "He said 'I have informed the mayor that the sheriff is unavailable. Can you confirm that status?'" Chris grinned with respect. "It made it damn easy to answer him."

"All right." Bobby started the car. "Still count on dinner. I'll call if I can't get all this handled by five or so." He looked past the others to the foot of the hill where Abby's stone rested. It was a beautiful spot for her. He cleared his throat hard and brought his focus back to his family. Nope, life didn't stop. Not for birthdays or dead wives or even family dinners. And maybe it was better that way.

Bobby didn't rush to get back to the station, but he didn't dawdle, either. While he and Hank Ramsey weren't close friends, Bobby'd been happy enough to vote for the man in the last three elections and didn't mind working with him when their paths crossed. At the same time, he didn't like Jimmy being bullied by anyone. He walked into the station fourteen minutes after signing off the radio and considered the point made.

Jimmy—Bobby smiled at the scene—was studiously shuffling papers at Bobby's desk. He could do a good impression of being busy when he needed to, all right. And by the looks of it, he had needed to. The mayor was pacing, so agitated Bobby could see the man's knuckles were white on the coffee cup he was holding. Well, whatever had Hank so worked up, they'd handle it.

Jimmy looked up at the sound of Bobby's steps and

relief flashed, momentary but there nonetheless, across his face. "Hey, boss." He stood up, giving Bobby access to his own desk.

"Sheriff!" Hank crossed to Bobby before he could even sit down. "Finally, I need to . . ."

Bobby cut him off with a raised finger. "One second, Mr. Mayor." He settled in behind his desk as Jimmy moved to the smaller one along the wall. "Anything urgent I need to know about before I handle this, Jimmy?" Bobby asked with a respectful nod toward the mayor.

"No, boss. Everything's quiet," Jimmy answered, using his most professional voice.

Bobby motioned for the other man to take a seat in the chair across from him. With an exasperated sigh, he did so.

"Now." Bobby kept his voice low and calm. "What do we have going on, Hank?"

"My office got a call from a New York City agent this morning. There's a writer who wants to do a comprehensive book on the Colonel and the history of Lambert Falls." Once Hank finally got to speak, the words came pouring out in a rush. "They thought they should speak to me, but I realized pretty darn quick it had to be you since your family still owns all the original documents in the library. He wants access to everything you'll give him and is even planning . . ."

Bobby stared at the man, raising a hand to silence him again. "Hold up there, Mr. Mayor." There was no emergency. No missing child. No threat. There wasn't even a police issue, hand to God. He spared a glance for Jimmy, who was looking at the mayor with undisguised anger. Bobby coughed and, with a look at his boss, Jimmy cleared his face. Once his deputy was shuffling papers again, Bobby looked away. But he couldn't blame the younger man. Truth was, he felt about the same as Jimmy obviously did.

Sensing the change in the air, the mayor leaned forward. "Bobby." His voice was what Bobby had always thought of as polished politician. "I know this may not strike you as important, but think of what it could do for the town. What I was trying to tell you was the author wants to do this right. He's hoping to come here for a few months, research the original documents. Shine the best light on the Colonel. On Lambert Falls." He paused and smiled. "On the Lambert family."

"What if I don't particularly want a light shone on me and mine?" Bobby kept his voice light, but his eyes had gone cold. Along the wall, Jimmy stilled.

Backpedalling quickly, Hank changed tacks. "I'm sure you and the girls can be as involved—or uninvolved as you want. You don't even have to tell him who you are if you don't want to. He's mostly interested in the Colonel anyway. The Colonel and the town."

"And why couldn't this have waited until I was back on shift tomorrow afternoon? Or even just a phone call to the house?"

Hank relaxed again and sat back in his chair. "I tried the house but you weren't home. And this agent wants an answer as soon as possible. This will be good for the town, Bobby."

Bobby leaned back and rubbed his eyes. Why hadn't he paid someone years ago to scan all that historical family information, to get it on the Internet? Or at least into a computer file. Then this writer could stay in New York . . . but he hadn't, and what was done was done. Or not, in this case, he thought wryly.

"All right," Bobby agreed. It probably—it definitely—could've waited until tomorrow, but, since he had lost his afternoon off anyway . . . "I assume you have the phone number?"

Hank smiled at him and pulled a yellow sticky note from his pocket. "Right here."

"Jimmy, handle anything. I gotta make a phone call."

"Sure thing, boss," Jimmy agreed, with another look toward the mayor.

Bobby picked up the phone, dialed and, with the receiver under his ear, spun so his back was to Hank.

"Erixon Agency. How may I assist you?" a lovely voice answered on the other end.

"This is Robert Granger, returning a call from Mr. Justin Erixon," Bobby replied.

"One moment, please."

Bobby caught Jimmy's eye while classical music played in his ear, and mimed drinking. With a nod, Jimmy moved to the coffeemaker. Before he could get the cup to Bobby, the music was replaced by a deep voice.

"Justin Erixon."

"Mr. Erixon." Bobby took his coffee from Jimmy with a nod of thanks. "This is Bobby Granger of Lambert Falls, North Carolina. Apparently, your office spoke with my mayor earlier today."

"Ah yes, Mr. Granger. About the Thomas Jefferson Lambert book. I'm glad Mr. Ramsey passed the message along. Thank you for getting back to me so quickly."

Bobby was impressed with the man's recall. "My pleasure. And call me Bobby. We're pretty casual down here. What can I do for you?"

"Bobby, I'm Justin. And your mayor tells me you own all of the original Lambert documents. One of my authors wants to do a book on the Colonel and we're hoping to get your and the family's cooperation."

His back still toward Hank, Bobby rolled his eyes. This

whole situation was going to take all of three minutes out of his life and he had given up Abby's birthday for it. "Whatever you need, Justin. I'm fine with it." Bobby didn't think his frustration was palpable. It wasn't the man's fault; he shouldn't take the blame for it, but hand to God . . .

"And do you think the Colonel's descendants will be willing to work with us? We can get started shortly after the new year and be out of their hair in three months."

Bobby started to tell Erixon the truth and then paused. He didn't want to be the focus of any research or written up in any book. Until he knew how all this would go, he would play his hand close to the vest. "I think that can probably be arranged, depending on what you need from them."

"Thank you, Bobby. I'll tell Howard it's a go. Now, will you be our local contact?"

Bobby spun his chair around. "Why don't y'all stay in touch with the mayor." Hank beamed and Bobby sighed. He was welcome to it. "I'll sign whatever you need so you can have access to the papers, but Hank has his finger on the pulse of the town."

Justin laughed. "And politicians enjoy this sort of thing far more than sheriffs do, right?"

Bobby snorted, grateful the mayor couldn't hear. "Thank you for understanding."

"Hey, boss?" Jimmy hurried down the street to catch up with Bobby. The sheriff had handed Mayor Ramsey the phone and walked out. Sure, he liked to keep his emotions to himself, but once Jimmy'd heard who the author was—well, he would've expected some reaction.

"Yeah, Jimmy?" Bobby stopped to allow his deputy to catch up.

"I was sorry to pull you in today, but I guess this is something else, huh?" He grinned, sharing in Bobby's excitement.

Bobby shrugged. "Honestly, Jimmy, seems kinda like a pain in the butt to me."

"You're kidding, right, boss?" Jimmy scratched his head. "'Cause I thought you'd be real excited about it."

"You too, Jimmy?" Bobby was surprised. "I wouldn't've expected you to get heated up about somebody wanting to write a book."

"Not me, boss," Jimmy explained. "You."

The two men stared at each other, equally confused, until Jimmy had a thought. "They didn't tell you who the author is, did they?"

"It didn't come up," Bobby answered honestly.

"It's Howard Michaels." Jimmy's smile was even in his voice. Bobby's eyes widened briefly before he caught himself. "Exactly." Jimmy nodded.

"Thanks for telling me, Jimmy." Bobby rocked back on his heels. "But it still sounds like a pain in the butt."

"Okay, boss," Jimmy said.

"I'll see you tomorrow." Bobby clapped Jimmy's shoulder. "I left you the squad car."

Jimmy watched him walk away. Whatever the boss tried to say, his stride said something different.

Bobby made it home in good time, but only because he wanted to get back to his family. That was it. He opened the door and hung up his coat.

"You home already?" Carter Anne called to him from the kitchen.

"I am," Bobby answered her.

Angie appeared in the doorway between the kitchen

and the entryway. "That didn't take long. Must've been a lame emergency. Chris and I are even still here."

"It was important, but no, it wasn't an emergency," Bobby explained.

"Well, then . . ." Angie started but Bobby held up a finger.

"I'll be right in and tell you everything," he said. Instead of going into the kitchen, he turned left into his TV room. Next to the set was a tall bookshelf. All the shelves were full, but Bobby knelt to get a look at the books on two of the lower shelves. Pulling one of them out, he stared at it. The same man had written all of the books on those two shelves. And Bobby had read them all, many times over. Howard Michaels. And he was coming here. To write about Bobby's family, Bobby's town.

Bobby carried the book into the kitchen and put it on the table in front of his family. "Guess who's coming to the Falls? To write a book on the Colonel himself?"

"Bobby!" Carter Anne squealed. "Are you serious?"

Bobby just gave a small grin. "Seems like it. That was the phone call—the man's agent. Needed to speak to me since we own all the documents."

"You said yes, though, right?" Angie pushed.

"I did," Bobby assured her. "Told the agent we'd give Michaels as much help as he needs."

"Bobby," Carter Anne said, "you're glowing."

Bobby waved her off. "Don't be silly, Carter Anne. It's important for the town, sure, but that's all."

"Okay, Bobby," Carter Anne teased with a look to her sister. Angie rolled her eyes in return. "You're just mighty pleased for the town."

Picking up his book, Bobby flipped it open. "I'll be in here." Whistling through his teeth, he headed back to the TV room. He really should be able to discuss the man's writings with him. To make the town look good.

Chapter 2

Bobby worked to keep the speed down on the car. Times like these, it was tempting to be in the cruiser, using the lights. But he couldn't do that. Business was business and this was . . . well, not business exactly and certainly not police business. Whatever it was, he would keep the sedan at the speed limit. Getting there faster wouldn't make the man's plane arrive any sooner anyway. It'd just mean more time waiting for it.

He checked his speedometer and raised his foot a bit, laughing at himself. He'd never really understood people's obsession with celebrities or the tendency to get starstruck. Seemed to him, people were just people, regardless of what they did. True heroes were people like Chris and his friend, Champ. Not movie stars and ballplayers. Carter Anne and her friends knew the tiniest details about everyone on television and in the movies, though, hand to God. Nope, he never had understood it. Until, if he was totally honest with himself, today.

It stung to admit it, but he was indeed excited about meeting Howard Michaels, getting to talk with him some, hear what he had learned that hadn't made it into the books. The girls' teasing had been right on target. And they knew it, too. That's partly why Angie had let him off the hook today and they had made him this sign. Still, even if they knew, and even if he had to admit it to himself, he certainly didn't have to admit it to them. That sting would be too much. A man deserved some pride, he added with a chuckle.

He eased his foot off the accelerator again until he was going a mere five miles an hour over the speed limit. That seemed like a reasonable compromise with himself, so he set the cruise control, obviously not able to maintain a safe speed on his own. Yeah, like it or not, Bobby was coming to understand being starstruck. With a shake of his head, he turned the radio on, hitting the search button until he found a news station. The drive to Greensboro would take as long as the drive to Greensboro took.

An hour or so after leaving the Falls—and it had only been about an hour, same as every other day—Bobby exited toward the airport. He glanced at the itinerary Mr. Erixon had sent him to double-check what airline Michaels was flying and found a spot as close to the Northwest baggage claim as he could get in short-term parking.

He looked at the sign. Only his girls would have made him this sign. Really, it was embarrassing. Purple ink. Michaels was a best-selling author and one of the best biographers in the nation, and here he had a sign made with purple ink. Maybe Angie hadn't completely let him off the hook after all.

There were plenty of quarters for the meter. According to the clock, he could probably get away with an hour. Still, if the plane was delayed or if it took awhile for baggage to come through, they might need a little longer. The purple ink caught his eye through the window as he fed the meter. Bobby sighed. Gritting his teeth, he grabbed the sign out of the car. He just wouldn't hold it up until the plane was announced as having landed and passengers started coming through security.

Bobby went inside and found the baggage claim for Michaels's flight, keeping the sign low, facing into his leg. Once the passengers appeared, he sighed and held up the purple-inked poster board. His practiced eye looked the crowd over, taking in far more than people realized in the one or two seconds before he moved on to the next face. A businessman, alert enough to be arriving for his meeting; another one just rumpled enough to be arriving home from his meeting. Couples, families, men, women . . . Bobby's eye landed on one particular woman and stopped.

She was one handsome woman, all right. Short black hair that framed her face, softening what, on another woman, would be a too-hard jawline; flawless makeup that didn't try to hide her age, but enhanced her beauty; a crisp white shirt with French cuffs, even; black-and-gold cufflinks that matched the necklace and earrings she wore; and black tailored pants that covered long legs, made even longer by patent leather high heels. Her clear blue eyes were scanning the crowd, and Bobby had just enough time to envy whomever she was looking for before her eyes met his. The corners of her mouth twitched in a small smile before Bobby looked away, back to the crowd.

With a shake of the head, he realized he'd been staring like a hormonal teenager. And worse, he'd been caught. Still, a woman like that had to be used to it, he rationalized. He supposed he could forgive himself for being human. Hell, might even allow himself another look before . . .

"Sheriff?" A voice to his right made him turn . . . and look straight into those crystal blue eyes of hers. They were even clearer up close, sharp and intelligent, but with a twinkle that said she knew he'd been looking. And, he realized, they were also level with his. Those legs of hers did go all the way up. Fighting the urge to check them out again, Bobby held her gaze.

"Ma'am." Bobby nodded, feeling the blush begin at his neck. If he was really lucky, she would ask directions. That sometimes happened when he was in uniform. And if he was really unlucky, well, he probably deserved the scolding he would get. "How can I help you?"

"I believe you're the man I've been looking for." The woman smiled and stuck out her hand. "Michaela Howard." A slight shiver went down her spine. It wasn't often she was met by such a good-looking man. She'd been met by old people, young people, men and women, but this tall man in the sheriff's uniform, with his salt-and-pepper hair and striking hazel eyes that seemed to take in everything, including her . . . well, yes, it had been a long time since she had been met by someone quite like this man.

"Nice to meet you, Miss Howard." Bobby tried to shake her hand gently, but her grip was firm. "But I'm afraid you have the wrong person."

"Not if you're Sheriff Robert Granger. Anyway, according to your"—she motioned to the sign and her lips twitched again—"very colorful sign, you're looking for . . ." Michaela's voice trailed off at the look in Bobby's eyes. She gasped with a laugh. "They didn't tell you, did they? Oh damn, I'm so sorry."

"Who didn't tell me what?" Bobby had a sinking feeling in his gut. Surely he was wrong.

"Justin didn't make it clear that I'm Howard Michaels," Michaela said, motioning to the sign again. "Or that's my nom de plume, rather." She looked into the blank eyes staring back at her. "My pseudonym? Pen name? The name I write my books under?" She tried a tease, hoping that would work. If he'd been handsome before, he was positively disarming when his slight blush colored his neck.

"I know what a nom de plume is, Ms. Howard. And a pseudonym." Bobby's voice was colder than he meant it to be, but hand to God; first she lies about being a man, then she embarrasses him, and now she's insulting him? Big city author or no, he had some pride. "We're not all hicks down here."

"No, I . . ." Michaela stammered. This was going very badly. She took a deep breath. "I'm very sorry, Sheriff. I didn't mean to offend or insult you."

"No." Bobby's voice was still hard. "I don't suppose you did. Mean to."

Their eyes locked. Michaela hated the way this had started, but damned if she was going to grovel just because this man had an ego as fragile as glass. Across the room, a loud buzzer announced the arrival of luggage, breaking the tension.

Bobby looked down at her single wheeled carryon and computer bag slung over her shoulder. "I assume you have more bags checked?"

Michaela nodded. "I do."

"This way then, Ms. Howard." Bobby led the way to the carousel in cold silence.

Had she thought him handsome just moments ago? Those cold eyes and that stalk as he led her away didn't belong to a handsome man. They belonged to an ass. Michaela found all three of her bags—another wheeled bag and two soft-sided suitcases—relatively quickly. She braced herself for a sarcastic comment from Sheriff Granger about having four bags plus her computer, but, surprisingly, he kept his mouth shut. Well, thank goodness for small favors. She started to stack the two suitcases on top of the two wheeled bags just as Bobby reached for them.

"Oh." Michaela juggled the bags, thrown from her routine. She was so used to traveling on her own . . . "It's not necessary, really." He didn't seem to have heard her. If he had, he certainly wasn't listening.

"I don't mind." Bobby looked at her. What kind of a woman didn't want help with her suitcases? Especially a woman who'd had to pack everything she would need for God only knew how long into four bags? He went to stack one of the cases on the larger rolling bag just as Michaela went to do the same with the second case. The larger bag tipped over. Michaela lost her grip on the duffel as she reached to keep the other suitcase from falling.

"I have this!" she snapped. Oh damn. This was just not going well. Michaela straightened up and closed her eyes, trying to regain her composure.

Bobby spoke before she could look at him again. His voice was, she was amazed to realize, even colder than before. "I apologize for getting in your way."

Michaela took a deep breath and relaxed her shoulders, then opened her eyes. "No, Sheriff. I am the one who is sorry. I appreciate your assistance." She took a step back from her bags with a slight nod of her head, her eyes never leaving his.

Bobby allowed himself a satisfied smirk and responding nod before reaching for her bags again. He stacked the larger suitcase on the largest wheeled bag and picked up the second suitcase, leaving her with only her carryons. Gritting her teeth and sighing quietly, she followed him to the exit.

Instead of heading to the parking lot, he led her to a car parked at the curb and opened the trunk. Okay. It had started badly, but Michaela was a professional. She could find a way to make peace with Sheriff Robert Granger. Even if it killed her. "It must be nice," she said in what Justin called her friendly author voice, "to be in law enforcement. You get to park anywhere." She smiled as he finished loading her bags into the trunk.

"Actually," Bobby replied, slamming the trunk shut, "you just gotta find an empty meter." He motioned to the line of them along the curb.

"You can still park at meters here? Even at the airport?" Michaela was amazed. How wonderful it must be to live in a place where people trusted each other, where the specter of violence didn't hang over everything.

"Quaint, aren't we?" Bobby had been raised better than to push by her to open her door for her—but it was a close thing.

Behind him, Michaela sneered. That was it. Screw him. She had to write the book; the contract was already signed. But she didn't have to put up with this shit. She'd go to Lambert Falls, she'd find Colonel Lambert's descendants, and she would write her book. Once the drive to town was up, she would just see to it that she and this sheriff stayed out of each other's way. Surely Lambert Falls wasn't that small. She managed to clear her expression just in time to keep Bobby from seeing it as he held open her door.

"Miss Howard." He motioned for her to get in.

Michaela answered with her warmest—fakest—smile. "Thank you, Sheriff." She crossed to the passenger door and slid in.

He didn't notice how the woman seemed to slink those three or four steps it took for her to get from the trunk of the car to her door. And he didn't notice the musky perfume she wore as she ducked under his arm to slide into her seat. And he certainly didn't notice how she folded her long legs into the car with a grace that was almost unnatural. Bobby slammed the door a little harder than necessary. Damned if he hadn't noticed all of it, all of her. Shaking his head, he stomped around to his side of the sedan. It was going to be a long ride back to the Falls.

Taking a deep breath, Bobby got into the car and was careful not to slam the door this time. "So." He looked for something to say as he pulled out of the parking space, but came up empty.

"So," Michaela repeated. Not helpful. Not helpful at all. She was a writer for God's sake. She should be able to come up with words. Even to say to a man who, for some unknown reason, had decided to hate her on the spot. What did they have in common? Everyone had something in common. Finally, she hit on it. "I'm looking forward to seeing Lambert Falls tomorrow."

"Town's small enough." Bobby nodded. "Shouldn't even take you all day."

Michaela listened for a sarcastic or bitter edge to his voice and, finally, this once, didn't hear it. She almost couldn't bring herself to correct him. "Actually, I meant the falls themselves."

Bobby looked at her questioningly. "What falls?"

"The waterfall," Michaela explained. "The town is

named Lambert Falls. I'd like to see the falls it's named after."

Trying not to roll his eyes, Bobby answered. Weren't writers supposed to do research? "There isn't a waterfall."

"There isn't?"

"Nope." Bobby watched the road. "The river got dammed up over the Virginia border back during the Depression. Lambert Falls hasn't had falls in over seventy years. There's a little lake on the other side of town, though."

He had to be doing it on purpose. No one could be this obstreperous by accident. "Then I'd like to see where the falls were," Michaela said through gritted teeth.

Bobby glanced at her, taking in her shoes, her hair, her nails, in a split second, and nearly snorted. Quickly he looked back at the road before he lost his manners completely, but the old falls were at least two miles out of town proper and another two through rough terrain. No way would she, with her high heels and manicure, make it that far.

In spite of his best effort, Michaela saw the look of distain in his eyes. Dammit, she had trekked all over three continents, slept in tents in sweltering heat and sub-zero temperatures. She could manage the terrain of North Carolina. "Sheriff Granger." Her voice was cold, but she didn't care any longer. "I'm not asking you to carry me there and back. I'm not even asking you to be my guide. I am simply expressing an interest in your town and the area that was settled by Colonel Lambert. Is the area accessible or not?"

What was it about this woman that was making him so crazy? Bobby had no idea. All he knew was he wanted to get back to the Falls and get her out of his car as quickly as possible. Until then, he would be polite. She wanted small talk, he could give her small talk. "Actually, it's not too bad." She started to protest his earlier sneer, but he kept speaking before she had the chance. "The path is really grown over, mind. Still, it's only about a two-mile drive out of town and from there, just about another mile or two in."

"You're right. That doesn't sound too bad," Michaela agreed, implicitly accepting the truce. "I assume the library will have a map?"

"Yep. You can pick one up when you check in with them. That's actually where you'll be staying while you're here. They've done up a couple rooms there like a suite, for weddings and small functions and stuff."

"Visiting dignitaries?" Michaela teased, beginning to relax. As soon as Bobby spoke, she knew she'd relaxed too soon.

"It's where the first lady and governor stay when they're in town visiting, actually." Why had he even bothered to try? "'Course, if you'd prefer the Super 8, there's one on the highway just outside of town."

"The library sounds lovely." Sighing, Michaela looked out the window. It was going to be a long drive to Lambert Falls.

"You have got to be shitting me." Michaela covered her eyes with one hand while the knuckles of the other turned white around her cell phone. This whole day was turning into a nightmare.

"I wish I could say I was, Mike," Justin answered from his office in New York. "But Robert Granger is the direct descendant of the Colonel. At least, according to the e-mail Teri sent me while you were airborne. I'm looking at it now."

"There must be someone else."

"According to this, there is," Justin agreed.

"See . . ." Michaela allowed her voice to become a little smug. But just a little.

"His nieces. Angela Lambert Kane and Carter Anne Kane." Justin's voice became smug, too. And just, she realized, a little more smug than hers had been.

"Kane . . . Kane . . ." Michaela thought quickly. "They have the same last name, so it's not a married name for either of them. That implies there is another descendant. Granger had a sister, if they're his nieces. Right?"

"Right," Justin agreed, but he continued reading quickly before she could get her hopes up. "But she's dead. Died several years ago when the girls were still infants. They were raised by . . ."

"Robert Granger." Michaela completed the sentence for him.

"You got it." Justin tried not to smile.

"Maybe Teri is wrong. Maybe she missed someone."

"Mike . . . come on."

Justin Erixon. Teri Pittman, her assistant. Her friends. Her trusted team . . . until today. Today, they were part of a grand conspiracy to piss her off.

"Justin," Michaela sighed, her exasperation bubbling over. First that damn sheriff. Now her agent. What was it with the men in her world these days? "I don't need descendants. Most of my subjects don't have descendants anyway. That's what research is for."

"That's true." Justin's voice was calm, but she knew him too well. She could hear him biting back his laughter. "But those subjects also had primary sources that weren't under the control of those nonexistent descendants."

"That sentence doesn't even make sense!" Michaela's voice rose, in spite of herself. Shit, she hated it when Justin was right. And he was right. All of the primary sources for Colonel Thomas Jefferson Lambert and most of the secondary ones were in the control of the Lambert Falls Historical Society Library. Whose board of directors happened to answer to the descendant of Colonel Thomas Jefferson Lambert. Who just happened to be the single most annoying man on the planet. So fine. She wouldn't write the book. The advance hadn't been spent yet and royalties for the others were doing well. She would renege on the contract. Dammit. She'd never reneged on a contract in her life. And double dammit, she wanted to write the book.

The other end of the phone line was silent as Justin wisely waited her out.

"Fine." Michaela's voice was low and hard. "I'll make nice with him. But I won't like it."

Justin gave in to his laughter. "You don't have to like it, Mike. You just have to write the book."

"And it's going to be a damn good one, too," Michaela added, illogically stubborn.

"No doubt, Mike. Call me tomorrow and let me know how it goes."

Michaela growled low in her throat and snapped her cell phone shut harder than necessary. If she broke the damn thing, she was billing Justin. Well, that was that. She would have to find a way to suck up to a closed-minded, arrogant, misogynistic Southern redneck of a sheriff. With a groan, she threw herself back onto the bed, feet dangling off the end, and was pleasantly surprised. The mattress was hard and the duvet was soft.

Propping herself up on her elbows, she ran a hand along the cover and over the pillow cases. Five hundred thread count or better—she'd bet on it.

When she'd first gotten to the room, she had been so irritated with the sheriff that she hadn't bothered to look around, just gotten upstairs as quickly as possible without creating collateral damage in the lobby, and called Justin. Now, the decision to suck up having been made—or forced upon her or something—she was beginning to calm down and notice her surroundings. The room was really lovely.

She wasn't sure what she had been expecting by "a couple rooms in the library itself," regardless of who sometimes slept there, but it hadn't been this. The suite consisted of two rooms and a full bath, and while the bedroom was smallish, the ceilings soared and the hardwood floors gleamed. The moldings had been polished to match the floors and bring out their natural shine. The other pieces of furniture—an actual wooden dresser and overstuffed chair—were of the same quality as the linens on the queen-size bed.

Curious now, Michaela got up and wandered into the second room she had stormed through, blindly, on her way to drop her bags on the bed and place her call. But now she couldn't imagine ever having missed this room. Michaela let out a low whistle. This was part of what she loved about researching a book: immersing herself in other cultures. And there was no doubt about it. She was in another culture. This was the old South.

Man, she must've been really pissed at Granger to have missed this. Built-in bookshelves lined the two walls of the room, carved ornately from the same dark wood from the bedroom. Large bay windows took up one wall, and a fireplace with an equally ornate mantle, the other.

The fine gentleman above it was, she knew from her own preliminary research, her man himself, Colonel Lambert. She crossed to him and smiled. "Nice to meet you, Colonel," she said, studying the portrait. He was handsome, that was certain. Strong, solid, and yet he had a twinkle in his eye and a lift to his lips that was rare in men of that time. Or at least in their portraits. Even portrayed by an artist, there was a charisma about him that made it obvious why people would have chosen to settle in his town, build their lives around him, follow him to war. That's what Michaela wanted to tap into, to discover, to share.

Gently, she reached out and touched the glass over the oil painting and sighed. If she had to suck up to the living Lambert in order to get to know this fine gentleman, well, so be it. She would just have to teach Granger that Northerners could be charming, too, if it meant getting what they wanted. With a final wink to the Colonel, Michaela turned back to the bedroom. It was time to unpack.

"Bobby, what has gotten into you?" Carter Anne tugged the remote away from him and turned the television channel back to his favorite police drama, in spite of his grumblings about poor procedure. "You have been grumping and snapping around here all night, more like a bear than a body, hand to God. What is wrong with you already?"

"Carter Anne, I haven't been grumping. Don't recall snapping at you once all night," Bobby answered, trying to keep his voice calm. He didn't like to take things out on his girls so he'd just kept quiet. And if Carter Anne wouldn't allow for that, then he'd wander over to the bar for a beer, if he had to. But he thought he was doing a pretty good job of keeping to himself. If she'd just let him, he'd keep on doing that pretty good job.

"Fine, then. You haven't been snappy," Carter Anne agreed, and Bobby was just about to let it lie when she continued. "You've been sullen. Which is just as bad and you know it. So you can either tell me why you're grumpy and sullen or you can sit there and be miserable, but please stop making me miserable while you're at it."

Bobby shook his head. So much for his pretty good job. "I'm sorry. I haven't meant to make you miserable, too."

"Well, I know that." Carter Anne sat back on the sofa. If she could just get him talking, he'd get it out and feel better. It had to have something to do with Howard Michaels. Bobby'd been fine when he left for Greensboro. Hell, he'd been giddy—at least, as giddy as Bobby ever got. With Bobby it was best to go at it head-on. "I figure something happened with Mr. Michaels. You haven't said a word about meeting him."

Bobby humphed down low in his throat.

Yep, she was onto something. "Angie and I knew you wouldn't come back bursting with stories, but we both expected to hear something about the man."

Her uncle cleared his throat again, harder.

After years of handling him, Carter Anne knew she was close. Grinning to herself, she tried again. "Didn't you like him? I thought for sure you would, seeing how you like his books so much."

"Carter Anne." Bobby's voice was tight. "As it happens, he's not a man at all. He's a woman."

That rocked her a bit, Carter Anne admitted to herself. "What?"

"Howard Michaels is really a woman named Michaela

Howard. He's not a he; she's a she. Now will you drop it?" Bobby took the remote off the coffee table where Carter Anne had left it and turned the volume up.

"But Bobby"—Carter Anne shook her head, puzzled—"she's a girl. So what? That doesn't explain why you're so all-fired upset."

"Because"—Bobby let the heat rise in his voice—"she's not just a woman, she's also a . . ."

Carter Anne raised an eyebrow at her uncle. No name-calling had been a hard-and-fast rule in their house since he had started raising them. If he was so worked up he was about to break that rule . . . well, a phone call to Angie was in order. And maybe even a meeting with this mysterious Ms. Howard.

Bobby caught himself just in time. "She's also a Yankee," he finished lamely. Hand to God, he didn't know why he was so angry at the woman; he only knew he was. Something about her just didn't sit with him, and he'd spent too many years listening to his gut to ignore it. All right, his gut didn't usually make him this angry or cause him to snap at one of his girls, but still. It was just . . . her.

Carter Anne gasped. "You were mean to her."

"What?" Bobby didn't even try to hide his confusion.

"You were mean to her," Carter Anne repeated. "Weren't you?"

Bobby didn't answer. Had he been mean to her? Surely not . . .

"Did it throw you that much for her to be a woman, Bobby?" Carter Anne asked, a little more gently this time.

Damned if it didn't, Bobby realized. Sure, the woman had been citified and condescending, but that wouldn't have gotten to him like she did. He was used to people's attitudes about his little town.

Bobby cleared his throat and rubbed between his eyes. Carter Anne recognized the motion. He was thinking something he didn't want to be thinking, all right. Angie did it, too, had picked it up from him. She waited, quietly, for him to grapple with whatever it was.

"I guess I owe the woman an apology." Bobby looked directly at his niece.

"If the way you've been acting around here is anything like the way you were acting around her, you do." Carter Anne's words were harsh, but her tone was teasing.

"Too late to do anything about it tonight. It's not the kind of thing you do over the phone, anyway, I suppose," Bobby thought out loud. "I'll head over midmorning while I'm doing rounds." He stood and stretched. Howard Michaels was a woman, hand to God. It was humorous, in a surreal way, now that he'd come to grips with it. "I'm going up. Turn off the lights when you go to bed."

Automatically, Carter Anne lowered her head to let him kiss the top of it. "Love you, Bobby."

"You, too," Bobby answered into her hair before he moved away. Carter Anne lifted her head and watched him go before looking over to his bookshelf. All the Howard Michaels, and she'd swear on a stack of Bibles he had every single one of them, had been pulled forward just a bit. Put on subtle display, in case the man ever showed up in this living room. Well, Carter Anne wondered. What did it mean now that the man was a woman? And what kind of a woman could've thrown Bobby that hard? She picked up the remote and switched the channel with a smile. What kind of a woman indeed? She would just have to find out.

* * *

Michaela wiped the sweat off her forehead with the neck of her T-shirt and pulled her New York Yankees cap back over her hair snugly. She really should go back in the private entrance of her suite rather than stop by the main desk of the library looking—and smelling—like this. Still, she wanted to ask where she would find the sheriff, and it wouldn't hurt to know what time the library staff made their appearance. It would be too easy to keep making excuse after excuse to not inquire about him. After today, she promised herself she would stay out of the public areas when she was finished with her morning runs. Anyway, it was only eight. The odds were good she would find the front entrance locked.

A gentle tug on the heavy wooden door brought it swinging outward easily. So much for finding the place still closed. Ah well. The front entrance was as grand as her suite. If the whole building was like this, it was going to be a pleasure working here. But before she could look around and take it in, her eyes locked on the figure standing at the desk in the middle of the room. His back was to her, but there was no mistaking him. The sheriff had come to her.

Wishing she had indeed showered before making an appearance, Michaela thought briefly about trying to sneak back out the front doors. There was no way she could get to the stairwell immediately behind the desk without him seeing her. It was no good, though. Running away wasn't her style. He was here now and so was she. She would deal with him now. She strode forward and was just about to speak when he turned around.

She was a punch to his gut. Mind you, she shouldn't have been. One look at her and he knew she'd been on a run, and a long, hard one at that. There was little sign of the perfectly put-together woman he'd left here late yesterday afternoon and yet . . . hand to God, if he wasn't reacting the same way he had in the airport when he'd first seen her. Shame he knew now she was a . . . Yankee. Bobby coughed. He was here to make peace, not continue the war. And he hadn't exactly given her a chance yesterday to be much more than he thought of her. "Miss Howard."

She wouldn't be suspicious of why he was here. Just because when they had left each other last, he had barely managed to be civil. Anyway, she needed the man, so his motives hardly mattered. She'd planned on making peace today. This was fortuitous. Not suspicious. Not at all. "Sheriff Granger." She stuck out her hand and tried to smile warmly. And if she braced her fingers for the inevitable macho, caveman squeeze, that was just learned behavior, not anything to do with him.

Bobby shook it, not nearly as surprised by the firmness of her grip as he was by the warmth of her smile. "I was just leaving you a note. Asking you to give me a call down at the station."

"And I was just coming in to ask where I might find you this morning. Great minds think alike, apparently."

"Apparently." Now that Bobby was face-to-face with the woman, he wasn't quite sure what to say.

Of course, having Grace Mason staffing the volunteer desk immediately behind him and not even trying to pretend she wasn't listening didn't help a damn bit. Every word would be repeated back to Betsy Abernathy and he knew it. Gossip was the nature of small towns but Grace and her friends had raised it to an art form. Well, might as well take on that complication first. "Have you met Grace Mason yet?" He stepped aside so the two women could see each other. "Grace, this is Michaela Howard, the author staying upstairs for a while. Writes under the name of Howard Michaels." He turned back to Michaela. "Miss Howard, this is Grace Mason. She's one of our best volunteers here at the library."

Michaela wasn't sure what was going on, why he was suddenly here and being nice, but it was certainly going to make her life easier. And maybe, if she was lucky, there wouldn't need to be quite so much sucking up. She studied him a moment longer before smiling at the woman behind the desk and extending her hand. "It's a pleasure, Grace. Forgive my appearance."

Grace shook hands with a tight smile. "Any relation to Clark?" she asked.

"Um . . . no . . ." Michaela answered, confused.

"Well, we're all pleased to have you in town, anyway. Anything any of us can do for you while you're staying with us, just let us know. We open at eight, but most visitors, when we get them, won't start showing up until nine or so." She moved her eyes pointedly up and down Michaela's running clothes.

"Thank you, Grace," Michaela responded. She managed to keep her voice light, but it wasn't easy. Seriously, who did these people think they were?

"Is there anything else you need from me right now, Miss Howard?" Grace asked.

Oh yes, Michaela realized. She had been dismissed. Well, two could play that game. "Not now that I've found Sheriff Granger. I'll have a private word with him and leave you to your library." She smiled at the other woman and waited. Grace looked at Bobby but he just looked back. Finally, with a brisk nod, she got up and crossed to rearrange fliers on a display table.

Bobby sighed. "Sorry about that."

Michaela joined him, shaking her head. "I should

probably be the one apologizing. After all, I'm the interloper."

"Don't see much reason for you to be the one apologizing because people in the Falls are being rude to you." Bobby scratched his neck and looked over at Grace. Even from here, he could see her straining to listen. "We really are a friendly town, in spite of what you've seen today." He squared his shoulders and looked Michaela in the eye. "And what I put you through yesterday. I am sorry about that."

The warmth that erupted in her stomach had nothing to do with being overheated from her run. Dear God, she was looking into the eyes of the man in the portrait upstairs. Only these eyes belonged to a living, breathing man, not one dead one hundred years. A man she hardly knew and wasn't even sure she liked . . . yet that warmth was spreading from her stomach to places it had no business spreading. Across the room, Grace Mason settled a display with more force than necessary, and thank God for it, too. It broke Michaela out of whatever strange spell those eyes were casting over her. Bobby cleared his throat harshly, seeming to come to reality as well.

"Thank you, Sheriff." She had to focus. He was making this easy for her; the least she could do was make it easy for him, too. Grace Mason wasn't his fault. "Honestly, I don't think either of us was at our best yesterday. I'll accept your apology if you'll accept mine." She smiled and Bobby felt the kick in his gut again.

"Then that's done. If you'd gotten my note and called me, I was going to ask if I could buy you a coffee to make up for it." Where had that come from? All he'd been planning on doing was apologizing over the phone and assuring her she still had his cooperation.

Michaela made a shocked noise through her nose,

causing Grace to turn her head sharply. Well, this was a surprise. "I was going to invite you to breakfast, actually."

"Those great minds again," Bobby said dryly.

"Of course, I was planning on having showered first," Michaela added. "How about you give me an hour to get cleaned up and then let me take you for breakfast?"

"Now, I'm not sure . . ." Bobby started, but Michaela interrupted him.

"I'll keep the receipt and take it as a business expense."

Bobby nodded. "I'll be back in an hour, then."

Michaela shot a glance at Grace Mason. "Perhaps you should just tell me where to meet you."

Bobby didn't even have to follow her eyes. "The diner's on the corner of Main Street, right off the town square."

"I bet I can find it," Michaela assured him. "I think I even ran by it earlier."

"Probably did," Bobby agreed. He put his hat on as he moved to the front doors. "And if you get lost, just ask." He turned back and smiled at her. "We're real friendly here in the Falls."

Michaela laughed richly and, ignoring the look from Grace Mason, headed up the grand staircase to her rooms.

The bell over the door jingled and Bobby looked up again, quietly satisfied when Michaela came in. She was punctual. He liked that. Not, he reminded himself, that it mattered what he did or did not like. It would just be easier to work with someone who understood that an hour meant an hour, not an hour and a half. He watched as she scanned the room, surprised to find himself sitting up a little straighter when her eyes finally lit on his.

Without seeming to notice the eyes that followed her, Michaela crossed the short distance to the booth where Bobby was sitting. The diner wasn't too crowded at this time of the morning and Michaela was grateful for it. Mostly, just a few people lingering over the last sips of coffee. Still, every eye was on her as she slid into the booth across from him.

"That only felt a little like crossing no-man's land," Michaela said under her breath, but with a smile.

Bobby felt his hackles rise but checked himself. He was supposed to be making peace. They'd even been able to joke a bit—at least he'd thought so—only an hour ago. Surely they could maintain a civil relationship longer than an hour. "Seems to me you'd be used to lots of people looking at you."

Now what did the man mean by that? Michaela swallowed down her retort. Sucking up. She was supposed to be sucking up. "Just the opposite, actually. In New York there are so many people, no one looks at you. It's very private, even in a crowd."

"There aren't many crowds here," Bobby agreed. "But not much privacy, either," he allowed.

"And so you get to cross no-man's land every time you walk into the diner?" Michaela asked.

"Only the first dozen or so times," Bobby reassured her with a grin.

Michaela grinned back. She thought that might have been twice he'd joked with her. Or maybe it was just wishful thinking that he could have a sense of humor about his town. "So, what's good here?" She changed the subject, just in case, looking down at the menu that was already on the table. Why push it?

Bobby shrugged. "It's diner food—but it's good diner food. Stick to any of the basics and you won't be disappointed."

"So long as the pancakes are good, I'll be happy."

"Then you'll be happy," Bobby guaranteed her with a nod to the young waitress hovering behind the counter. She was at the table, coffeepot in hand, before Michaela could lower her menu.

"More coffee, Sheriff?" She poured without waiting for his answer. "And a cup for you?" Again, Michaela hardly had time to right the mug in front of her before the eager young woman was pouring coffee.

"Thanks, Sarah," Bobby spoke, putting cream in his mug. Michaela noticed she had left him room to add plenty, and he did. "Sarah," he continued, "this is Michaela Howard. Michaela Howard, this is Sarah. Serves the best pancakes in town."

Sarah beamed at Michaela. "So nice to meet you. Are you related to Clark and Langdon?"

"Um . . . no . . ." Michaela answered again, still confused, and lifted an eyebrow at Bobby, who spoke up.

"Ms. Howard is the author writing about the Colonel," he explained to Sarah.

She looked from Bobby to Michaela and back again. "But I thought . . . I mean . . ."

Michaela chuckled. "I know. I'm supposed to be a man. It's okay."

"I'm so sorry." Sarah giggled nervously, covering her mouth with her hand.

"I'm not a man and I'm not related to Clark or Langdon, but I would love a short stack of the best pancakes in town, if that's possible," she said as gently as she could.

"I can do that." Sarah nodded, obviously relieved to be back on familiar ground. "And you, Sheriff? The usual?"

"Not today, Sarah. Bring me two eggs, hard, an English muffin, and bacon."

She nodded and headed back to the kitchen. Bobby waited until she was out of earshot before speaking.

"You handled that well. I should've warned you there were Howards in the area."

Michaela almost choked on her coffee. "That sounds ominous. What does it mean?"

"It means"—Bobby took a sip of his—"you'll be asked if you're related to Clark and Langdon Howard every time you cross no-man's land."

"Thanks for the warning," Michaela snorted. "I guess I could always just carry a sign."

"No." Bobby shook his head seriously. "Then you'd stick out."

Michaela laughed outright. "And I wouldn't want anyone to notice me, not when I've managed to be so discrete up until now."

Bobby shrugged, but the corner of his mouth twitched in amusement.

"So, what's your usual?" Michaela asked, before it could become uncomfortable between them.

"Wheat toast and coffee," Bobby said.

"You live on the edge, Granger."

He patted the gun holstered on his hip. "Part of the job."

Michaela leaned over the table and looked. "Is that even loaded?"

"Is that a problem?" Bobby asked.

"I'm from New York City," she reminded him. "If someone has a gun, you expect it to be loaded."

"Well, you can expect them to be loaded down here, too," Bobby said. "I just think you'll find more hunting rifles here than you will up there."

"Yeah, there aren't many deer wandering Manhattan."

Bobby chuckled. He was enjoying himself. Actually enjoying himself. When had that last happened with a woman? The conversation lagged and Michaela sipped at her coffee. Bobby cleared his throat.

"So . . ." He looked for something to talk about. It had been too long since he'd tried to make small talk with a woman.

Michaela looked over at him. Unless she was mistaken, he needed a little help. It was, well, endearing. "I'm looking forward to writing about the Colonel." It wasn't much, but she had to throw him something.

"We're honored you want to. It's a big deal here in the Falls." She didn't need to know it was a big deal to him, that he'd read all her books. A man didn't have to gush, after all. "And I'm pleased that, if anyone is writing about him, it's you." Hand to God . . .

"Have you read my stuff?" Michaela asked, honestly surprised.

Bobby nodded. Surely he wasn't blushing. Surely. "I have, actually."

Michaela looked at him, slightly wide-eyed. "You may be the only person who has ever read my stuff who isn't an anthropologist, a historian, or a relative of mine."

"Somehow I doubt that, Michaela," Bobby said softly.

A shiver ran up her spine and she gasped lightly.

"I do . . . I do okay. In sales." Had she really thought looking at him was like looking at the cold, dead painting of the Colonel? She'd been wrong. Very, very wrong. The Colonel had nothing on this man, with his eyes deep and a strong hand wrapped around his coffee, so close to his lips, and that slow Southern drawl, saying her name that way . . . She looked away and regained her composure quickly. "Seriously, sales are all right. I make

"You know, I really don't." Grace shook her head and pursed her lips into a tight smile. "I wish I did."

"I do, too." Michaela matched Grace's expression. "Is there someone who might be useful? With the Internet, I mean."

Grace's smile tightened even further. "Betsy might know something. She's the president of the volunteer committee."

Michaela waited but . . . nothing. The woman didn't move. For God's sake, this couldn't possibly be real. Swallowing hard, Michaela spoke through a tight jaw. "Would you call Betsy, then, please?"

With a sniff, Grace picked up the phone and dialed.

"Thank you, Grace," Michaela said coolly. "I appreciate it."

"Betsy, it's Grace," she said, once the other line had been picked up. "Oh, we're fine. Pretty quiet today, although the sheriff was in earlier this morning."

Michaela managed—barely—to not tap her fingers on the desk while Grace listened to Betsy's end of the conversation.

"No," Grace continued, "I think it was just to make sure everything was fine with Miss Howard." She paused again.

Michaela gritted her teeth. Good Lord, she could've wired herself a network by now.

"Well"—Grace's eyes flicked toward Michaela and away again, just as quickly—"now's not the best time for that. We are a little busy. See, I have Miss Howard right here with me waiting for some information." She sent Michaela a simpering smile. "Yes, she has a question and we're hoping you know the answer."

Michaela wanted to scream. They could gossip about

her all they wanted, just get her hooked up to the Internet first, dammit.

"Yes," Grace continued, "I thought you would. Well, Miss Howard was wondering if the research room or the suite has . . ." She moved the phone away from her mouth and addressed Michaela. "What did you call it?"

"Wi-Fi," Michaela enunciated.

"Wi-Fi," Grace repeated into the phone, before waiting. Again. "Okay." She nodded as if Betsy could see her. "Thanks, Betsy. Oh yes, tomorrow. Wouldn't miss it for the world. Bye now." She hung up the phone before turning, very deliberately, to Michaela. "Betsy says she's not sure, but you can always check with Kerri Bartholomew. She tends to know these things."

"Wonderful." Michaela breathed a sigh of relief. "And how do I get in touch with Kerri Bartholomew?"

"She'll be in on Saturday," Grace stated.

"Saturday." Michaela could only stare.

"Saturday," Grace repeated.

It was decision time. Michaela crossed her arms and rested a hip on the edge of the desk, smiling to herself as Grace's eyes grew wide. "You know." It was a risk, but it was one she was willing to take. It was either this or live under Grace Mason's thumb for the next several weeks. "I once spent three months writing about the territorial wars among the indigenous peoples of Africa. Didn't even have plumbing or electricity, let alone Internet access." She shook her head. "Wrote eight hundred pages longhand, footnotes and citations included. Had to get back to New York before any of it got onto a computer, never mind into an e-mail." She smiled slightly, as if remembering, then looked square at Grace. "Saturday's great. Saturday's nothing. Thank you for your help."

She gave in to a moment of satisfaction when the

Chapter 3

"I'm sorry there aren't pictures of the two boys who died with the Colonel in the war." Michaela looked over the table of books. Every book was open to reprints of photos of various Lambert family members. "If those boxes you've got in your attic are the gold mine you've promised"—she grinned over at the sheriff—"I'll have images of everyone but them."

"You've found everybody else already?" Bobby asked. "I'm not sure Betsy Abernathy herself could've put her hands on all this so fast."

"Ah, Betsy Abernathy. Her reputation precedes her," Michaela said, looking back at her books.

"Betsy is . . ." Bobby thought a moment. He liked Michaela. Liked her far more than he'd expected to, but she was an outsider. And a Yankee to boot. "In charge of the Lambert Library volunteers," he finished. That was a diplomatic enough answer. The truth, just not the whole truth.

"So, she is the one I need to worry about?"

Bobby looked over at her, eyes wide. Her eyes were twinkling with a mischievous understanding. Her lips were curved in the slightest knowing smile. This woman was something else, all right.

Granger's hazel eyes were locked on her lips with an intensity she didn't know he had in him. That laid-back, good-old-boy persona he put forth might not be all there was to him, after all. She should feel uncomfortable under that stare. And realistically, she did—just not in the way she would've expected. "So—" Her voice caught. Clearing her throat, she tried again. "Do you think that those boxes will be what I need?" She shifted in her chair, crossing her legs.

Bobby had to practically shake himself. They were talking about pictures. The pictures in his attic. "I've been meaning to get them down here, actually," he answered, pulling himself back to reality. "This will be a good excuse. And yes, we've got the photos you're looking for. My grandparents, right through me and Abby and the girls."

"I'm going to have to build a family tree, and fast," Michaela laughed. "I didn't remember the girls' mother being named Abby."

"Oh. No." Bobby shook his head. "The girls' mother, my sister, was Laura. Abby was my wife."

"Was?" Michaela asked. "Who would've let you go, Granger?"

"Laura and Abby both passed," Bobby answered plainly.

"Passed as in . . . died?" Michaela was mortified.

"As in." Bobby nodded.

"Oh shit, Granger." Michaela closed her eyes. So much for whatever progress she'd made with him the last couple days. "I'm sorry."

"It was a long time ago," Bobby tried to reassure her. "Laura and her husband, Evan, went in a car accident while the girls were still very little. That's how Abby and I got them. Then Abby was gone just a few years later." He shrugged. "But again, it was a long time ago now."

"You don't have to talk about it, if you don't want to," Michaela said. It was easier when there were no descendants. So much easier.

"It was faster than anyone'd expected," Bobby continued. "Longer than I would've wished on her."

"Cancer?" Michaela asked.

Bobby nodded. "Osteosarcoma." He smiled with sympathy at the blank look on Michaela's face. "I didn't know what it was either. It's fancy for bone cancer."

"Oh." Michaela wasn't sure what to say.

"She went from diagnosis to passing in about six months. It was . . . hard," Bobby admitted.

"What happened?" Michaela asked.

"She'd been achy. Thought it was early arthritis. One day, I hugged her. Broke one of her ribs." He shook his head. All these years later, he could still hear the crack. "I took her straight to old Doc Montgomery."

"Was that . . ." Michaela searched for the name she'd heard Bobby mention and found it. "Chris's dad?"

"No, his grandfather," Bobby clarified. "He took X-rays." Bobby looked up at Michaela, sighing. "From there, it just snowballed. Turns out, she'd been more than achy for a while, just didn't want to worry me. We got her to the University of Virginia. And Duke. Everybody was great and did what they could. But . . ." He shrugged. The ending was what it was.

"You did all that while raising two girls who were going through their own grief already." Michaela couldn't imagine.

"It was a tough time, all right," Bobby admitted.

That had to be the understatement of the century,

Michaela knew. The whole family already grieving two deaths and then Abby gets sick. She studied the man sitting across from her.

"I still don't know how my girls turned out as well as they did." Bobby shook his head. "They're both more okay than they've got any business being."

Michaela snorted. "I think I have a pretty good idea."

Bobby looked over at her. "Oh, well." He sounded thrown. "I did okay. I know that. But I also had a hell of a lot of help."

Michaela rolled her eyes. "Yeah. Okay."

"You know"—Bobby leaned forward, his elbows on the table—"people have always tried to make what I did with Abby and my girls something special or heroic. But it wasn't. It was"—his gaze was distant—"necessary. They were so little and I was all they had left." He looked back to her. "And they were all I had anymore." Why did he say that? He hardly knew this woman. It was one thing to tell her the facts of Abby's death. Everybody knew those. But the rest? He'd have to watch that, or he'd end up telling her far more than just the Colonel's history.

"Call it what you will, Granger," Michaela spoke gently, "it's still amazing that you raised two girls on your own." Amazing and very heavy. "I'm looking forward to meeting them."

"Or at least seeing their pictures," Bobby joked, lightening the mood.

"How about both?" Michaela joked back.

"It's a small town," Bobby assured her. "Meeting them is practically a given."

"And seeing their pictures?" Her eyes twinkled.

Bobby stood. "I'll find those boxes for you."

"Oh." Michaela stood as well. "I didn't mean you had to find them right now."

He chuckled. "No, I know that. However"—he reached for his hat, sitting on the table—"I do still have a job. Should probably make an appearance at the station."

"Of course," Michaela said. "Thank you for your help today."

"It was my pleasure," Bobby assured her. He had to get to the station. But it had been nice spending the morning here. "I'll bring the boxes by tomorrow?" he suggested.

Michaela tried to hold back her smile and, but for a tightening around the corners of her mouth, succeeded. She knew it was only because the sheriff was a bit starstruck—now that he'd gotten past her gender—but still, she'd enjoyed his company. The afternoon wouldn't be nearly as interesting. But maybe tomorrow could be.

"That sounds great, Granger. And thanks."

Bobby headed out to the station, grateful he hadn't brought the car. The walk felt good. Who knew the anticipation of looking for old pictures could put such a spring in his step?

The rest of the day had gone as well. Even Jimmy had noticed his mood. Of course, in some ways it made him wonder if he was usually a grumpy ass the rest of the time. Still, it just wasn't every day a man got to assist his favorite author on a book about his own family. By the time his shift was over, he was still eager to get home and look for those pictures.

"Carter Anne!" he called into the house as he hung up his coat on the rack just inside the door.

"Be right down, Bobby!" Carter Anne called back.

He headed into the kitchen. The coffee pot was rarely full in the evenings since Angie had moved out, but Carter Anne still did a good job of keeping the refrigerator stocked for him. Sure enough and bless that girl, there was both beer and Dr Pepper in the fridge for him. Technically he was on duty tonight; the answering service would be calling him rather than Jimmy after the deputy got off at eleven. Even with a six-hour window, he bypassed the beer and pulled out a soda. By the time he had popped the top, Carter Anne was in the kitchen, too.

"Did you make up yet?" she asked.

"Yesterday," Bobby assured her.

"Good man." Carter Anne crossed and kissed him on the cheek.

"Spent this morning with her, too, making sure she knows she's welcome here. You've got class tonight, right?"

Carter Anne was surprised, but let it go. "I do," she confirmed. "I can't decide if I like this professor or not, though, but it doesn't really matter." Bobby lifted his eyebrows for clarification. "The class is a requirement," she explained, "and he's the only one who teaches it, so I have to take him if I like him or not."

Bobby nodded in sympathy, but offered up a silent prayer that the girl would come around to liking the professor. He loved her, but she could be hell to live with when she didn't like a course or a professor.

"How 'bout you?" Carter Anne asked. "What are you up to tonight?"

"I have to find a couple boxes from up in the attic," Bobby said, opening the refrigerator again.

"Why do you need boxes out of the attic?" Carter Anne asked, suspicious of the answer.

"Michaela wants some pictures of more recent family," Bobby explained, studying the contents of the fridge.

"Really?" She'd been right to be suspicious. "The two

of you really have made peace. There's leftover meatloaf in there if you want it."

He found the Tupperware she was talking about and pulled it out.

"Real peace," Carter Anne pushed, "not just a truce, if you're willing to brave the mess in the attic for her. You've been putting that off for how long?"

"For the book, Carter Anne," Bobby corrected her, but she simply rolled her eyes. "Okay," Bobby allowed. "We might've gotten off on the wrong foot, but honestly, I'm learning she's actually everything I'd expected her to be."

"Except female," Carter Anne pointed out.

"Right," Bobby agreed.

"And a Yankee," Carter Anne added.

"But I'd expected that."

Carter Anne made a face.

"You're the one who scolded me for being rude," he reminded her.

He was right; she had. But that was before he had started being this nice.

"You don't win all of them, Carter Anne," Bobby said with a twitch of his lips.

"I'm sure she's lovely," Carter Anne snipped, "and you *were* being rude."

"Don't you need to be going?" he asked.

"Damn." The clock on the microwave over his shoulder told her she was running late. Because of the Yankee woman. "Eat your meatloaf," she said, pointing her finger at him.

"I raised you, remember?" Bobby teased.

She made another face but knew he was right. With a sigh, she turned on her heel. The man could get on her very last nerve, hand to God.

* * *

The little red convertible squealed around the corner just down the street from Bobby. One of these days he was going to have to ticket that girl. Maybe that would slow her down. Maybe. Carter Anne whipped the car into the parking space next to where he had stopped to wave to her as she passed.

"Bobby." She jumped out and hurried over to him. "Are you going over to work with Miss Howard?"

"Now what makes you think that?" Bobby asked. Michaela's phone call inviting him to help had only come through that morning. Of course, Jimmy had taken the call . . . and Kirk Deal had been in about a parking ticket . . . and Mary Jones had been asking about a car she didn't recognize parked in the lot of the Food Lion . . . He rolled his eyes. Lots of people could have spread the word. Giving in to the inevitable, he answered her original question. "But yes, I am heading over to give her a hand."

"Ooh. Can I come, too?" Carter Anne put on her best smile. "I want to see her."

"She's not a zoo exhibit, Carter Anne," Bobby scolded her.

"Fine." Carter Anne corrected herself. "I want to meet her. You know that's what I meant anyway."

"This is work, honey." Bobby sighed. He wasn't at all sure he trusted her motives. Still, they would meet eventually. At least he could be there when it happened, see if he might protect Michaela a bit. "We'll probably break for lunch about one, I imagine. Stop by then and I'll introduce you."

Carter Anne rolled her eyes. "I'm on my lunch now,

Bobby. I have to be back at work by twelve-thirty." She
sidled up to him and linked her arm into his. "Please?"

He sighed again. Normally, he was immune to Carter
Anne. He'd had to be in order to counteract a town that
seemed to give her everything she'd ever batted her eyes
for, or else have a spoiled brat on his hands. This time,
though, well, it was different. How could he deny her
what he'd been so excited about as well? "All right.
Come on."

"Thank you, Bobby." She leaned up and kissed his
cheek. "I even promise not to stay too long."

He watched as she grabbed her purse from the car
and dug through for change to put in the meter. No way
would Jimmy ticket her if he came by, but still, it pleased
Bobby to see her being responsible. He'd done all right
by her. She jogged back over to him and put her arm
through his again for the walk.

"You're a good girl, Carter Anne." Bobby leaned down
and kissed her head.

"Why . . . thanks, Bobby. What brought that on?"

"Nothing particular." He shrugged.

Carter Anne wasn't sure what to say so she just snuggled in closer to her uncle. She'd caught up with him
close to the library, so the walk was short. Bobby pulled
on the large door and held it for her. Margaret Jones was
at the volunteer desk, keeping an eye on a school field
trip group that was staring at the domed entry, only half
listening to their teacher. Their entrance took away
whatever attention the teacher had, as the children
waved and giggled at the sheriff and Miss Carter Anne.
With a quick wave back and an apologetic shrug, Bobby
moved Carter Anne through the little crowd as quickly
as possible and over to Margaret at the desk.

"Morning, Margaret," he greeted her, taking off his hat and tucking it under an arm.

"Morning, Sheriff, Carter Anne." She smiled at them both. "Are you here to meet with Miss Howard?"

"I am, actually." Bobby didn't even bother to ask how she knew this time. "And I thought I'd introduce Carter Anne while I'm at it. Do you happen to know where she is this morning?"

"Well"—Margaret pointed at the ceiling above them—"I haven't heard footsteps in the suite for a while, so I think she's probably in the Lambert Room or the little research room. She's out of her suite, that's for certain."

"What's she like?" Carter Anne leaned in and whispered to Margaret.

"Now, Carter Anne, just stop." Bobby spoke before Margaret could answer. "If you're that curious, come meet her."

"Well, I was planning on that, Bobby," Carter Anne replied, but her grin was for Margaret. The two women laughed and Carter Anne had to scurry to keep up with her uncle as he walked away. She caught up with him on the stairs and they made their way to the third floor in comfortable silence.

As they entered the Lambert Room, they saw Michaela, a stack of books in one arm, cell phone in her other hand. She saw Bobby and Carter Anne and nodded before turning to cross into the research room. Bobby followed, but Carter Anne wasn't sure she liked the assumption that they would just come along behind her.

"I've gotten them scanned"—Michaela spoke into her phone as she walked—"so that's not the problem. As soon as I can, I'll get them to you." She dropped the books on the table, next to a laptop and portable scanner. "Unfortunately, it's not that simple. There have been"—

she looked up as Bobby and Carter Anne reached the room behind her, and frowned—"complications. I'll explain later."

Carter Anne stayed a step or two behind Bobby as he entered the smaller room. So this was Michaela Howard. With a quick eye, Carter Anne took in the white silk blouse, charcoal pencil skirt, and patent leather pumps. Fine. The woman could dress. She looked impressive. But except for the nod, there had been no indication she had even seen them. She had just walked away, toward the research room, without so much as asking the other person to hold on a minute. And why would Bobby showing up, when he'd been asked to come, be a "complication"? Important author or no, rude was rude. Looking over at her uncle, she started to say something about it until, hand to God, the man was looking at Miss Howard's legs. Admittedly, the skirt and pumps showed off those legs nicely. And when she turned, the blouse was cut to a teasing depth without being trashy, but still. Bobby was looking at a woman's legs. A rude, Yankee woman's legs at that. Well, what was she supposed to do about this? Keeping an eye on her uncle, she stood, waiting in the doorway.

Michaela rifled through a stack of papers, holding her phone with her shoulder before throwing her hands in the air and dropping into the closest chair. She rolled her eyes broadly at Bobby and Carter Anne with a resigned shrug, and waved for Carter Anne to come into the room. Lifting her finger to ask for a moment more, she wrapped up her conversation. "No, Teri. Not yet. Saturday, hopefully. But you don't have to get to it until Monday, so no checking your e-mail over the weekend." She laughed at something Teri said. "Listen, I need to run." She flashed a smile that encompassed both Bobby and Carter Anne. "My descendants just got here. I'll call you later tonight. Bye."

Flipping her phone closed, she stood and crossed directly to Carter Anne. "You must be Angie or Carter Anne."

"I'm Carter Anne."

Bobby was by their side in a heartbeat. "Michaela Howard, my niece, Carter Anne Kane. Great-great-great-great granddaughter of the Colonel."

"And so much more, I would imagine." Michaela extended her hand.

"Pleased to meet you, Miss Howard." Carter Anne shook hands. She was surprised at the warmth of the woman's smile and handshake.

"Please, Carter Anne, call me Michaela."

"All right, Michaela," Carter Anne agreed. "We're real honored you're writing a book about the Colonel."

Michaela laughed richly. "Oh please. I'm honored you're letting me." She turned her smile on Bobby before moving them all to seats around the table. Carter Anne couldn't help but notice that Michaela looked at Bobby the same way he'd looked at her. Well, this just kept getting more and more interesting.

"I'm sorry I was on the phone when you got here," Michaela continued, once they were all seated. "That was my assistant, Teri, wanting to know if I had found some of the old deeds that were top on our list of research items."

"So that's where you start?" Bobby asked. "With a list of research items you're looking for?"

"Sometimes," Michaela explained. "Usually there's more information to begin with than I've got with the Colonel, but even then I like to have an idea of what information I need to find first, like your pictures." The two exchanged smiles. "After that"—she shrugged—"you have to stay flexible because you never know what you're going to learn or where your research is going to lead."

"So." Carter Anne stepped in. "What made you decided to write about the Colonel?"

"I didn't start out to, honestly," Michaela answered. "My publisher has been after me for a while to write something on the Civil War, so I'd planned on writing a book about one of the Northern generals. A man named Robert Johnston."

Carter Anne made a noise in her throat.

"I'm sure a Northern general would've been interesting for you to research, too," Bobby said, shooting Carter Anne a look.

"True," Michaela agreed with a nod. She bit back a smile at the younger woman's reaction and kept talking. "However, early on in my research, I'm reading about this one battle that my guy lost horribly. It easily could've been a turning point for the South if they had been able to take advantage of it, or if the North had been as badly broken as the loss warranted." Michaela couldn't quite read Carter Anne, but Bobby seemed genuinely interested. And it was so easy to talk to him when he looked at her like that. Trying to focus on her story, Michaela continued. "There wasn't a lot written about the Southern officer who beat him, though. Just a footnote that read 'Colonel Thomas Jefferson Lambert would be the only officer to hand General Johnston such a decisive loss in Johnston's entire career.' I was hooked." Michaela shrugged. "But I couldn't find anything else on him. Just the one footnote and the occasional mention of his name, but only as a part of the bigger picture of Johnston's story. A quick call to my agent and the first book was shelved. And here I am."

"Not writing about a Northern general," Bobby noted.

"No," Michaela admitted, "but chasing down a far more interesting character."

"So much for Johnston," Bobby said. "Seems our Colonel is still beating him."

"Poor man." Michaela smiled.

Carter Anne had been watching. Oh, she'd been listening as well, but mostly she'd been watching. And my, my, my, what she had seen. A call to Angie was definitely in order. "So," she said simply, reminding the other two people that she was in the room. Bobby cleared his throat hard and turned to his niece. "Were you able to find the deeds that your assistant was asking about?" Carter Anne asked.

"I have," Michaela assured her, pulling herself back to the room and all its inhabitants. She wasn't sure how much more she should say, but Carter Anne took the matter into her own hands.

"But you can't e-mail them until Saturday?" she asked, frowning, with a nod toward the laptop on the table between them.

Michaela hesitated. Navigating the politics of a new place was always difficult until one learned the alliances. "We're having some difficulties with wireless access up here." She waved it off. "It should be resolved by Saturday."

"Who've you talked to about it?" Carter Anne pushed.

"I mentioned it to Grace Mason earlier this week. She put in a call to someone named Betsy Abernathy."

Bobby and Carter Anne exchanged a look. Bobby shook his head with a low chuckle. Carter Anne sighed. If Michaela was already having to deal with Betsy Abernathy, maybe she deserved a break. Besides, Bobby seemed to like her.

"But really," Michaela rushed to add, "someone named Kerri is supposed to be coming by on Saturday and I'm told she'll be able to help."

"Kerri Bartholomew?" Carter Anne asked. Michaela nodded. "Kerri would be mortified if she knew you were waiting on her. Hold on." She pulled her phone out of her purse and flipped it open.

"You really don't have to . . ." Michaela started, but Carter Anne ignored her.

"She's on a mission now," Bobby whispered. "There's no stopping her."

"Hi, Bev? It's me, Carter Anne," she spoke rapidly into the phone. "Would you leave a message for Kerri, asking her to call me when she goes on break this afternoon? I'll be at my desk all day. I've got a favor to ask her." She paused. "Thanks so much." And clicked her phone off. "There. Kerri's the English teacher over at the high school. I'll send her over once school lets out for the day."

Michaela sat back. There were some women it just wasn't worth arguing with. "Thank you, Carter Anne."

The younger woman stood. "I have to be getting back to the elementary school myself. My head secretary covers my desk during my lunch, and I don't want to keep her waiting," she explained, picking up her purse. "Michaela, it was nice to meet you." Carter Anne was surprised to discover she actually meant it. Michaela was, well, nice. She stuck out her hand. When Michaela shook it, Carter Anne leaned in. "And don't let Betsy Abernathy push you around. She only thinks she owns the town."

Michaela laughed as Carter Anne leaned down, kissed her uncle, and was gone. She wasn't even on the first floor yet when she pulled her phone back out and hit the speed dial. Angie answered after the first ring.

"A Touch of Home, Angie spe—"

Carter Anne interrupted. "I just met Michaela Howard." She spoke low, just in case.

"What's she like?" Angie didn't even try to hide her excitement.

"I didn't like her at first, I have to be honest," Carter Anne confessed. "But she grew on me."

"Really? What changed your mind?"

Carter Anne lowered her voice even more as she stepped into the grand entryway of the library. She waved toward Margaret Jones and kept walking. "You're not gonna believe it," she giggled.

"Believe what?" Angie urged. "What changed your mind?"

"The way she looks at Bobby," Carter Anne stated plainly.

"What?" Angie gasped.

"And"—Carter Anne paused for effect—"the way Bobby looks at her."

"No!" Angie sighed. "Seriously?"

"Seriously!" Carter Anne exclaimed. "They've got this . . . thing . . . going on. At one point, it was almost like I wasn't even there."

"When'd they meet?" Angie asked, laughing. "Two days ago?"

"Well, Ang, honey, not everybody moves as slow as you do," Carter Anne teased.

"But still, two days ago, Carter Anne." Angie was still laughing.

"You know what they say about New Yorkers and how fast they move." Carter Anne joined in the laughter. She got to her car and slipped behind the wheel. "Listen, I've got to get back to the school. My lunch is almost over. But call me tonight, okay?"

Angie agreed and they hung up. Turning the radio up, Carter Anne sped off toward her work, thinking. It had been an even more interesting hour than she'd expected.

Chapter 4

Michaela looked at her watch. Finally. It was nine a.m. She could call Teri. Generally, she tried not to call her assistant on the weekend at all, but when she had to, she at least made sure it wasn't too early. Teri answered the phone. Michaela tried not to be too pushy.

"I need you to send me those three books on General Johnston that we found before I switched subjects."

"Good morning, Michaela," Teri said dryly.

"Good morning, Teri." So much for not being pushy. "Sorry. Now—I need you to send me those three books . . ."

"On General Johnston that we found before you switched subjects," Teri finished. "Got it. I know exactly where they are."

"You're the best, Teri. Thank you."

"What's your address there?" Teri asked.

"Shit," Michaela muttered, "I don't know. I'll call you back." She disconnected without even saying good-bye.

As often as she was up and down these stairs, she was going to be able to shorten her morning runs. She started down the main staircase, into the lobby.

"Kerri, what is . . . oh." The young woman at the desk wasn't Kerri Bartholomew. She got to the bottom of the steps and crossed to the volunteer desk, hand extended. "Hi, I'm Michaela Howard."

"Langdon Howard." She shook Michaela's hand, weakly.

"Ah"—Michaela smiled—"of the Howards I'm not related to."

Langdon just looked at her. So much for bonding through levity. "I thought Kerri worked Saturdays."

"She comes on at noon," Langdon clarified. "I guess you just . . . haven't been down early enough to know."

Michaela looked at the other woman. It was like that, was it? "That's what happens when you work hard, I guess. You don't always get a break until lunch or later."

"Mmmm." Langdon gave her a pursed-lipped smile. "What can I do for you, Miss Howard?"

"My assistant is sending me a package from New York. What's the address here?"

"I don't know that we can accept mail here, Miss Howard." Langdon's smile tightened even more.

The Internet. The yellow pages. Hell, the front of the building. She could've gotten the address from any of those places but no, she had to try to be polite.

"How do we find that out?" Michaela asked, forcing herself to stay calm.

"I could call Grace Mason," Langdon offered. "She might know."

"Thank you, Langdon." Michaela leaned a hip up against the desk, pointedly ignoring the horrified look the action brought to Langdon's face.

With a sniff, the younger woman dialed the phone. She and Michaela exchanged tight smiles until Langdon spoke into the receiver.

"Grace, it's Langdon. Do we accept mail for others here at the library? . . . Yes, Miss Howard . . . right here with me . . . yes, you were right . . . okay, I'll tell her. Bye, Grace." Langdon hung up and looked at Michaela. "She says she and I aren't authorized to make that decision."

Michaela sighed. "And who can make that decision?" she asked, but it was a formality. She knew the answer.

"Betsy Abernathy," Langdon answered, as Michaela knew she would.

"Can we call her?" Michaela prodded.

"She's probably over at the church, setting up for tomorrow night's potluck," Langdon answered. "I can try her, though, if you'd like."

"That's okay." Michaela stood and flashed a smile.

"Miss Howard?" Langdon called after Michaela as she headed out the front door. "Miss Howard, where are you going?"

Screw this, Michaela thought. She walked out and studied the front of the building. There. Running down the side of the door was the house number. Smiling for real now, she marched back into the library and went straight to the desk.

"My assistant is sending a package here for me. No one will need to sign for it. No one will need to track it. No one will even have to be here. So there's no reason for us to even bother Betsy Abernathy."

"Well . . ." Langdon wasn't sure how to respond.

Michaela turned and headed back up the stairs, speaking over her shoulder. "No need to thank me, Langdon. And feel free to take the credit. It's fine."

She had to call Teri back with the address—and to warn her. The residents of Lambert Falls were crazy.

* * *

"Miss How—" Kerri caught herself. "Michaela?" She'd insisted Kerri stop calling her Miss Howard while they had dealt with the computer mess. Kerri hadn't expected to like the author from New York as much as she did. Now it was exciting to be on a first-name basis with an author, even if her students would have been more impressed with Stephen King.

Michaela closed her eyes and took a deep breath before turning around. Kerri Bartholomew was her favorite of the volunteers. How was she supposed to know now was a really bad time to be interrupting?

"Yes, Kerri?" She turned to see the younger woman standing in the door of the research room.

"It's after five and I really need to be closing up."

"Is it really?" Michaela looked at her watch. Sure enough, it was nearly five-thirty. "You go right ahead. Do you have any plans this weekend?" Since she had been interrupted anyway, she could at least be friendly.

"That's actually why I need to close on up. I'm due at the old Montgomery place at six. I'm in Angie Kane's wedding and we're looking at more dresses tonight."

Michaela smiled. Ah, to be young and in love. "The sheriff mentioned she was getting married this summer. How exciting."

"It is," Kerri agreed. "Especially for her and Chris. They almost broke up a couple months back."

"Really?" Michaela knew she shouldn't pry, but she couldn't quite help it. She loved a good story. It was . . . research. Into the family. "What happened?"

"Oh!" Kerri moved into the room and took a seat next to Michaela. "It's okay to tell you because it all ended well, but it was a close thing. I suppose you know Chris used to be a Green Beret?" Michaela just nodded, so Kerri went on. "Well, he was planning on coming here to settle down. He's a Montgomery of the old Montgomery place. That's when he and Angie first fell in love. Only then he got an offer to go back to train other soldiers or something in Colorado. Was talking about leaving."

"Really?" Michaela was surprised. Sure, she hadn't been in town for quite two weeks but she and Granger had talked a lot. He had never even hinted that the wedding between his niece and her fiancé almost hadn't been.

"Really," Kerri confirmed. "He was set on going and she was set on staying. It nearly killed her, but she's stronger than she thinks. Then, while he was away that last time, he realized his life was with her. He hasn't been away since."

"That's really beautiful." She had to admit it. Even her heartstrings had pulled a bit at the story.

"I wouldn't have wished it on her, but it's how we became friends, so I can't fault him," Kerri finished with a sympathetic shrug. "Plus, he did wise up. Anyway"— she glanced at her watch—"that's why I need to go ahead and close up. We still haven't found the dresses." She smiled. "Otherwise, I wouldn't mind staying."

"Don't be ridiculous," Michaela insisted. "You go on. I appreciate you staying this late. You really didn't have to."

Kerri was stunned into silence, then rolled her eyes. Leave it to Betsy to pull this kind of a stunt. "I take it Betsy Abernathy hasn't spoken to you yet?"

Michaela shook her head. "I actually haven't met Betsy yet. Is there a problem?" No, she hadn't met the woman yet, but she had heard. Had she ever heard.

Kerri sighed. "Betsy has decided that you're not supposed to have run of the library when we're closed." Her voice was dry, bordering on sarcastic.

"When no one's around to keep an eye on me, you mean." Michaela's tone matched Kerri's.

"That's what I think she means. I couldn't care less. But yes." Kerri sighed again. "It's stupid . . . but yes."

"Well." Michaela looked at the chaos the table had become during the day. There was no way she could move all this into her suite.

Kerri followed her gaze and shook her head. "You know what? Never mind. If it's that important to Betsy, she should've told you herself. You stay here as late as you need. I'll lock everything up and set the alarms. All you'll need to do is turn off this light and not open the windows. Same as every other night. It'll be fine."

"No." Michaela ran her fingers through her hair and over her face. She'd handled the elders of an aboriginal tribe. She could handle Betsy Abernathy. "That's not fair to you, Kerri. Although I do appreciate it." She smiled at the other woman. "No reason to get Betsy on both of our bad sides."

"Or," Kerri continued, "just tell me you're calling it a night and come back up once I'm gone."

Michaela laughed. Oh yes, she liked this woman. "Now, that's tempting. But no. I'll get this figured out without you being in the middle of it. Thank you, though."

Michaela stood and stretched her lower back. It was probably time to move, anyway. Kerri followed her down the flight of stairs to the door of her suite. With a wave, the two went their separate ways. Michaela was certain to lock the door to her suite from the inside, in case tomorrow's volunteer had been told to check it.

Who the hell was this Betsy Abernathy, anyway? And what the hell was she supposed to do now? She'd been on a roll, dammit. How was she supposed to work when she wasn't allowed to work? It was almost six. Justin should still be in the office for a few more minutes. Grabbing her cell phone, she placed the call.

"Justin Erixon."

"I have been run out of the research facility," Michaela said without preamble.

"At least you weren't run out of town," Justin said.

"I have never been run out of town," she replied icily.

"I know." He sighed. "But I can hope, right?" The image of his sarcastic smile and tousled brown hair helped her regain perspective. She couldn't help it; as always, she laughed.

"There you go," Justin reassured her. "Now, tell me what happened."

Michaela explained as calmly as she could, grateful nonetheless that no one could overhear her.

When she was finally done, Justin spoke up. The tease was out of his voice. "I'll get you access again. The mayor keeps calling here, wanting to know if you've told me how it's going."

"You can tell him I'm unimpressed with Southern hospitality," she snipped, then bit her lip and closed her eyes. "That's not true, Justin. It's a nice town with nice people. It's just this same group of old hens who seem determined to remind me I'm an outsider, far too modern, and a Yankee."

Justin guffawed. "A Yankee? That's new. Are you serious?"

"Completely," Michaela answered. "You have no idea. This Betsy Abernathy woman is the worst of the lot and we haven't even met yet. I only know her by reputation."

"And is Betsy Abernathy likely to be at the local bar this evening?" Justin asked.

"Oh God, no!" Michaela exclaimed with a laugh.

"Then that's where you need to go tonight," Justin explained wisely. "Get out. Have a beer. Relax. It won't be Barrymore's or The Divine Club, but it will be good for you anyway."

"You're right, Justin. Thank you."

"That's why I'm here, Mike. I'll give the mayor a call tomorrow. Get you run of the place again. For now, take a night off."

They said their good-byes and Michaela hung up feeling better. He was right; a night off would be good for her. She'd heard good things about the Italian place, Sartini's. And no, it wouldn't be Barrymore's and it certainly wasn't going to be The Divine Club, but if they had a good beer and a decent marinara sauce, she'd consider herself lucky. Stripping as she walked, Michaela headed into the bathroom for a shower.

Sartini's was absolutely no surprise. It was, in fact, everything she'd expected, right down to the checkerboard tablecloths and Frank Sinatra over the sound system. Looking into the restaurant part of the facility, Michaela was surprised to see several of the tables full. Not bad for a Tuesday night. But the bar area looked more interesting.

"Are you waiting for someone?" the man in the tuxedo at the host's station asked her.

"No, I'm alone," Michaela answered. "Is there dinner service at the bar?"

"Of course, madame." The man motioned her into the other room. "Sit anywhere you'd like."

That was a nice change. Michaela was used to responses ranging from pity to scorn when she said she was alone at restaurants. Who would've expected a little

Italian place in Lambert Falls, North Carolina, to be more respectful? She wandered into the other room. The bar itself was empty except for a man sitting at the far end of it, closest to the emergency exit, studying his own menu.

Michaela took a seat midway down the bar and was met by the bartender.

"Good evening." He smiled warmly. "What can I bring you?"

"A menu and a recommendation of a good local beer, if you've got one," Michaela answered, beginning to relax. Justin was a brilliant man.

The bartender reached under the bar for a menu and handed it to her. "As for the second one"—he turned to the wall of bottles behind him—"I'd recommend any of the Natty Greene's along here." He indicated five bottles lined in a row. "They're all good. They're brewed down in Greensboro. And they've got a flavor for every taste. What do you like?"

"Maybe a little sweet, with a clean, bitter finish."

"Really?" Simon raised an eyebrow, impressed. The lady knew her beer. "Then I'd recommend the Buckshot Amber Ale." He pointed to one of the bottles.

"You really taste the hops?" Michaela checked.

He grinned at her. "You won't be disappointed."

"Excellent." Michaela nodded.

He poured the glass, creating a foamy head, and placed it in front of her. "Let me know what you think. And flag me when you're ready to order."

The man at the end of the bar had been watching her out of the corner of his eye. He didn't think she'd noticed, but he'd been wrong. City instincts didn't disappear in a handful of days. Harmless, she decided. Curious. With maybe a thing for older women. She studied her menu, ignoring him until he started to move. Looking up, she was amazed to see he had gotten within two stools of her so quickly. But he had left a stool empty between them.

"You must be Michaela Howard, the visiting author." The man's stare was intense through those blue eyes, but his smile was pleasant and his voice friendly. He stuck out his hand. "I'm Chris Montgomery. You know my fiancée's uncle, Bobby Granger."

"Of course, Chris. It's nice to meet you." Michaela shook his hand. "I've heard a lot about you."

"And not just from Bobby, I imagine." Chris added. Michaela shrugged noncommittally and he laughed. "It's a small town."

"So I'm learning," Michaela agreed.

"How hard have they been on you?" Chris asked.

It was Michaela's turn to laugh. "Not too bad. All things considered."

"All things considered," Chris agreed with a knowing nod. "How are you holding up?"

Michaela waved him off good-naturedly. "I'm used to any number of reactions. Some people are great about my presence. Others . . . not so much. I do my best to fit in, be gracious to the ones who are nice, and win over the ones who aren't so. But in the end, I go away and life goes back to normal for everyone concerned." She paused. "I guess that sounds cold."

"Not really," Chris assured her. "I made a lot of places home temporarily, too."

"Ever tempted to stay in one place?" Michaela asked.

"Only once." Chris smiled at her.

"I do hear there's wedding planning going on at your house tonight." Michaela made it seem like a question.

"See?" Chris toasted her with his glass. "Small town."

Michaela lifted her glass to his and took a sip. It was good. Chris swallowed, then continued.

"I love Angie. And I can't wait to marry her. But I could do without all the wedding." He smiled again. Talking about Angie, Michaela saw his eyes light up. No wonder he'd stayed for her. "So I've given the house over to her and her bridesmaids and come to Sartini's for dinner alone."

Michaela gestured with her menu. "Would you like to have dinner with me?" She was intrigued, she admitted, by someone who knew Granger so well. Getting to know him could only help her understand the sheriff better.

Chris thought about it. People were talking about how much time Bobby was spending with this woman. Perhaps some intelligence gathering wouldn't be amiss. "I'd be pleased to. Thanks."

"So what's good here?" Michaela asked, taking another sip of her beer. "Aside from the local brew?"

"Really anything," Chris answered honestly. "The Sartinis are actually Italian. Some of the recipes have been in the family for years. But the braciole is really something special. Of course, if you want something a little simpler, the stuffed shells are damn good, too."

"As tempting as the beef is," Michaela decided, "I came in craving a good marinara, so I think I'll go with the shells."

Chris waved the bartender over. "Simon, allow me to introduce you to Michaela Howard."

Simon wiped his hands on his towel before extending his right one. "I figured as much. Nice to meet you, Michaela."

Did everyone in town know who she was? "Nice to meet you as well. You were right about the ale. Thanks."

"Glad to hear it. Are you ready to order?" Simon

asked, reaching for a scrap of paper. They placed their orders and he disappeared into the kitchen.

"So," Chris spoke before the silence could get uncomfortable. "What made you decide to write about the Colonel?"

"I didn't start out to, honestly. I had just finished up a book that kept me traveling throughout the UK and I thought some time in my own bed would be nice."

Chris nodded. "I know that feeling."

Michaela nodded back. "I thought you might. Anyway . . ." She shrugged and explained again about finding Colonel Lambert in a footnote. "So, here I am." She paused while the bartender delivered their meals and refilled their glasses. Taking a bite of her shells, she was pleasantly surprised. The pasta was perfect and the cheese piping hot. And damned if the marinara wasn't as good as anything she could find in New York. Pulling herself back to her story, she continued around bites of her dinner. "Turns out, the Colonel is as fascinating as I'd hoped he would be."

"But you're away from your own bed, again," Chris noted sympathetically.

"I am," Michaela admitted with a sigh. "Still, I think he's going to be worth it."

"So you're finding everything you need over at the library?" It was quick and it was subtle—but Chris caught Michaela's eyes darting away at the question. "Ah. You don't have to answer that if you don't want to."

"I don't want to give the wrong impression," Michaela said. "Granger has been great about access to information and a terrific source of family lore that didn't always make it into the written stuff."

Chris took a bite of his dinner. Not the sheriff or even Sheriff Granger. Granger. Interestingly intimate. And reluctant to speak badly about anyone. He admired that. Still, he decided to push a little. "Sounds like there's a 'but' coming after that."

"No 'but,'" Michaela assured him. "He couldn't have been more accommodating." She wasn't sure, but she thought she saw a shift in the man's eyes. As if she had passed a test of some sort. It was time to go on the offensive. "What about you, though?" Michaela changed tacks. "What do you do?"

Chris shrugged. "Right now, I plan a wedding."

Michaela laughed and Chris joined in before continuing. "After it, though, I'm planning on opening a private security firm. Use my military training, get some of my guys in on it. There's real potential here."

"In Lambert Falls?" Michaela couldn't quite believe that.

"In the surrounding cities," Chris clarified.

"So, if that's what you want to do, why come to Lambert Falls in the first place?"

"My grandfather left me the house when he died. I wanted to check it out."

"The 'old Montgomery place'?" Michaela confirmed.

Chris nodded. "I came because of the house. Stayed because of Angie." As he told their story, he began to understand why Bobby was spending so much time with this woman. She had a way of drawing people out, making them want to talk about themselves. At least, she was drawing him out. Angie and her family were the only people he'd been this comfortable with before now and hell, he'd just met this woman. Poor Bobby . . . he was screwed.

"And so we're getting married in June," he finished with a bashful smile.

Michaela sighed. If the story had been romantic when

Kerri had told it, it was twice so in Chris's own words and voice. "Congratulations." She lifted her glass and clinked it to Chris's. "Seems you've managed to be accepted."

"The key"—Chris motioned to her with his fork—"is Bobby. The mayor and Betsy Abernathy like to think they run the town. But Bobby's the heart of it. You get on his good side and you'll be welcome." He hesitated. "Eventually."

Michaela laughed. "Well, I hope you're right."

"It does seem you're on his good side," Chris said.

"Well, I'm . . . well." What was she supposed to say to that? And why on earth would it make her stomach fill with butterflies? Chris Montgomery was far too observant for her own good. "That's good to know," she finished. It sounded lame, even to her own ears. Oh, it was definitely time to change tacks again. "Do you ever find Lambert Falls small, though? After everywhere you've been?"

Chris thought about it for a moment. "Honestly, I do. When it gets to be too small, though, Greensboro and Danville are close. Mind you, they're not Singapore or Rome," he added with a chuckle.

"But nor, I imagine, are they Mogadishu or Tikrit," Michaela noted.

"And thank God for that." Chris swallowed deeply on his beer, but shook his head when Simon motioned to refill it. "You haven't actually been to Mogadishu or Tikrit, have you?"

"Missed out on the Middle East so far, but I've been to most of the African countries," Michaela told him. Something else shifted in the man. Yes, he was observant, but so was she. She was definitely winning points here.

They spent the evening finishing their meals and comparing notes on their favorite places. Chris would never understand why women loved Paris and Michaela finally threw up her hands in mock exasperation trying to comprehend the allure of Berlin. They agreed Mardi Gras was overrated and Carnivale, under-so. It wasn't until Simon told them it was last call that they realized how late it had gotten.

"It's eleven, already?" Chris looked at his watch. Sure enough. He'd spent nearly five hours talking to this woman. Bobby probably had no idea how much time he was spending with her. Chris certainly hadn't. It was too easy to lose yourself in the sharp, witty conversation.

"Just the check, please, Simon," Michaela spoke for both of them. She indicated Chris's plate as well. Simon acknowledged it with a subtle nod, but looked discretely at Chris for confirmation. Chris's head barely moved, but Michaela caught the motion nonetheless.

She turned to him. "I did ask you to join me, after all."

"But I was the one honored by the invitation," Chris countered. "Everyone all over town has been buzzing about you. I'm the one who gets to say I've actually had dinner with the famous author."

"Ah!" Michaela lifted a finger. "But I'm the one who gets to take it off my taxes as a business expense."

She'd trumped him. "You win," he conceded with a grin.

"I always do." Michaela winked at him.

Oh yeah, Bobby was screwed. Chris turned to Simon, who had been waiting patiently for a decision. "The win goes to the lady, Simon." Chris shook his head and slumped his shoulders. "Give it to her."

"First time I've seen a man unhappy about not having to pay the bill." Simon slipped the check next to Michaela and started clearing the plates.

Michaela was shocked at the total. It was nearly half what she would've paid back home. For a dinner that was every bit as good and service that was probably better. She settled up, thanked Simon, and allowed Chris to walk her out.

"Would you like me to walk you home?" he asked. Michaela noticed that he didn't zip his coat, either.

"Thank you, Chris, but I'll be fine," she assured him. "It's been a pleasure meeting you. I hope we run into each other again."

"You as well, Michaela." Chris shook her hand. "I'm sure we'll meet up again. After all, it's a small town." They both chuckled. "And I'd like you to meet Angie."

"I look forward to it. Good night, then."

Chris touched his finger to his forehead in a mini salute as Michaela turned away with a smile. She could feel his eyes on her as she walked away. Not in an uncomfortable way but . . . protective. He might be letting her walk home alone, but he was going to keep an eye out. Michaela looked up into the clear night sky and then turned back. Sure enough, Chris was there, standing guard. She waved and he waved back. What a surprising evening it had turned out to be, especially considering how it had started. An excellent dinner, a really fine restaurant, a bartender who knew her preferences and, well, yes, a new friend. Maybe Lambert Falls wasn't going to be such a bad place to spend a few months, after all.

Angie couldn't help but smile when Chris opened the door to the diner for her. The sounds, smells, and sights were the same. She hadn't been away from the years of waiting these same tables and these same customers long enough for it not to bring back memories. This was where she'd met Chris for the first time. Her uncle had sent him in for a good cup of coffee. Chris seemed to read her mind, as he slipped his arms around her.

"They still make a pretty good cup of coffee, even if the best cup in town is now poured in my kitchen." He kissed the top of her head.

Angie leaned back against his broad chest, pulling his arms even tighter around her. "There're two stools open at the counter, if we want 'em."

"I'd rather wait for a booth," Chris said, before leaning down and putting his mouth to her ear. "I like you right here, and I'm willing to wait for dinner if it keeps you here longer," he whispered.

Sarah stopped by before Angie could do anything but giggle in response. "Hey, you two. I think the Thompsons are about done, if you want to wait for a booth. They've paid out and everything. Or you can grab up those two stools."

"I think we'll wait for the booth," Angie answered. Chris subtly pushed himself against her. "If that's okay," she finished with a catch in her voice.

"Fine with me," Sarah agreed.

"Why are you here tonight?" Angie asked her, trying to ignore Chris's strong chest behind her. "You got the day shift when I left."

"I did a swap. Maggie has a big test tomorrow and wanted to study tonight," Sarah explained. "When the Thompsons leave, make sure you give me a chance to wipe the table down," she added, before heading to check on a table.

Sure enough, the Thompsons were standing. With a wave in Angie and Chris's direction, they started gathering their coats.

"Shame about the short wait," Chris muttered to Angie before releasing her and following her down the length of the diner, hand on her lower back. They passed the family and exchanged pleasantries before moving on to the table; Sarah had just finished cleaning it and was replacing flatware on the thin paper napkins.

"I'll be right back with coffees for y'all, unless you know what you want?" she asked as they slid in on either side of the booth.

"Bring the coffees and we'll decide," Chris answered. With an efficient nod, Sarah moved on.

"Can you see what cakes they've got?" Chris asked, trying to look behind him into the dessert case.

Angie shook her head. "Tonight's Thursday. You'll want to stick to the pies or ice cream. The cake baking is done on Fridays so whatever's left is starting to stale," she explained.

Chris reached out and took her hand. "You're an interior designer now, babe. Sought after by world leaders and heads of state. You don't have to keep up with the baking schedule of the diner anymore."

"I may be an interior designer," Angie countered, "but I still like my desserts to be fresh. What's the point otherwise?" she added. "And I would hardly call the governor of North Carolina a world leader." Still, she smiled.

Chris shrugged. "It's only a matter of time. So, the pie?"

"Looks like pecan and apple." Angie strained to see over his shoulder. "Shame the pumpkin's already gone."

"The pecan will do," Chris decided, just as Sarah reappeared with their coffees.

"Y'all decided?"

"What specials do you have left tonight?" Angie asked.

"I've got meatloaf and chicken pot pie. The chicken and dumplings went fast," Sarah said.

"Who made the crust for the pot pie?" Angie asked.

"Alvin," Sarah reassured her.

"Then I'll have the pot pie," Angie decided. "And save me a piece of the pecan pie."

"And I'll have the meatloaf," Chris added. "Also with a piece of pecan, please."

"This won't be but a second," Sarah said and headed into the kitchen.

Chris reached out and took Angie's hand, twirling the ring on her left hand. This beautiful woman was going to be his wife. Some days it still amazed him. "I called Champ today."

Angie entwined her fingers with Chris's. She would always have a special place in her heart for his former commanding officer. First, he saved Chris's life, then he made it okay for Chris to settle down, build a life outside of the military. How could she not care about him? "Tell me he can make the wedding," she said eagerly.

"He thinks he can make the wedding," Chris answered with a smile.

"And?" Angie urged.

"And yes, he'll be my best man."

She tried not to squeal and almost succeeded.

"He's put in for leave already and was told it looks good," Chris continued, "especially considering the reason for it."

"The general always did like you." Angie stopped trying to hold in her excitement. "I can't believe we're finally gonna meet!"

"Who're you meeting?" Sarah appeared at the table, plates in hand.

"Chris's old commanding officer," Angie explained.

"Oh." Sarah sighed. "I thought you meant Michaela Howard. Have you met her yet?"

"Not yet." Angie shook her head. "But Chris has."

"I was shocked when she turned out to be a woman,"

Sarah stated plainly. "But she was real nice once I got over that bit of information."

"You've met her?" Angie couldn't believe it.

"Sure." Sarah crossed her arms, thinking. "Probably the first day she was in town. Came in with your uncle for breakfast. She's been in a couple times since."

Chris chuckled but Angie just stabbed at her chicken pot pie.

"What's so funny?" Sarah asked.

"Angie's out of sorts that everyone has met Michaela but her," Chris explained with a twinkle in his eye.

"Well, I am," Angie pouted. "Even you've met her." She waved her fork at Chris.

"She's real nice, isn't she, Chris?" Sarah winked at Chris conspiratorially.

"A lovely woman," Chris agreed. "And Carter Anne speaks highly of her, as well."

"You know," Sarah continued, "the Jones sisters say she's smart and funny, too."

Angie shook her head. "Just bein' mean."

Chris and Sarah laughed. "In all seriousness, though," Sarah continued, "she does seem nice. She and the sheriff have been here a couple times since then and they're always talking nonstop."

"Really?" Angie perked up. "About the book?"

Sarah thought for a moment. "Sometimes. But sometimes, it doesn't sound to me like they're talking about the Colonel or even the town. Sometimes, it just sounds . . . like they're talking. About normal stuff."

Angie turned to Chris, with a grin and a raised eyebrow. "See? I told you what Carter Anne had said."

"You can't be surprised," Chris sighed. They'd been round and round about this already. "The man's read everything she's ever written. He's probably the only one in town who's read any of it. Of course they talk."

"According to the Jones sisters," Sarah interjected before Angie could speak up, "he's spending as much time at the library as he is at the station these days. You know one of them volunteers there almost every day, so they see him coming and going."

"Really?" Angie leaned her chin on her hand, elbow on the table. "I knew he was helping, but I had no idea. What does Miss Abernathy think of that?"

"Well, I don't really know." Sarah leaned down to get closer to Angie. "But I've heard she's making it hard for Miss Howard. You know how she can be."

"Especially with—" Angie started, but Chris interrupted her with a light touch of his hand.

"Angie." His voice was low but his meaning was clear. There were enough people in town talking about Michaela Howard.

"I know, I know." Angie waved away Chris's admonition. She sat back and Sarah straightened up. "It's just I miss so much, bein' so busy an' all, 'specially now I've moved out."

"Anyway," Sarah wrapped up, "she's real nice. You'll like her when you meet her. Y'all give me a wave if you need anything. I've got those pies back there when you're ready."

"Thanks, Sarah," Chris responded. He turned to Angie. "Will you let it be, now?"

Angie looked up from her dinner and batted her eyes at him. "Let what be?" she asked innocently. "I'm just eating my dinner."

Chris laughed loudly. God, he did love her.

Chapter 5

Carter Anne flipped open her cell phone, as she turned her little car into the driveway. "Hello?"

"Hey, it's me." Angie was on the other end.

"Hey."

"Have you pulled anything for dinner yet?"

"Nope," Carter Anne answered. "I was just about to. Why?"

"Why don't you and Bobby come up here for dinner tonight?" Angie asked. She continued quickly before Carter Anne could say anything about her cooking. "Chris is actually doing ribs on the grill. Figure we'll add cornbread and throw together a salad."

Carter Anne thought about it for a moment as she headed into the house. "Want me to bring the cornbread?"

Giggling, Angie responded, "Well, I was hoping you'd offer. But I am getting better at that one if you want to see."

"I'll bring the cornbread. It's all right." Rolling her eyes, Carter Anne moved into the kitchen and opened the cupboards. Please let her have everything. With relief, she ran her eyes over all the ingredients, already there, waiting in the cupboard.

"Does six-thirty give you enough time?"

"Sure," Carter Anne reassured her sister. "I'll call Bobby now and let him know, grab a shower, and start the cornbread. We'll be there."

"Bye then."

Carter Anne heard Angie click off, then thumbed the button on her own phone quickly. She dialed the station as she poured herself a Diet Pepsi. Jimmy answered on the second ring. "Hey, Jimmy, it's Carter Anne. Can I talk to Bobby, please?"

"Hey, Carter Anne. He's not here right now. Want me to radio him?" Jimmy offered.

"He out on a call?" Carter Anne would just leave a message if her uncle was out on official business, but if he was just on rounds, she'd accept the deputy's offer.

"Actually"—Jimmy lowered his voice, as if there was someone who could overhear—"he's over at the library with Ms. Howard, working on the book."

"Really?" Carter Anne put down her drink without ever taking a sip of it. Wasn't this an interesting development. "But he is on this afternoon, isn't he?"

"He sure is." Carter Anne could hear the smile in the man's voice. Oh yes, an interesting development indeed. "But he's got his radio if I need him."

"You know what? I'm out running errands anyway." A little white lie didn't hardly count as a lie, after all. "I'll just swing by there on my way home. When he checks in next, just make sure we didn't miss each other for me, will you?"

"Sure thing, Carter Anne," Jimmy agreed. "You have a good night, now."

"You, too, Jimmy." Carter Anne hung up, grabbed her keys and headed back out the door.

She drove the few blocks to the library faster than Bobby would've liked, but at least she knew where he was and that he couldn't be writing her out a ticket. The only space on the street was designated handicapped, and Carter Anne's own conscience wouldn't let her bend the rules that much. The lot behind the library was almost empty though, so she whipped into a space and walked around to the front of the building.

Margaret Jones was behind the information desk and looked up, smiling, as Carter Anne walked in. "Good afternoon, Carter Anne."

"Good afternoon, Miss Jones." Carter Anne couldn't help but smile back at the older woman. "How's your afternoon?"

"Almost over," Margaret said, with a sly look at the clock up high on the wall. "Less than half an hour before closing time."

"And do you have big plans for the weekend?" Carter Anne leaned on the desk.

"Mary and I are going into Danville for the evening."

Carter Anne straightened up, hoping her surprise didn't show. "Are you really?" It wasn't that big a deal that the Jones sisters were going out for the evening—and all the way to Danville at that—she had just . . . well, she'd never thought they would.

"We are indeed. We're going to dinner and then watching a show and then we thought we might finish off the evening with a cup of tea, if we can find a Starbucks that's still open. If not"—Margaret's eyes twinkled at Carter Anne—"we'll have to settle for wine."

Carter Anne laughed along with the other woman, but she wasn't completely sure if a joke had been told.

Before she could ask, Margaret continued. "But I don't think you're actually here to ask about my weekend. Are you looking for the sheriff and Miss Howard?"

"I am." Carter Anne nodded.

"They're upstairs in the research area just off the Lambert Room." Margaret gestured gracefully toward the grand staircase. "You can take the elevator if you'd prefer, though. That is on the third floor."

"The stairs are fine, Miss Jones, but thank you," Carter Anne reassured her.

"And will you be long, dear?"

"Oh, that's right." Carter Anne looked at the clock herself. They were five minutes closer to Margaret getting to head out for her big night. "I'll hustle Bobby along, if you'd like me to."

"Oh no," Margaret fluttered. "I wouldn't want that."

"Then why don't Bobby and I just go out the private entrance to Michaela's suite. I'm sure she wouldn't mind," Carter Anne offered. "That way you can lock up here if either one of us is longer than fifteen minutes."

"You're a sweet girl, Carter Anne." Margaret grinned at her. "Thank you."

"Anytime, Miss Jones. You have fun tonight." She couldn't resist. "Don't drink too much wine." With a wave, she headed up the stairs.

She climbed the grand staircase, making her way up into the less formal parts of the old building. One of these days, she really needed to come and spend some time looking around. This wasn't just the history of the town, it was her history as well. For now, though—Carter Anne shrugged—she'd leave it to Bobby and Michaela. Turning the corner, she started up the last flight of stairs.

The Lambert Room was a large room at the top of the building with a soaring rotunda. The research room next to it had always struck her as a letdown, even a bit depressing. If she was going to spend hours researching, she would much rather do it in the beautiful, light-filled main room than in what might have originally been a closet or pantry. One would be inspiring, the other— well, the other just seemed depressing.

But as Carter Anne entered the Lambert Room, the voices from the smaller room struck her as anything but depressed. Unless she was mistaken, Bobby was . . . giggling. As quietly as she could on the hardwood floor, she moved beneath the rotunda to the open door across the room. From this angle, she could just see her uncle and Michaela. The table was large enough to hold several books, a scattering of documents, and at least three individual laptops comfortably, yet the two of them were sitting shoulder to shoulder, heads almost touching, as they examined the pages in front of them. And yes, Bobby was giggling at something the woman had said. Her uncle. Giggling. Hand to God . . . Michaela's laughter, fuller and less restrained, joined his as they both looked up at the same time, into each other's eyes. Bobby cleared his throat hard and looked back down at the papers—but he was still smiling.

Biting her own smile back, Carter Anne took several quiet steps backward, putting some distance between herself and the room's occupants before calling out, "Bobby? You up here?"

"Right in here, honey," Bobby called back.

The creak of the chairs as the two people in them jumped back and away from each other was unmistakable and Carter Anne had to fight even harder to keep from smiling. Still, she'd give them credit; by the time she was in the doorway, they had several inches between them.

"Hey there, you two," she said, leaning against the

door. "Y'all look busy." Was Bobby blushing? Maybe a little, but Michaela just looked right back at her, eyes happy.

"We are," Michaela agreed. "The Colonel is a fascinating man."

"What brings you by, Carter Anne?" Bobby asked.

"Just wanted you to know that we're going to dinner up at Angie and Chris's tonight. 'Bout six-thirty."

Michaela looked back at her work, giving them as much privacy as possible for the personal conversation, but looked back up just as quickly as Carter Anne continued speaking.

"Of course, we'd love if you'd join us, Michaela." Carter Anne didn't think her uncle himself even realized how much his eyes had lit up at her suggestion. It had been spur-of-the-moment, but it was obviously the right thing to offer.

"Oh. Well . . ." Michaela hesitated. "Thank you, but I wouldn't feel comfortable showing up at a family dinner unexpected."

Bobby nodded, but his eyes lost a little something. Nope. This wouldn't do. "Oh hush." Carter Anne brushed away the other woman's concern with a wave of her hand and a smile. "By the time you get there, you'll be expected. Chris is grilling, which means there'll be enough food to feed his old unit anyway.

"We're meeting up there at six-thirty. The old Montgomery House. You can't miss it." She bulldozed through, unwilling to give Michaela another chance to protest. Turning back to her uncle, she continued on without slowing. "I've gotta scoot because we're bringing the cornbread and it's not even in the oven yet. Oh, and Bobby." She looked at her watch. It was right up five. "If you're staying, you need to go out through the suite because the Jones sisters have a big night planned and Margaret wants to head out right now. In fact, I'll be lucky if I get down the stairs before she locks up." Carter Anne straightened up and started to turn but Bobby's voice stopped her.

"Go on down. Tell Margaret I'm on my way. I'll catch a ride back to the house with you."

Carter Anne smiled. "Will do." Turning to Michaela, she continued. "See you up at the house, Michaela. And bring your appetite." With a final wave, she scurried out, hoping to catch Margaret Jones.

"Well." Michaela exhaled sharply. "I guess I'm coming to dinner tonight."

Bobby chuckled. "You haven't really ever been on the receiving end of Carter Anne when she's decided she wants something, have you?"

"That young woman is a force of nature." Michaela looked out the door, following Carter Anne's path.

Nodding, Bobby agreed with her. "She certainly can be. I don't want you to feel obligated, though. She didn't really leave you much choice . . ."

With a sarcastic laugh, Michaela held up her hand. "Oh, I'll be there. First, it will be nice to have a home-cooked meal. But second, I'm not about to get on the wrong side of Carter Anne."

More satisfied than he cared to consider too hard, Bobby stood up and picked his hat up off the table. "Then I guess we'll see you at six-thirty."

"I guess so," Michaela agreed. She looked into those eyes for the hundredth time that day and for the hundredth time felt her stomach turn over. The silence between them lengthened.

"Well." Bobby spoke first. "I'd better get down there."

"You don't want to keep Margaret waiting," Michaela said.

"Right." Bobby paused a moment longer than necessary before tugging his hat into place and walking away.

Michaela turned back to the table. She should work for another thirty minutes, at least. She should. Unable to hold it any longer, she allowed herself to grin, then smile, then laugh. Oh, work was done for the evening, who was she kidding? Even if it wasn't exactly a date it was . . . something. She knew that. And she thought Granger did, too. With that thought, she shut everything down and hurried to her rooms, still smiling.

"Angie, babe, relax." Chris moved in behind her and started rubbing her shoulders. "She'll be here when she gets here. It's not even quite six-thirty. Bobby and Carter Anne haven't even arrived yet."

"I know, I know." Angie lowered her head and let Chris's fingers work their magic on her neck. "It's just so excitin', finally gettin' to meet Miz Howard. And to have her here at the house and everything."

"Angie." Chris kissed her hair before turning her around to face him. Her arms instinctively wrapped around his neck. "You are becoming friends with the first lady of North Carolina. Michaela is a nice woman, but she's just a writer."

"I work for Lydia. We're not friends," Angie protested.

Chris just rolled his eyes. "Did she or did she not take you to lunch as she came through on her way up to Virginia last month?"

"She did," Angie agreed reluctantly. "But that's not the point," she continued before Chris could change the subject entirely.

"Then what is the point, babe?"

"This is Howard Michaels, Chris. Okay, fine, she's really a lady, but the point's the same. She wrote the books that were scattered all over the house the entire time I was growing up. Carter Anne and I didn't ever get a chance to get Bobby her most recent title because he had always bought it for himself within a day or two after it came out. And now the person who wrote all those books, well, she's comin' to my house for dinner. And it's excitin', is all."

Chris chuckled and kissed her nose. "I do love you, Angie."

"I love you, too," Angie replied with a squeeze and a wink. "But we don't have time for that right now."

Chris's laughter was interrupted by the door chime.

"Oh my God, she's here." Angie tried to pull away from him, but his arms wrapped around her tighter.

"And she's lucky to be meeting you." He looked at her with an intensity that Angie had come to know, come to trust and depend on.

"You're right." Angie smiled back at him. "Now let me go so I don't keep her waiting."

Rolling his eyes, Chris released her and watched her head down the hall. He did enjoy the view from here.

Angie reached the door and, with a steadying breath, opened it wide. She wasn't sure what she had been expecting, but it wasn't the woman standing in front of her. Oh, she was beautiful. There was no denying that. Even dressed casually in jeans, a crisp white shirt, and leather bomber jacket, she had an air of sophistication about her. But, hand to God, she looked as nervous as Angie felt. Angie liked her already. Smiling, she reached out her hand.

"Miss Howard? I'm Angie Kane. I'm so glad you could come tonight."

"Nice to meet you, Angie." Michaela transferred a brown bag from her right side to her left and shook hands. "Please, call me Michaela."

"Come on in." Angie stepped out of the doorway to allow the other woman to move through it. "Can I take your jacket?"

"Sure." Michaela juggled the bag again before holding it out to Angie. "Um . . . I brought ice cream. I hope that's all right. If you have dessert planned already we certainly don't have to eat it this evening. It was just very short notice and I wanted to bring something."

"Why, thank you, Michaela," Chris spoke from immediately over her shoulder. Michaela jumped slightly. "It's nice to see you again."

"You get used to him just appearing like that," Angie assured Michaela with a grin. Chris leaned in to take the bag. Michaela released it with an air kiss next to his cheek.

"You as well, Chris. Thank you."

"I'll get this in the freezer, then I need to check the grill." With a nod to Michaela and a wink to Angie, he was gone as quietly as he'd arrived.

"He does seem to just appear and disappear, doesn't he?" Michaela asked.

Angie laughed. "You have no idea. Now, let me take your jacket."

Michaela maneuvered out of it with a grace Angie envied. She couldn't ever be in the same room with Michaela and Lydia; she'd feel like a bull in a china shop.

"The young woman at the ice cream shop helped me with the flavors," Michaela added, thumb over her shoulder, pointing down the hall to where Chris had gone. "I've got pints of rocky road, vanilla yogurt, butter pecan, and mint chip."

"Amy must've been working tonight." Angie hung up the jacket, grinning. "But which flavor is yours?" she asked, leading Michaela across the hall into the parlor.

"I plan on having a little of all of them. If we have them tonight, of course," Michaela added quickly. She sat down on the loveseat and draped an arm across its back. Then brought her hands back together in her lap as she crossed her legs. "Bobby and Carter Anne aren't here yet, I take it?"

Angie watched the woman fidget. Perhaps Angie really wasn't the only one nervous, after all. "Not yet." She sat down next to Michaela and put on her warmest smile, hoping to put her at ease. "But I'm sure they'll be here any minute. Carter Anne's usually real punctual."

Seriously, she just needed to relax. "And Bobby? Is he usually really punctual, too?" Michaela asked, trying to buy herself some time to get her head together. It was just dinner with the descendants. That was all. Nothing to be nervous about. In fact, it was commonplace. Dinner with the descendants. So what if it was a lie. It was a workable lie. She could live with that. Feeling more in control, Michaela turned her focus back to Angie's answer.

". . . But it's hard sometimes when he's on call. Lambert Falls is small, but it still sometimes needs its sheriff. 'Course when he's off duty . . ." Angie's thought was interrupted by the sound of the door opening and Carter Anne calling out.

"Hey y'all! We're here."

"When he's off duty, they're both real punctual," Angie finished with a grin as she stood up. "Hey, y'all," she called back.

Michaela followed Angie into the foyer. She'd never seen anything quite like it. Chris had appeared from somewhere, which made five of them, but even so—there were only the five of them and yet . . . As she watched, coats were removed and hung up, a large pan of something was passed around until it finally ended up in Chris's possession, and it seemed as if everyone got hugged at least twice. Even after years of learning to observe and to listen, she couldn't keep up with the conversations and who was saying what to whom or answering which question. They were even including her. Carter Anne gave her a quick squeeze and a kiss on the cheek, Chris managed to pat her on the back as he walked by and she thought, although she couldn't be one hundred percent certain, someone had asked her a question. She also thought someone else had answered it, so at least she was off the hook there. It was noisy and busy and . . . comfortable. Before she knew it, all five of them were heading down the hall, in a cloud of conversation. She felt a gentle touch on her elbow and looked over. Bobby had fallen in next to her, behind the rest of them.

"Sorry you beat us here," he said, his voice low. "It can be kind of awkward to be the first to someone's house."

"It was fine. Angie was very nice about it," Michaela assured him. "You look good in civilian clothing, Granger." She realized she hadn't seen him in anything but his uniform until now. As much as she enjoyed a man in uniform, jeans and a chambray shirt were equally pleasing on the right man. Apparently, Granger was the right man. She grinned at the sight of the blush that started at his neck.

Chris raised an eye at the knowing grin on Michaela's face—and the very subtle blush at his friend's jawline—

but Bobby just gave that cough of his. Neither Angie nor Carter Anne had appeared to notice, which was fine by Chris. If Michaela was making Bobby blush, it might not be such a bad thing. Getting teased by his girls might be, though. Especially this early. "Michaela," he spoke to his guest, "come on in and have a seat." He motioned to a chair at the table. "We're pretty relaxed around here. Bobby, can you help me with the meat?"

Bobby gave an appreciative nod and followed Chris out the back way while the three women settled into the kitchen. Michaela was in good hands.

"So." Chris spoke as he opened the grill and tended to the ribs. "How's the book coming?"

Bobby nodded. "Well, I think. Of course, you'll have to ask Michaela to be sure, but I think it's going well. Even I'm learning about the Colonel, and I thought I knew just about everything there was to know about him."

"It's taking up a good deal of your time." Chris spoke calmly.

Bobby squared his shoulders. "Do you have something you want to say to me, Chris?"

Chris hardly even looked up from the grill. "You know me better than that, Bobby. You also know your town well enough to know that people are noticing how much time you're spending on the book. And with Michaela. If it doesn't matter to you, it certainly doesn't matter to me." Next to him, Chris felt his friend relax again. "And I really don't blame you for spending time with Michaela, book related or not. She's an interesting, intelligent woman."

"That she is," Bobby agreed.

"Not to mention a damn fine-looking one," Chris added.

Bobby chuckled. "I can't say you're wrong. The conversation's good, but looking at her's not the worst part of my day, either."

Chris laughed with his friend. "Of course, you don't have to mention to Angie that I noticed."

"Hell, Chris." Bobby's chuckle became a full-out laugh. "I'd just as soon you not mention to Angie that I've noticed."

"So we're in agreement. Michaela is unattractive and a nuisance to have in town and we can't wait for her to leave." Chris pulled the ribs from the grill and stacked them high on a tray.

"At least as far as the girls are concerned. That works for me," Bobby agreed. "Not that either of them would believe it of us."

Chris grinned at the older man. "They don't have to believe it of you."

Shaking his head with a laugh, Bobby opened the door for Chris and followed him in.

"Hope you ladies are ready," Chris announced. "Because the ribs are."

Bobby's quick eye had taken in the scene as they'd come in. What he'd seen made him smile. Michaela leaning, apparently relaxed, against the refrigerator holding a bottle of beer, while Carter Anne put the finishing touches on the salad and Angie pulled the plates from the cupboards.

"Good, because I'm starved," Angie said over her shoulder, as Chris walked on through to the dining room.

"Let me take those." Michaela moved in to Angie to help with the plates.

"Nonsense," Angie answered plainly. "Tonight, you're

company. Bobby, come grab my beer and get a couple for you and Chris if you want them."

"Don't let her fool you, though," Bobby teased. "You come back a second time and she'll have you working as hard as I do."

"Then I'll have to be sure to get another invitation," Michaela parried, picking up Angie's beer anyway. She watched Bobby move from the door to the refrigerator and bend over to get the other beers from the bottom drawer. Yes, well-cut jeans worked as nicely as a uniform, thank you very much. Neither she nor Bobby noticed Carter Anne wiggle her eyebrows at her sister or Angie grin back.

Angie led the way into the dining room, where Chris was waiting. Aside from the plates and salad, the table had been set. Michaela was struck at the simplicity and warmth of the meal. Nothing fancy for a visiting author. She truly had been invited to a family dinner. The general chaos as everyone began settling in and finding space on and around the table confirmed it. The thought pleased her. Bobby held out a chair for her and, once she was seated, placed a full bottle of beer down next to her already open one.

"Thought you might like another," he whispered in her ear. She barely had time to whisper a thank you before he had straightened up and passed another bottle over to Chris.

Finally everyone was seated and, with a minimal amount of additional fuss, plates served. Next to him, Bobby was pleased to see Michaela take several ribs and extra sauce, as well as a large portion of salad.

"All right, you two. Tell us about the book." Angie waved a rib at her uncle and her guest. "Michaela wouldn't talk about it unless you were around, Bobby, so it's time." Turning her attention back to Michaela, she asked, "What made you decide to write about the Colonel, anyway?"

Michaela grinned. "He was actually a footnote." She related the story again for the whole family, as everyone ate and asked more questions. And as the conversation moved on from her work, she was happy to let it do so. It gave her the opportunity to just listen and watch the dynamics around the table. Chris, quiet but watching, attentive and astute. Angie and Carter Anne, practically boiling over with curiosity, talking over each other in the loving but abrupt way sisters can. And Bobby. Sitting next to her. Even at Chris's table, the head of the family. He managed to be talkative and taciturn all at once, although how, she wasn't quite sure. None of his words, no matter how many of them there might be, were wasted or unimportant. The descendants of Colonel Lambert were as interesting and unique in their own rights as the Colonel himself.

She was enjoying herself so much that she tried to hide the yawn that escaped in spite of the good time and good company, but Bobby caught it out of the corner of his eye. The twitch of a grin at the corner of his mouth gave him away.

"I hate to be the one to do this," he said with a stretch, getting to his feet, "but I need to be getting home. Carter Anne, are you going to stay a bit longer or come on home?"

Carter Anne looked to Angie, then to Chris, who lifted his empty beer bottle and waggled it gently.

"It's Friday night . . ." Angie agreed with Chris's unspoken invitation.

"I think I'll stay, Bobby," Carter Anne decided.

"Michaela"—Angie turned to her guest—"you're more than welcome to stay. We'd love you to."

"Thank you, Angie," Michaela said, standing up. "But I think it's time to leave the evening to the younger generation."

In spite of it just being the two of them going, Michaela was amazed to learn that the leaving process was as much a production as the arriving process. Apparently all three of the others had to come and see her and Bobby out. Then everyone had to hug them both. And remind each other to call or stop by or be in touch tomorrow. And Carter Anne to lock up when she got home. Then hug each of them again. By the time Michaela stepped outside beside Bobby and the door finally closed behind them, the cool air felt good. She took a deep breath and looked up into the sky. There were a few clouds moving in. It would probably be fully overcast tomorrow, but for tonight, there were stars around and between the clouds.

"It's a bit chilly," he said. "Would you like my jacket for the walk?"

"Mmm. No. Thank you, though," Michaela replied, tugging at her own lapel. "I think this is probably warmer than I need." She looked back at the front door, now closed behind them, and shook her head.

Bobby took one look at her still dazed expression and chuckled. "I take it it's not like that up in New York."

"We just don't need to hug every person in the room a dozen times before letting them go for all of twenty-four hours, I suppose." Michaela shrugged and fell into step next to him as they started down the driveway.

He was learning to read her, hear the meaning behind her words, and was grateful for it. Two weeks ago, he would've been insulted. Now? Well, now he knew

Michaela and her ability to make an observation without making a judgment about it. Still, he could tease her a little. "Yep, some people just aren't the friendly type, I guess. I'd heard that about Yankees. Been trying to give y'all the benefit of the doubt, 'til now."

"It's not that we're not friendly, Granger," Michaela explained. "It's just that we don't like anybody."

Bobby's chuckle turned to a bark of laughter, which became a sharp cough as Michaela slipped her arm into his. Apparently it had been longer than he'd realized since he'd had a good-looking woman so close because, hand to God, she felt good there.

It would never work between them, she knew, but oh, she could certainly enjoy the solid muscle beneath the soft shirt. He tucked her arm firmly against his side and covered her hand with his.

"Do you mind if we take the long way? I'd like to have one last look around town before dropping you off and heading in for the night," he asked. It wasn't necessary. He could just as easily loop the town after dropping her off. Well, she could always say she was too tired. He'd take her straight home then.

"You're walking me home?" Michaela asked, eyebrows raised.

"Of course." Bobby looked down at her, puzzled.

Michaela smiled and squeezed his arm. Yes, she could enjoy the feel of a strong man at her side. At least for now. "Then no. I don't mind taking the long way at all."

Bobby turned them left at the end of the driveway, refusing to consider how pleased it made him. Eventually he'd have to deal with it, think about it. But not right now. "Another difference 'tween y'all and us, I take it?" He grinned down at her. "Yankees aren't so gentlemanly?"

Michaela flattened her lips but her eyes twinkled. How could they not, looking up into his? "They're gentlemen. They're just gentlemen enough to not make the assumption women need walking home at night."

Bobby nodded. "Yep. That's what I said. Yankees aren't so gentlemanly." Her confidence threw him. It was either tease her back or kiss her right here. If she'd been as arrogant as he'd first thought, there'd be no problem. But she wasn't. She was strong and confident and assured . . . and pressed up against him. Thank God the night was cold and the walk was long.

Michaela elbowed him, but laughed nonetheless. As they walked, Bobby waved to a few cars as they drove by and checked a gate or two, making sure they were locked. Still, he was relaxed about it, almost nonchalant. There was none of the hyperawareness she was used to in the city. It was different and nice, in an unexpected way. He was different and nice, in an unexpected way. There was something undeniably sexy about his casual professionalism.

"Is it always so slow on a Friday night?" she asked, trying to keep her mind from the other train of thought.

Bobby shrugged. "Sartini's is probably busy. Same with the diner and the ice cream parlor for the kids who have midnight curfews. A lot of them will have headed up to Danville and the movies there, though. Although—" He motioned toward the curve in the road ahead of them. A footpath led into a park. "We'll probably run into a few of them over there."

They crossed the road and headed up the footpath, around a small pond. Was this the "little lake" he'd mentioned the first day they'd met? She supposed it counted, if you stressed "little." A few lights reflected back at them in its clear waters. She hadn't even known it was there.

Michaela looked around; on the other side of the water was the statue of the Colonel. How they'd gotten here, she wasn't quite sure, but yes, it was the Colonel himself. They must have come up a back way. Sure enough, she looked out toward his other side and there was the little footbridge and, just through the trees starting to get bare, the lights of Main Street.

"I always try to make a round through here, especially on weekend nights," Bobby said to her. He stopped Michaela, put his finger to his lips, took two steps away from her and cocked his head. Michaela listened, but couldn't hear anything. She had opened her mouth to ask, when she heard it—whispering and a giggle or two.

"Evenin'," Bobby called out. There was a rustle and Michaela looked in the direction of the noise. Hidden at the base of a large tree, totally shadowed this time of night, was a stone bench. An occupied stone bench.

"Um . . ." a young man's voice spoke up. "Evening, Sheriff Granger."

"Johnnie Thompson, that you?" Michaela saw Bobby's lips twitch in a smile, but knew the young man would only hear the sternness of his voice.

"Yessir, it is." Johnnie stood up and stepped out into the brighter area.

Bobby saw the movement also blocked the girl on the bench. Not completely, but enough for Bobby to appreciate the effort the boy was making. "Bit cold to be outside, isn't it, son?"

"I guess so, Sheriff."

"Might be warmer over at the diner."

"Yes sir, it probably is," Johnnie agreed.

"And what time's your curfew?"

"I'm seventeen now and don't have one," Johnnie said, with a bit of defiance in his voice—that shriveled under Bobby's look. "But she's gotta be home by eleven."

Bobby looked at his watch. "If you start walking now, you can take your time and still get her home in time to say good night."

The younger man gave Bobby a lopsided grin. Michaela choked back a laugh, making him look at her for the first time. "Sheriff . . . ?" Johnnie started, his eyes going wide.

Bobby interrupted him before the question could be fully formed. "Get her on home, son. And give her your jacket for the walk. It's a might bit cold. Be a gentleman and treat a lady right." Michaela was startled by that comment, given Bobby's earlier offer to her, but far too amused by Johnnie to think on it.

The young man dragged his eyes away from Michaela and looked back to Bobby. Michaela wasn't sure, but she thought there just might be something new in the young man's eyes. Shock, yes, but there was something else, too. Admiration or possibly heightened respect. She bit her lips and lowered her head to keep from laughing out loud. With another grin to Bobby, Johnnie turned to the bench and took off his jacket. As the two teenagers made their way through the shadows, Bobby called out one more time. "You go straight home, Amy."

The two of them froze for a moment before the young woman turned to Bobby. "Yes sir, Sheriff." Then, with a giggle, she added, "Good to see you again, Miss Howard," before taking Johnnie's hand and leading him away.

Michaela raised her hand and laughed. "Nicely handled, Granger."

"Why, thank you, Miz Howard," Bobby drawled. "We'll have tongues wagging come morning. You should be ready for that."

Michaela shrugged. "Everyone's been nice enough so far." Bobby raised an eyebrow, making Michaela smirk. "More or less, anyway. I don't see how my being here with you tonight is going to change anyone's opinion, for better or worse."

"Well." Bobby tipped back on his heels, looking away from her. "You see what this place is usually used for in the evenings. Once Johnnie and Amy tell their folks, well, word'll spread and assumptions will be made." He looked over at Michaela, who was just smiling at him. One of her damned confusing, impossible-to-read smiles, too. Bobby simply stopped speaking. Sometimes it was better to just stop. Now was one of those times and, hand to God, he was old enough to recognize it.

"You know, Granger." Michaela walked around him until they were face-to-face. Was she really about to do this? She looked up into those eyes and felt her stomach turn over. Yes, she was. "Those kids were cute and young enough to care about gossip and what the sheriff might be doing down here with the Yankee." She grinned. What about this man made this so difficult? He was so different from the men in New York. What if she was wrong? Surely he couldn't be that different. Surely she hadn't read him so badly. Taking a deep breath, she jumped. "Luckily, we're a little past that. If two adults want to be down here, enjoying the evening and . . ." She moved closer to him. "Each other, well, that should be okay. Right?"

"I suppose so." Bobby's hands were on her hips, his thumbs stroking her waist gently. When had they moved? Truth was, he couldn't remember.

"We're both adults, Granger," Michaela continued, wrapping her arms around his neck. "We should be able to go into this, eyes open . . ." Her voice was low and husky.

"Seems to me"—Bobby's voice was no more than a whisper itself—"so long as both people understand each other . . ." He looked into her eyes and saw the heat he was feeling reflected back in them.

"Then no one gets hurt," she finished. The last two weeks of wanting had her breath coming in short gasps. Why didn't he just kiss her already, dammit?

Her breasts were pushed against his chest. Somewhere, a voice argued with him that they should discuss this, negotiate it, make sure they both really were in agreement about how this would all work and how it would end. But all he could hear was her breath and a rushing in his ears. All he could feel were those long legs of hers pressing up against his thighs. Then her fingers fisted in the hair at the back of his neck.

"Kiss me, Granger. We'll figure out the rest later." Her voice was sultry with need.

Bobby had no idea which one of them moved first, but knew it didn't really matter. What mattered was the taste of her, finally, as her lips opened under his. What mattered was the feel of her shirt clenched in his hands and the heat from her skin he could feel through it. What mattered was the way she pulled him to her, responding with her own built-up passion.

Neither of them noticed as the clouds that had been forming seemed to move off, barely outlining the moon, but never crossing it, as the Colonel looked down from his horse. Bobby felt Michaela begin to pull away and so let her. But damn, he didn't want to. Still, they couldn't stand out here all night.

She looked up at him, a wry smile on her face. "I guess we're on the same page, then, huh?" she teased.

"I suppose so." Bobby grinned back at her. He couldn't help himself.

"It's cold, Granger." Michaela turned and snuggled in, her arm through his. "Take me home."

Bobby fell into step beside her. This is when the complications started. One kiss was easy enough. The rest, though . . . Well, hell, she was right. They were both adults. They both knew she was only here until the research was done. The rest wasn't complicated. The rest just . . . was. He could live with that. Especially when it felt as good as she did.

They walked toward the library. If Bobby wasn't quite as attentive to his town as usual, well, he figured he could be forgiven this once. They reached the library and went around to the back of the building where an outside stairway led to the private suite. Michaela held his hand, leading him to her door and unlocking it. Bobby followed her in, grateful to her for making her preference clear. It was too cold a night to be standing outside wondering.

"May I get you some wine?" she asked, hanging up their coats. "I haven't picked up beer yet, but I've got seltzer, a nice white wine that's already chilled, and a not-quite-as-nice red that will need to breathe a bit."

"I'm not a fan of whites, to tell you the truth," Bobby answered honestly. "Spent too much time eating steaks to ever really get the taste of them. I don't mind waiting for the red if you don't."

She smiled her answer and went to the kitchen. Bobby looked around, awkward for the first time in his life anywhere in this building. He was relieved when she came back very quickly, wine and bottle opener in one hand, two stemmed glasses threaded between the fingers of the other. "Would you do the honors?" She

handed him the bottle and opener before leading him
through to the sitting room.

"It'd be my pleasure," Bobby replied, following her
to the loveseat. He opened the wine with a practiced
hand and set the bottle next to the glasses on the coffee
table before taking a seat next to her. "We'll give that ten
minutes or so."

Michaela reached out, stroking his arm, but not meeting his eyes. Was she nervous? His implacable Yankee?
"Michaela." His voice was quiet and low. He took her
hand in his. "We don't have to do anything but have a
glass of wine if you don't want to."

"Oh, Granger." Michaela almost laughed. "Always the
gentleman." She entwined her fingers with his. "It's not
that. Believe me. If I'd had any doubts, I wouldn't have
started this." She looked at him then and he saw the
honesty in her eyes. "It's just . . . oh, sometimes I think it
would be easier to be younger and have grown up in
today's world." She dropped her head back on the settee
but didn't let go of his hand. Staring up at the ceiling,
she spoke. If he hadn't known her, the matter-of-fact
tone would have put him off. For all her reassurances,
this wasn't easy for her. Bobby squeezed her hand.

"At our age, we don't have to worry about pregnancy
any longer. That's the plus. But there are . . ." She struggled to find the words. Somehow she didn't think this
was a conversation Granger had had recently. "Other
considerations," she finished.

Bobby nodded. Hand to God . . . Still, if she could do
it, so could he. "Sexually transmitted diseases are on the
rise among our generation. And it's, well, it's been a
while for me, but there's no reason for you to trust that.
Not really."

"And"—Michaela glanced over at him, eyes twinkling—"I can't imagine it's been that long."

Bobby cleared his throat hard and Michaela laughed. "You don't have to answer that. A gentleman never tells, I know." She sat up and faced him. "I just wanted you to know, beforehand, that I bought them just a few days ago. I didn't bring them with me. I just . . . I guess you could say I hoped."

Bobby laughed outright at that. "I don't know if I should be flattered that you thought so much of me, or insulted that you didn't think I'd take care of you." Swallowing hard, he continued as she smiled. "I'll choose flattered if you will. I hoped, too." Reaching in his pocket, he pulled out his wallet. With the flush of embarrassment rising on his neck, he pulled out the condom and offered it to her. Then he knew he'd screwed up. Screwed up in a big way. Michaela was staring at the small, blue square in his hand as if she'd never seen one before. Trying not to let his hands shake or fumble with a wallet he'd maneuvered every day for years, Bobby started to put the condom away.

"Don't. You. Dare." Michaela's voice was steely but her smile was huge. She reached out and took the packet out of his hand, eyes twinkling. Instead of sitting back, though, she stretched her body out over his. "So you'd hoped, too, huh?"

Bobby didn't need any further encouragement. It had been a long time, but Michaela was right; it hadn't been that long. He leaned up and, taking her face into his hands, pressed his mouth to hers. A small sound came from Michaela and she opened her lips to him.

She tasted sweet and clean. This close to her, Bobby could smell her hair, her skin. His body began to respond as Michaela reached for the buttons on his shirt.

As each button released, she scraped a nail teasingly along his skin. It was Bobby's turn to growl deep in his throat. He deepened the kiss, but Michaela's fingers were relentless until his shirt hung open. With a wicked grin, she lowered her mouth to one of his nipples and rolled it between her teeth.

"Michaela," Bobby groaned. He gripped her shoulders and pushed her back until she was prone on the loveseat.

Laughing, she reached up and slid his shirt off his shoulders. He shrugged out of it and dropped it on the floor. Michaela wasted no time in pulling him back down to her. She tried to spread her legs so he could settle in between them, but the back of the loveseat was in her way. He tried to stretch out, but ended up kicking its arm.

"This isn't . . . it's not . . ." Bobby sat up in frustration. This damn couch wasn't going to beat him.

Michaela followed him up in a fluid motion. "Come on." Without missing a beat, she picked up the condom from the table where it had ended up, and took his hand. "Come on."

Bobby wrapped her up and kissed her as they moved into the bedroom, laughing, stopping only when their legs hit the side of the bed.

"My turn," Bobby whispered. He popped the button on her shirt with skilled fingers. The look in his eyes had Michaela's skin burning under his gaze.

Her nipples were hard, nearly pushing through the lace of her bra. Bobby lowered his mouth to one of them, flicking at it with his tongue.

"Granger," she choked, but he just chuckled low.

Michaela reached for his pants, while Bobby focused on her other nipple. By the time she was squirming under his delightful torture, she was slipping out of her jeans. Once she was naked, Bobby stepped back and looked at her.

"You're beautiful, Michaela."

"Well, it's not what it used to be." Michaela blushed. "Things have started to . . ."

Bobby cut her off, reaching for her. "You're beautiful, Michaela."

Before he could wrap her up again, Michaela stretched out on the bed. "You're not so bad yourself, Granger."

He tried not to blush as he moved onto the bed. Without the arm of the loveseat in his way, settling himself between her legs felt . . . right. If he'd been a romantic man, he'd even say it felt like coming home. Since he wasn't, he'd settle for it felt comfortable. Far more comfortable in here than on the loveseat. As Michaela began to stroke him, the debate no longer seemed important.

He was soft and solid at the same time. And Michaela couldn't help but smile to herself at how he filled her hand. Their mouths came together hungrily. Bobby's hands continued their own exploration, alternating between a firm grip and a feather touch that was setting her nerves on edge.

Nudging her legs apart with a knee, Bobby smiled as Michaela murmured his name. She released him long enough to tear at the condom wrapper. Rolling the condom onto him, she guided him into her. Bobby paused a moment, holding his breath. Below him, Michaela closed her eyes, lips parted. He waited until her hips started to move underneath him. Finding her rhythm, he met her with long, slow strokes.

Holding himself up on one elbow, he reached low with his other hand. Without missing a stroke, his fingers made circles that brought Michaela's eyes wide open, and she gasped.

He watched her, felt her body respond, and knew she was close. Michaela lifted her hips, pulling him deep inside of her. Following her lead, Bobby thrust deeper, pushed harder with his fingers. Michaela's nails dug into his shoulders. Her back arched as she gave in to the orgasm that washed over and through her body. Bobby moved slowly until her body relaxed and her breathing was almost back to normal. Before her eyes were open, her hands were on his hips, encouraging him to move again, move faster. If he'd needed more encouragement, the look in her eyes when she finally opened them was more than enough.

She put her hands on his face and brought him to her for a kiss. Her tongue in and out of his mouth matched their rhythms. Bobby's hips thrust and he groaned into the kiss with a shudder.

He wanted to collapse, pass out, stop breathing. But first . . . he kissed her, went into the bathroom and came back out again.

"You okay?" Michaela checked. She had gotten under the covers while he'd been up.

"Just taking care of business," Bobby replied. Michaela was on the right side of the bed. The covers on the left had been turned down. Accepting the implied invitation, Bobby slipped in next to her.

"Speaking of"—Michaela rolled over—"we don't need to use the condoms again. At least"—she hesitated—"not for me. It's been . . . long enough to not be an issue."

"You could've said so before." Bobby rolled his eyes. "There are no issues here, either."

Michaela defended herself. "I was distracted earlier, and you didn't say anything, either."

"Fair enough," Bobby conceded. He settled down on his back.

Michaela turned off the light and snuggled into him. "Hey, Granger?" she whispered.

"Yeah, Michaela?"

"You still got it."

He kissed her hair. "You, too, Michaela."

She batted at him but smiled into the dark.

Bobby's dream was soft. And pinkish. And smelled good. Only . . . he couldn't remember ever dreaming in color before. Or in scents. Yet both were here. The soft moved further down his chest. Oh yes, both were definitely here. A trumpet blast and orchestral swell blared next to his head and the arm over his chest wasn't quite fast enough to keep the alarm from jarring him fully awake. Michaela.

He smiled as she collapsed diagonally across him, hand still draped over the alarm clock, breasts pressed flat against his chest. She let out a soft groan as he kissed her head.

"Good morning," he spoke into her hair.

"It's early," she muttered, bringing her arm back under the covers and wrapping it along his side. Bobby folded his arms around her and let her nuzzle into him.

"Can you sleep in?" The thought was alluring.

"I wish," Michaela muttered. She sighed and lifted her head. "Morning." She smiled at him.

"'Morning." Bobby smiled back. He leaned down and kissed her gently. "Did you sleep?"

"Oh yes," Michaela practically purred. Rolling off

of him, she stretched, lifting her arms over her head, exposing her breasts. Bobby trailed a finger down her stomach. It made her toes curl. She could so easily spend the day right here, letting him touch her like that. If only. "Did you?" she asked, trying to keep her thoughts on waking up.

"Mm-hmm," Bobby responded with a lazy nod. Watching her stretch like that was making him wake up in ways he wouldn't have thought possible so soon after last night. Still, he needed to check in with Jimmy. And with Carter Anne. That was going to be an interesting conversation. But the thought of responsibilities was warring mightily with the look of Michaela, stretched out, naked, next to him.

"If you don't stop looking at me like that"—Michaela interrupted his thoughts, laughing—"all sorts of bad things will happen."

"Like what?" Bobby asked, fingers tracing her skin.

"I won't go for my run and I'll get fat."

"There are worse things than a woman with some meat on her bones," Bobby muttered. Michaela's back arched as his fingernail found one of her nipples.

"My book won't get written. I'll lose my contracts and my reputation. End up living in squalor."

"A smart woman like you?" Bobby watched, pleased, as her nipples hardened under his touch. "Bet you've got plenty saved."

"The town," Michaela gasped as he pinched gently. "Lambert Falls will collapse into anarchy and organized crime without its sheriff."

"Jimmy could do my job already. The boy's solid." Bobby leaned over and took her other nipple in his mouth, nipping playfully.

Michaela's nails dug into the sheets, giving in. It was

official; her weight, her job, and the town of Lambert Falls were doomed. It was inevitable. Except . . . shit. "Wait, Bobby."

He recognized the playfulness of her tone was gone and stopped. Sitting up, he let his hand go flat on her tummy and looked at her. "What is it, Michaela?"

"We've got about forty-five minutes before you'll have to walk by whoever is manning the volunteer desk downstairs," she sighed. "Even if you go out the back way, somebody is probably going to notice."

"Damn." He ran his fingers through his hair. "Your staying at the library seemed like a good idea at the time." Bobby smiled at her. Michaela's responding laugh was light and easy.

"And I've enjoyed it. Until now." Swinging her feet out of bed, she pulled on her robe. "How are you with a coffee pot?"

"I taught my girls everything they know."

"Then you make the coffee," Michaela said with a definitive nod before disappearing into the bathroom.

Bobby watched her go and allowed himself a moment to appreciate the skin-hugging satin of her robe before standing himself. What a turn of events this was. He shook his head but couldn't stop grinning. Looking around, he found his clothing . . . except for his shirt. Where was his shirt? And his grin became a full smile. His shirt hadn't made it to the bedroom with them. He and Michaela had given the Colonel a bit of a show before changing rooms. Okay, maybe not much of a show by today's standards, but enough of one by his own standards. He pulled on his clothes and headed to the sitting room. Sure enough, there on the table next to the open and still untouched bottle of wine, was his shirt. All of Michaela's clothes had made it into the bedroom. Maybe they'd do something about that next time. Grinning wickedly, he slipped the shirt on and headed in to make the coffee.

The brew had just finished when Michaela appeared in the doorway. Her face was scrubbed clean and she was wearing a running suit, sneakers already laced up. Bobby tried not to feel silly with his shirt hanging open and almost succeeded. Almost. It was different now, in the daylight, both of them dressed. Well, almost dressed anyway. Instead of pouring the coffee, he went to work on his buttons.

Michaela crossed the room in three long strides and covered his hands with hers. Carefully threading the buttons through the holes, she was also deliberate about caressing his skin as she moved her way down his shirt. "There," she said with mock seriousness. "Now you're ready to face the world. Respectable again."

Bobby rubbed his hands up and down her arms and looked hard into Michaela's eyes. "I won't say I've done anything disrespectable yet." He paused and thought for a moment. "Is that even a word?"

"It is." Michaela laughed and wrapped her arms around his waist. He pulled her in until her head was resting on his shoulder. "But even if it wasn't, I'd take the compliment." She sniffed the air. "And some coffee, too."

Bobby poured two mugs full and hoped she had sugar somewhere and not just the artificial stuff Carter Anne insisted on using. If not, well, caffeine was caffeine. Michaela just took a long swallow. "Oh, that is good, Granger. Compliments and coffee. What a way to start the morning." She took another drink before remembering. "I do have sugar somewhere. That's how you take it, right?"

Bobby nodded with a surprised expression. Michaela answered his unspoken question as she pulled a small box of sugar out of the cabinet and a spoon from the drawer. "I'm a writer. I get paid quite a bit of money to be observant."

"I'll remember not to try to be sneaky." Bobby took a swig of his own coffee and was grateful as the hot drink made its way into his system. "Speaking of sneaky . . ." He downed his coffee in a long swallow, his throat immune to its heat after years of guzzling on the run. He put his mug back on the counter. When was the last time he hadn't wanted to leave somewhere? Still, their window was closing. "I should go."

Michaela nodded. "I know." What the hell was she supposed to say now? "Don't forget your coat." Oh please. Don't forget your coat. Like he wasn't a grown man. She rolled her eyes at herself but reached into the closet, passing it over.

He opened the door. "Well."

"Well."

To hell with this. Bobby closed the door again and reached for her. Michaela had no memory of moving, just of being pulled into his arms and being suddenly, demandingly kissed. She kissed back with all the passion she had. Sooner or later, they would wear each other out, but it hadn't happened after only one night. Not in the least. And damned if she would let him think it had.

He set her back on her feet, grateful to hear her breathing come a little ragged, too. "I'm working the graveyard tonight so won't be around today. Need to get some extra sleep." He saw her eyes twinkle at the memory of why he needed extra sleep, but with an effort he thought should be praised, kept his hands to himself.

"But if you want a late dinner, I can ask Carter Anne to put up another plate."

Michaela didn't hesitate. "What time?"

"'Bout eleven."

"I'll see you then, Granger." Michaela smiled at him. "Now get out of here. If I'm having dinner that late, I definitely need my run or I will get fat."

Giving her a last, quick kiss on the cheek, Bobby headed out into the day. It was cold, still, and clear. The clouds from last night had moved on. Tucking his hands in his pockets, he rounded the building. Grace Mason was coming up the walk.

"'Morning, Grace," he called to her.

"Why, Sheriff, you're up and about mighty early this morning."

"And so are you, it seems," Bobby replied. It was closer than he or Michaela had intended. The key was to keep her from having a chance to ask any questions. He spoke before she could. "Opening up early today?"

"Not formally." Grace shook her head. "We just like to get here in time to make sure Miss Howard doesn't need anything in the mornings."

"That's awful nice of you, Grace." Bobby reached out and patted her arm. "I'm sure you and Betsy and the other girls are taking good care of her. I'll leave you to it, then."

Grace thanked him and moved on down the walk. He wouldn't look back. Nothing would give them away faster than looking back. Trying to look casual, Bobby walked through town, and thank God, didn't meet up with anyone else who might want to know why the sheriff was out so early.

He got to his door and opened it quietly. It had barely

closed behind him when a voice bellowed from the kitchen.

"Bobby Granger! That had better be you and you had better be dead because hand to God, if you aren't dead, I'll kill you myself!" Carter Anne wasn't happy.

"Carter Anne, honey, it is me," he called back as he hung his coat on the rack. "I'm not dead and you won't be killing me." On some level, he deserved her anger. That was true. He should've called. On another level, it was hard to take that tone of voice directed at him in his own home. He moved into the kitchen with his hands already out, but his protests and explanations died on his lips.

Carter Anne stood at the coffee pot, grinning ear to ear. She poured him a mug and added some sugar to it as she spoke in that same tone she used with her girl-friends. "You spent the night at the library, didn't you?"

Bobby leaned against the doorframe and crossed his arms over his chest. "Now, Carter Anne . . ."

"I'm not asking for details," she reassured him, as she brought him the mug. "In fact . . . ew." She gave a dramatic shudder and sat down in front of her own coffee. "I just want to know"—she batted her eyes at him—"if you spent the night with Michaela."

"A man's private life should be private, Carter Anne," Bobby teased back. "Didn't I always teach you that a boy who would tell on you wasn't worth seeing twice?" He took a sip of coffee and turned on his heel. "I'm on the overnight tonight so I'm going to sleep now. Try to be a little quiet when you leave, please." He stuck his head back through the door. "And I would appreciate it if you would put up two plates of whatever you're making me for dinner tonight."

"What?" Carter Anne exclaimed. "Two plates? You're having dinner together tonight?"

Bobby didn't say a word, just grinned. After all, some things were private. Whistling through his teeth, he headed upstairs.

Chapter 6

"Well, some people around here still feel strongly about the War of Northern Aggression." Bobby reached over and pulled the sheet up over Michaela's bare shoulder.

"The what?" Michaela asked with a laugh. She raised herself up on an elbow. Her shoulder stayed covered but a breast came bare. Bobby smiled.

"The War of Northern Aggression," Bobby repeated.

"Is that what's commonly known as the Civil War?"

"Just because it's common doesn't mean it's accurate," Bobby explained.

"Are you serious?" Michaela tried to keep the laugh out of her voice. There was something in her eyes, though. Bobby just shrugged. "Bobby." Michaela sat up and looked over at him. He sat up as well, bringing their eyes level. "I've heard you call it the Civil War. You know it's the Civil War."

"Sure," Bobby agreed.

"But . . . ?" Michaela asked.

"But," Bobby spoke simply, "some people around here still feel strongly about the War of Northern Aggression."

Michaela shook her head, trailing a finger lazily down

Bobby's bare arm. "Why is something that happened so long ago still so important?"

"Did your family come over on the Mayflower by any chance?" Bobby asked.

"Nope." Michaela shook her head. "We're pure Irish. Got here during and because of the potato famine. Almost everyone headed on up to Boston, but I had an aunt who stayed in New York. She . . ." Her voice trailed off in response to Bobby's knowing look. "Got it," she nodded with a sigh.

Silence fell, the first awkward one since that initial ride from Greensboro. Michaela wanted to say something—anything. If she could only remember what they'd been talking about before, although that had gotten them here . . . The phone rang, making her jump, but thank God for the distraction. She fumbled on the bedside table for her cell.

"Yep?" she asked into it.

Bobby swung his legs over the side of the bed and rubbed his face. He looked over his shoulder at Michaela, but she was concentrating on her phone call already. He made a drinking motion and she nodded distractedly.

"You're right," she spoke to the person at the other end of the line, "I had forgotten."

What had she forgotten? Not that it was any of his business, of course. Conversations like this one served to remind him of just that fact. Mindlessly, he pulled glasses from the cabinet and filled them with ice.

In fairness, he did call it the Civil War. Calling it the War of Northern Aggression was outdated and disregarded the causes of the conflict. Still, it was different somehow for her to laugh at it like that.

He poured the seltzer Michaela preferred and added a squeeze of lemon before filling his glass from the tap.

With a grin and a shrug, he added a squeeze to his own drink. It wasn't a horrible taste; he'd give her that much.

It wasn't right for Michaela to scoff at something that mattered to some people. It might not matter to him, but it mattered to his people. Some of them, anyway. Ah well. It didn't really matter. Not really. Sighing, he tried to ignore the sinking feeling in his gut as he headed back into the bedroom.

Michaela pulled the notepad she always kept next to her bed over onto the sheets. She was taking notes on whatever the person on the phone was telling her. Her glasses were perched on the end of her nose. They and a look of concentration were still the only things she was wearing. Bobby stopped short in the doorway, momentarily stunned. Even after the last hour, he could still feel a pull for her.

She looked up, saw the expression on his face and smiled, wickedly. Reaching out for her glass, she motioned him into the room.

"Okay, Teri." She spoke into the phone, but her eyes watched Bobby cross the room. Looking at the man was no hardship, even after spending all afternoon doing more than just looking. "Assure them I'll be there. And thanks for catching this one. I'll talk to you tomorrow."

Bobby sat on the edge of the bed, sipping his water and waiting. Michaela flipped her phone closed.

"So," she said, taking a sip of her seltzer. "Want to come to New York with me this weekend?"

Bobby swallowed, grateful he managed not to spit water on her. "New York? This weekend?"

"Sure." Michaela took off her glasses and leaned back against the headboard. "I've got an event Saturday night. Thank God Teri reminded me, because I'd completely forgotten about it. It was booked almost a year ago now."

She waved it away. "Anyway, the event is a silent auction for a historical society I support some. They think my presence might make them a little more money than usual." Her shrug both dismissed and acknowledged the possibility at the same time. "You should come with me. Give me a chance to show you my hometown."

She wanted him to go to New York with her. This weekend. What the hell was he supposed to say to this?

"Michaela," he started, searched for his words, and started again. "This weekend is short notice. I'm on. Jimmy hasn't had a weekend off in a while." He reached out and took her hand. She squeezed back.

"It's okay, Granger," she assured him. "Sometimes I forget people have regular jobs with regular schedules. Besides"—she took a sip of her seltzer—"Teri only got me one ticket."

Bobby forced a smile for her. It was the right decision. Surely it was. "I should shower before we head over to Angie and Chris's for dinner."

"Is it that late?" Michaela asked, surprised.

"Well—" Bobby paused, a twinkle in his eye. "We weren't exactly watching the clock."

"No." Michaela grinned back at him. "We weren't."

She threw the sheet back and they both stood up. As she reached for her robe, Bobby picked up his pants and started to dress.

"Nights are getting colder. Want me to pick you up? We can drive over," Bobby offered.

His definition of colder was very different from hers, but what the hell? "Sure," she accepted.

"Then I'll see you in about thirty minutes?" he confirmed, buttoning his shirt.

"Sounds like a plan." Michaela leaned in and gave him

a quick kiss. "But that means you have to go if I'm going to be ready that fast."

He grinned and turned on his heel. Michaela listened to him whistle until the tune was cut off by the closing of the door. What the hell had she been thinking, inviting Granger to New York like that? She took both glasses into the kitchen before padding into the bathroom and starting the shower. The steam began to build and she stepped under the stream of water.

At least he'd turned her down. This wasn't about him meeting her friends or seeing her apartment or being on her arm at any kind of fund-raiser. This was about some interesting male company while she was away from home. Not about taking that male company into her world. The hot water felt good over her body. It might have been her second shower of the day, but considering how she'd spent her afternoon—she smiled at the memory—it was as necessary as the first one she'd taken after her morning run.

It had been a lovely afternoon. She closed her eyes and let the water move over her the way Granger's hands had not too long ago. A lovely afternoon, indeed. No wonder she'd lost her mind and invited him home with her. Still, it was best he'd turned her down. It was.

Thirty minutes after he left, Bobby pulled back up in front of the library. Michaela stood at the curb and watched as he got out of the car, walking around to open her door for her. Why was she relieved he wasn't coming to New York with her? Because she was, she insisted to herself as she moved to the car.

"Thanks for the ride, Granger." She smiled up at him and slid into her seat. "Where's Carter Anne? I guess I expected her to be with us."

"She went over early. Dinner will be . . . better . . . that way," Bobby answered as he closed the door.

The walk to the old Montgomery house was short, so the drive was over in moments, even with Bobby doing the speed limit through town. Michaela had almost gotten used to the organized chaos that went with the comings and goings of this family. At least it wasn't as overwhelming as it had been that first night. Not completely anyway. Still, she couldn't have told Teri exactly how she'd gone from entering the house with Bobby's hand on her elbow to sitting at the kitchen table. Somehow, Angie and Carter Anne had also returned to the stove, Bobby was next to her, and Chris was getting drinks from the refrigerator. It might not be as overwhelming. It was just as fast.

Chris put a beer in front of Bobby. "Michaela?" he asked. "Seltzer with lemon or a beer?"

"How did you . . . ?" Michaela looked over at Bobby, but he was studiously looking away from her. She turned back to Chris, who only nodded, so slightly she wasn't sure she'd seen it. "I'm done working for the day. I'll take a beer, thanks."

Chris pulled a bottle for her and another for himself. He took a moment to drop a kiss on Angie's shoulder before joining Bobby and Michaela at the table.

"How are the wedding plans coming?" Michaela asked.

Angie turned from the stove, grinning. Chris smiled over his beer back at her.

"Oh, it's goin' so well. The ballroom is going to be beautiful. I think the girls have found their dresses." Her gaze moved to Chris and lingered. "Chris has even agreed to come to the tasting with me at the caterer's."

"Of course I did," Chris assured Michaela, then laughed. "There's food involved."

Angie laughed and rolled her eyes at Michaela, who laughed back in understanding.

"Carter Anne and Kerri are coming, too," Angie continued. "Why don't the two of you come along? The food should be really great."

Michaela saw the glance between the two sisters. It was nice that they wanted to include her. But to be a part of the wedding planning . . . She looked over at Bobby, but he was no help, studying his beer. Steeling her nerve, she took the strongest course of action she could find. She stalled.

"When is this happening?" she asked.

"Saturday," Carter Anne answered over her shoulder.

Michaela hoped her relief didn't show. It wasn't that she didn't want to go. It was just . . . she didn't know. Luckily, it was moot anyway.

"I've got to head back to New York this weekend," Michaela explained. "There's a fund-raiser I booked months ago."

"Really?" Carter Anne perked up.

"Just for the weekend?" Chris asked.

Bobby looked hard at his friend but Michaela answered.

"Just for the weekend. I leave late Friday and get back Sunday."

Chris looked at Bobby, but he just looked back. Shrugging, Chris let it go. Carter Anne picked it up.

"What will you be doing?"

"Well—" Michaela turned to her.

"Wait," Angie interrupted, "tell us while we eat. I think dinner's ready."

Carter Anne turned to the stove, checked the pot, and smiled. "Hope everybody likes beef stew."

Angie stepped back, chewing on a nail, while Carter Anne spooned up the bowls.

"It's okay." Carter Anne winked at her sister. "Grab the bread out of the oven before it burns, though."

Michaela took her bowl and leaned over to Bobby. "What's the big deal?"

Bobby cleared his throat. "Well—" He hesitated. How to answer this? "Angie's still learning how to cook."

"I see . . ." Michaela looked down into her bowl.

Chris leaned across the table. "She's getting a lot better." He lowered his voice. "And Carter Anne kept an eagle eye on her tonight so . . ." He sat up quickly as the girls joined them with their bowls and the bread.

"I heard that, Chris Montgomery," Angie scolded him. Then she grinned. "But she did, so hopefully we'll be okay."

Michaela had to give it to Chris. The rest of them took small spoonfuls to start, but not Chris. With confidence, he filled his spoon and took the whole bite into his mouth. Not even he, though, could hide the look of shock as he started to chew.

"Angie, babe, this is really good," he announced.

"Well, it's about damn time, hand to God," Angie sighed with relief.

The whole table laughed and tucked into their meal. Michaela took another bite of her stew, wondering what she was missing. It wasn't bad, but it didn't merit the gusto with which everyone else was eating it. It was just beef stew. Still, she wasn't sure how to ask without being rude. Before she could think of a way to find out, Carter Anne brought the conversation back around to what was really important.

"So, New York this weekend?"

Michaela nodded. "This weekend."

"What will you do?" Carter Anne asked eagerly. "A whole weekend in New York."

Michaela laughed. "Check my mail. Catch up with my best friend. Sleep in my own bed. Remember"—she reached for a slice of bread—"as exotic as it sounds, it's just home to me."

"I don't know." Carter Anne shook her head. "I don't think living there would be like living here." She motioned to the house. "I don't think I could ever find it ordinary."

"Anything can become ordinary after a while, Carter Anne," Bobby said around a bite of stew.

"Of course," Michaela interjected, "it would have been more interesting if your uncle had agreed to come with me."

"What?" Angie and Carter Anne both gasped.

"You asked him to go to New York with you?"

"You're not going to New York with her?"

They spoke at the same time. Michaela laughed and Bobby held up his hands.

"Yes, she asked me," Bobby confirmed, "and no, I'm not going."

"How can you not be going, Bobby?" Carter Anne was incredulous.

"Have you ever been?" Chris asked.

"Not you, too." Angie batted at Chris's arm. "If he doesn't want to go, he shouldn't go."

Chris looked from Bobby to Michaela and back again. She was amused. His friend, though, looked as uncomfortable as Chris had ever seen him.

"Of course," Chris continued. "It's just that New York is one of those places everybody should see at least once."

Bobby snorted and looked at Michaela. "Did you bribe him or something?"

Michaela choked back a laugh. "Not me."

"Obviously, it's your decision," Chris continued nonchalantly, "but New York is a great town."

"And," Carter Anne added, "you get to see it with a local."

"Leave him be," Angie said, taking more bread. "If he doesn't want to go, he doesn't want to go."

"How can he not want to go?" Carter Anne turned on her sister.

"It's not that I don't want to go," Bobby stressed to Michaela. Damn woman was just sitting there, eyes twinkling, lips pursed like she was trying not to laugh. He had been a cop for nearly forty years, a poker player longer than he liked to admit, and he'd raised two girls on his own. Trusting his instincts had gotten him through more than one rough spot. And now, his instincts were telling him he was in trouble here. Even Chris thought he should go. But honestly, why wasn't he going? Why had he said no in the first place? Looking at the wry amusement in Michaela's eyes, he truly couldn't remember.

"Anyway," he sighed, "I can't say I'm still invited." He raised an eyebrow at Michaela.

She grinned at him. "I think something might still be arranged."

Carter Anne kicked her sister under the table and stirred her stew.

"Hey, Bobby." Carter Anne tapped her knuckles on Bobby's open door and stepped into his room. "I was thinking about . . ."

He turned from his bed and looked at her when her voice trailed off. "What's up, Carter Anne?"

"Is that"—she pointed to the half-packed suitcase open on the bed—"um . . . is that what you're taking to New York?"

Bobby looked back at the suitcase. Two pairs of jeans, good ones. Three nice shirts. A pair of Dockers pants. Somewhere he had a tie he was planning on packing. And he knew he still needed shoes and underwear, but it was a good start. "Yes?" he asked, knowing it was the wrong answer.

"Oh, Bobby!" Carter Anne crossed into the room and pulled out the Dockers. "These?"

"They look nice. They fit. They're comfortable," he explained. "What more do I need?"

"Bobby," Carter Anne sighed. "Has living with me taught you nothing? After all these years?"

"I can pack my own suitcase." He took his pants back from her and folded them carefully. "What brought you in here in the first place?"

"Nothing as important as this." Carter Anne took his Dockers back and went to hang them in his closet. "Where's your suit?" She flipped through his clothes.

"I'm not going to win this one, am I?" Bobby asked, sitting on the edge of his bed. He'd raised her. How'd she get so stubborn?

Carter Anne's only response was a grin over her shoulder before turning back to his hanging clothes. "Bobby!" She pulled out a pair of gray woolen slacks. "These are gorgeous. Why haven't I ever seen you in them?"

Bobby shrugged.

"Why do you even have them if you never wear them?"

"I'm not a total hick," Bobby sighed. "There just aren't that many places to wear them here in the Falls."

Carter Anne tipped her head in agreement but pulled them out. "Not in the Falls, no, but in New York? Yes." She laid them out on the bed. "Why didn't you pack them?"

"Those"—Bobby pointed to the Dockers hanging back in his closet—"are comfortable."

"You mean you're comfortable in them," Carter Anne corrected.

"Isn't that what I just said?" Bobby asked.

"Not at all." She squinted at him. "And you know it." With a purse of her lips, she turned back to the job at hand. It wasn't shopping, but it was close enough. "Here." Turning around with an armful of clothing, she gave orders. "Unpack those." She indicated his suitcase with her chin. "Pack these." She laid the rest of the clothes on top of the gray pants.

"Carter Anne—" Bobby started, but she silenced him with a raised finger.

"You're not winning. Besides"—she spoke gently now—"you know I'm right."

Bobby's cough couldn't hide the blush that started at his neck. "What were you going to say when you came in?" He changed the subject.

"Right. I'm heading over to the college for a study session. You can handle dinner?"

"I think I can manage," he assured her.

With a kiss on his cheek, Carter Anne headed out. Bobby sat a moment longer, staring at the pile she had created. He was a grown man. He'd been packing for years. He sighed. There was only one thing to do; he just didn't want to do it. Hell, he'd been avoiding doing it. That's why he'd given up and packed his usual civvies. Damn woman . . . With another sigh, he reached for the phone.

Michaela answered on the second ring. "Yep?"

"Hi, Michaela." This was a stupid conversation. He was

just fine in jeans and Dockers. He should just ask her to dinner and be done with it. She'd never know. "What . . ." He coughed again. "What will we be doing this weekend? Exactly?"

"You mean besides the fund-raiser?" Michaela asked.

"Well, yes . . . and the fund-raiser . . ." Dockers had been fine. He'd been happy with Dockers.

"Bobby, what exactly are you asking, really?"

And he thought Southern women could be blunt. "What should I pack?" He had not just asked that question.

"Oh." Michaela was thrown just a bit. "Well, the fund-raiser isn't quite black tie. A suit would be fine. Then, I thought we might go out afterwards but we should have time to change clothes because it won't be as dressy." Who would've imagined she would ever be having this conversation with Granger? "Is all that manageable?"

"Of course," Bobby assured her as he emptied his suitcase. "I know exactly what to pack now." He paused. "Thank you, Michaela."

She paused. That had cost him. "You're welcome, Granger."

There was a silence between them that Bobby really didn't want to examine.

"Would you like to go to dinner?" he asked, to avoid thinking about it.

"Chinese food this time?" Michaela offered. "One of the Jones sisters mentioned it the other day and I've been craving it ever since."

"Chinese food means it was probably Mary," Bobby told her. Looking at his now empty suitcase, he ran a quick calculation. "I can pick you up in twenty minutes. Is that enough time?"

"Bring your appetite, Granger," Michaela agreed. "I'm starving."

Chapter 7

It was childlike, bordering on childish, and she knew it. She just couldn't help it. As the plane came around for its final approach, Michaela looked out her window. No matter how many times she made this trip, the sight of her city always sent a tickle of warm satisfaction through her.

"Feels good to be home, huh?" Bobby leaned around her to look outside, then looked back to her.

"Does it show?" Michaela asked with a smile.

"Maybe a little." Bobby patted her knee. Michaela squeezed his hand and held on. He bit back a smile and looked back out the window with her.

The city was huge. And dirty. He wasn't just a small-town boy. He'd traveled. He'd been to cities before. But New York was nothing like anything he'd ever seen. And that was from up here. He stole a glance at Michaela. There was no mistaking the glow of happiness in her face. The place was huge and dirty and Michaela loved it. Bobby shook his head. It sure wasn't Lambert Falls.

The plane landed and, with Michaela navigating the crowds, Bobby found himself at the bottom of the escalator leading to baggage claim. Michaela raised her hand in a wave and broke out in a huge smile. Bobby looked ahead of them. A lovely woman approached them, arms open. Michaela moved into them easily.

"Teri!" she said, wrapping her friend in a strong embrace.

"Welcome home." Teri hugged her back. She stepped away and eyed Bobby up and down. "You must be Robert Granger. I see why Michaela brought you home." She stuck out her hand.

Bobby shook it. "Call me Bobby." It was all he could think to say. A few weeks ago, he would've been put off by the woman's grip, but that was before he met Michaela. Now, he was only stunned by her statements. Not even Michaela was that blunt.

"He also answers to Granger." Michaela patted his back with a grin.

Maybe she was that blunt. "Call me Bobby," he repeated, but with a grin this time.

"Granger," Michaela continued, "this is Teri Pittman, my assistant you've heard so much about. She keeps me organized, sane, and on schedule."

"Speaking of which," Teri interjected, "do you have bags or can we go on? You're free tonight but tomorrow is busy."

"All right," Michaela sighed, "and no, no other bags."

Teri looked at Bobby, who lifted his small suitcase.

"In that case . . ." Teri turned on her heel and strode toward the doors, maneuvering with ease through the crowd.

Michaela started to follow, then paused, reaching for Bobby's hand. He took it, hoping he didn't appear as grateful as he felt for the connection.

"It may be a busier weekend than we'd expected," Michaela said as they hurried to catch up with Teri.

"This is your time," Bobby assured her. "I'm just along for the ride."

Michaela smiled at him and squeezed his hand. They stepped up to Teri, who was waiting at the curb next to an impressive town car. She started to speak as if there had been no interruption in the conversation.

"If you want any time to see the city, tonight's the night. You're having a working lunch tomorrow. Bobby, you can give him your bag. Justin has some good news. PBS is showing an interest in adapting *The Motherland Wars* into a documentary."

Bobby jumped as a hand clamped down on his suitcase. A man in a navy suit nodded at him. "I can take this, sir."

Michaela passed her bag around in front of Bobby, hardly taking her eyes off Teri. "Thank you, Steven," she said quickly, not interrupting her assistant's flow of words.

Bobby released his suitcase. The suited man—Steven—took Michaela's bag in one hand and accepted Bobby's with the other before placing them both on the curb by the car.

"I appreciate it," Bobby said, looking the man in the eye. "Thanks."

"You're welcome, Sheriff Granger," the man replied.

Bobby watched him open the back passenger door. Teri slipped into the town car, hardly missing a beat.

"He thinks he can get them to commit to a two-picture deal, minimum, but he wants to talk to you about it first." Her voice faded as she moved deeper into the car.

Michaela turned to Bobby and grinned with a sigh. "Welcome to New York."

Bobby let the two women talk, tuning them out as the car moved through the city streets. Michaela kept her hand gently on his leg, under his hand. It was a soft reminder that he wasn't alone. The car pulled over in front of a large brownstone. Michaela leaned over to Bobby.

"This is us," she whispered.

"And"—Teri took a final breath and closed the folders in her lap—"if you have a little extra time, I'd love to have a cup of coffee with you. I'm thinking Sunday before your flight out." She turned to Bobby. "Maybe give you a chance to talk."

Steven opened the door from the outside and Bobby stepped out. The other man paused, but Bobby smiled.

"I can help the lady, Steven."

Steven smiled back. "Yes sir," he acknowledged, and moved to the trunk to retrieve their bags. Michaela took Bobby's proffered hand and stepped out onto the curb. The driver started to put the bags at their feet, but Bobby took them from him. With a nod, Steven addressed both of them.

"Will you be needing me again this evening?"

"Thank you, Steven, but no. Our plans aren't set for tonight." She waved to Teri and turned toward the door of her building. It might only be for a weekend, but she was home. Pulling the keys from her purse, she let Bobby carry their bags up the front steps. He paused in the entryway and looked around, but Michaela crossed to the elevator and hit the button. She turned to see Bobby examining the building.

"Bobby?"

He looked over to her. "Mid–eighteen hundreds? Expert renovations, obviously, but still no later than eighteen ninety, right?"

"How'd you know that?" Michaela asked.

Bobby shrugged. "You're not the only author I read." He grinned over to her.

The elevator doors opened behind Michaela so he crossed the space, a bag in each hand.

"Probably," he continued, as the doors closed after them, "a single family home originally."

"Converted in the fifties," Michaela confirmed with a nod.

"How many condos?" Bobby asked. Five floors, including the lobby, in the building. As big as the place was, there could be as few as eight, as many as twelve.

"Four," Michaela answered, eyes on the floor indicator lights above their heads.

"Four?"

"Four," she repeated, glancing over at him.

The elevator opened to a small entryway. The door to the stairwell was immediately next to them and another antique oak door was directly in front of them. A discrete, wrought-iron 3 was below a small square that the occupant inside could slide open and look through.

Michaela still had her keys out and used two on the ring to open a deadbolt and the knob lock. Bobby watched silently.

"It must seem excessive to a man who doesn't even lock his door." Michaela glanced at him, then looked away. "It's just . . . New York, you know . . . it's not . . ."

"I lock my doors," Bobby interrupted. "Taught my girls to do it, too."

Michaela smiled her gratitude and opened the door.

"Oh, God, it's good to be home," Michaela breathed as she moved into the condo. "Come on in. I'll show you around."

Bobby took two steps in when it hit him. It smelled

like her. There was no one particular scent he could
identify. It was just . . . Michaela. He recognized it from
her rooms at the library, but that was faint, almost an
echo, compared to this.

She strode into the room and opened thick tapestry
curtains, revealing a view of the skyline that would only
be more impressive as night fell. The whole place would
only be more impressive. Maybe Carter Anne was right;
maybe some places never became ordinary.

"This is, obviously, the living room." Michaela indicated the room around them. She sighed. It had only
been a few weeks, but it felt like much longer since she'd
been surrounded by her things. All she really wanted to
do was light her candles, maybe a fire, open a bottle of
wine and curl up on her couch, in her home, with her . . .
friend.

"Michaela?" Bobby looked concerned. "You okay?"

"Sure." She shook herself. "Just tired. Come on." She
moved into the bedroom. "You can drop the bags in
here."

The room was large enough to hold her king-size bed
without being crowded. The pillows and comforter were
as luxurious and beckoning as the overstuffed furniture
in the other room. The walls were a warm, subtle coral
color that complemented the dark wood molding and
hardwood floors. The piece that drew Bobby's eye,
though, was a cream velvet chaise longue. He remembered finding a piece similar to it when they were cleaning out the old Montgomery place for Angie and Chris.
Carter Anne had draped herself along it, in her best
Scarlett O'Hara impression. Somehow, he could see
Michaela in a similar position here, only the image in his
head looked right, not like his niece playing around. She
would read there, dressed in a long satin nightgown,

glasses perched on her nose. Or maybe take notes, curled up in pajamas and fuzzy slippers. He'd never seen her like that, but he could. Easily.

"So." Michaela rubbed her hands together. Maybe this hadn't been the best idea. Granger was standing in her bedroom, studying it as if it were a crime scene. "Teri came by yesterday. Put clean sheets on the bed. Made sure the towels weren't dusty." Dear God, she was justifying herself. "Anyway—" She straightened her back, determined to move on. "You can hang up clothes in here." She crossed the room and opened the closet. Bobby tried not to gasp. Her closet was the size of his bathroom back home. "Bathroom's in here." She opened the door next to the closet.

Even this room showed her sense of elegant sophistication. Cream-colored marble with thick coral-colored towels and accessories. Candles lined the edge of the oversize tub.

"Nice," Bobby said honestly. "I think this is what Carter Anne and Angie always hoped for when they would pester me about redoing their bathroom."

"What'd you give them?" Michaela asked.

Bobby grinned. "Let 'em paint it pink."

Michaela laughed. This was her friend, Granger. The location might be different, but the man was the same.

"Come on." She took his hand. "We don't have a lot of time, unfortunately, not if I'm going to show you around at all."

Bobby started to speak, but Michaela was already moving on. She led him through the rest of the condo.

"Carter Anne and Angie would love to host a party here," Bobby said when they got to the formal dining room.

"So long as Carter Anne did the cooking," Michaela added with a laugh.

Bobby nodded emphatically. "Angie designs the table, though. Trust me on this one, too."

"Well, maybe she can . . ." Michaela stopped talking. "The kitchen is through here." She spoke quickly, trying to cover her slip. What had gotten into her?

Bobby walked under the stone archway separating the two rooms. Had he ever seen a stone archway in anyone's home?

The kitchen was as impressive as the rest of the home. Stone tiles with copper accents and stainless steel appliances. More copper, pots this time, hanging over the island in the center of the room. Windows across the back showed a view only slightly less breathtaking than the one out the front.

Bobby whistled through his teeth. "I take it back. This is where Carter Anne would want to be."

"Somehow," Michaela said, "I think *that*"—she pointed out the window to the city below—"is where Carter Anne would want to be."

Bobby chuckled. "You've got her pegged."

"Keep your fingers crossed." Michaela crossed hers and opened the refrigerator, stooping to inspect the contents. "Oh, Teri! This is why you are worth every cent I pay you." Michaela stood up, holding a cold bottle of champagne. "Flutes are behind you." She pointed over Bobby's shoulder.

"Champagne?" Bobby asked, but pulled the flutes off the wineglass rack hanging under the cabinet behind him. "Shouldn't we save that for after your shindig tomorrow?"

"There's another bottle in there if we want it then," Michaela assured him. She opened the bottle with a practiced hand.

Bobby held out the glasses and she filled them. He

handed her one. Michaela put the bottle on the counter and tipped her glass to him. "Welcome to my home, Granger."

Bobby clinked his glass to hers. There she was. There was his . . . his friend . . . Michaela. In that wry smile and that teasing tilt of her head. He exhaled, comfortable for the first time since they landed. "Nice to be here, Michaela."

They wandered into the living room. That view was breathtaking. What would that view cost her, never mind the space? He couldn't imagine.

"You know what I want to do?" Michaela asked with a sigh.

"Somehow, I don't think it's race around town, showing me what's still open this late," Bobby responded with a smirk.

"It's not late for New York, but you'd be right." Michaela propped herself on the back of the couch, looking out at her city.

Bobby sipped his champagne—good Lord, champagne—thinking. "A club?"

Michaela shook her head. "That's tomorrow, after the auction."

"Your favorite restaurant? Some place that isn't Sartini's or mediocre Chinese food from Chow's?" Bobby tried again.

"Still no. But closer," Michaela conceded.

Bobby leaned up against the couch next to her. "Then what?"

"All I really want to do tonight is curl up right here, turn on an old movie, and order in Indian food." Michaela sighed again. "Just be at home."

"Indian food?" Bobby asked.

Michaela shrugged. "Or grinders. Or much-better-than-mediocre Chinese food," she laughed. "But stay here, with some good food, that whole bottle of champagne, and two of us, curled up on the couch."

Reaching out, Bobby smoothed a curl of her hair. "That sounds really nice, Michaela. But it seems we came an awfully long way to do something we could've done in the Falls."

Michaela chuckled and shook her head. "Not quite."

Bobby nodded. "I know."

She breathed deeply and leaned her head into his palm for a moment. "However . . ."

Bobby stroked her cheek with his thumb. "Is there any reason we can't do just that?"

"We have a night in New York City and you want to hang out in my apartment?" Michaela was incredulous.

"Michaela—" Bobby settled himself on the couch back. "I'm here with you. I meant it when I said it. Not to take a whirlwind tour of New York."

She gave him a tired, grateful look. "Seriously?"

"If I'd really wanted to see the city, I'd've come up before now," Bobby assured her.

"Oh, Granger, you're the best." She stood up. "I'd like you even if I didn't need your help with the Colonel."

Bobby laughed. "You're not so bad yourself"—his eyes twinkled—"for a Yankee."

Michaela finished the last swallow of her champagne. "In that case, let me go shower. Wash the airplane air off of me. Will you be okay while I'm in there, or should you join me?"

Bobby chuckled low. "As tempting as that is, I'll be fine. You relax. I need to check in with Carter Anne, anyway."

Michaela leaned over and kissed Bobby quickly. "I won't be too long. And I'll save you some hot water."

Bobby watched her head into the other room. It was a nice view. Once she was out of sight, he stood up and looked out the window.

It was beautiful. He thought there were probably more lights just outside her window than there were in all of Lambert Falls. Of course, there were no stars, either. This would be a great city to visit; he could definitely understand why Chris and Carter Anne had encouraged him to come. But Michaela was welcome to it full-time.

Thinking of Carter Anne got him up away from the couch and away from the window. His phone was in the bedroom, in his coat. He could hear Michaela singing through the closed bathroom door. A particularly flat note made him grin—and decide to place the call from the living room. Carter Anne answered on the second ring.

"Hi, honey," he said as way of introduction.

"Bobby!" his niece squealed. "Are you there? Is it wonderful? What's her apartment like?"

"Slow down, Carter Anne," Bobby said, intentionally calm. "Yes, we're here. I don't know if it's wonderful, but it's big. And her apartment's very nice."

"I still can't believe you're in New York City," Carter Anne gushed. "What're you doing now?"

"Talking to you."

"Bobby—" Carter Anne pouted. "You know what I mean."

"You're right. I'm sorry," Bobby said, laughing. "Michaela's in the shower. Tonight we're just going to be here. Order in some dinner."

"You're staying in?" Carter Anne gasped.

"Yes, Carter Anne. We're staying in."

"But you'll be busy tomorrow, right?"

"Starting with a business lunch with her agent," Bobby assured her.

"And after that?" she asked. She sounded as excited for his trip as if she were here herself.

"The auction we're here for, and then Michaela mentioned something about a club."

Carter Anne sighed. "A New York club. Sounds wonderful."

"But tonight, it's an easy night here in the house," Bobby repeated.

"All right," Carter Anne sighed. Bobby laughed. He could practically see her rolling her eyes at them. "Just remember to have some fun."

"I'm sure we will," he assured her.

"And come home ready to tell me everything," Carter Anne bubbled. "Wait. Maybe not everything."

"Now, Carter Anne," Bobby scolded, but his niece just laughed.

The water in the other room went off. It was time for him to shower. "Honey, I need to go. I want to get dinner ordered."

"I'll tell Angie you made it safe," she assured him. "Tell Michaela I said hi."

"We'll see you in a couple of days," Bobby said. He waited until Carter Anne had disconnected before hanging up himself. Listening hard, he couldn't hear Michaela in the bedroom yet, so figured he had just enough time. He and Carter Anne kept the menu to Chow's in the phone desk. Angie and Chris kept Chow's and one for a pizza place in Ashby that Chris liked, in a drawer in the kitchen. There was a desk close to the front door. He checked there first. Sure enough, there was a stack of menus. The one on the top was an Indian place. The dishes were a mystery. He looked around the corner, but the bedroom door was still closed. The next menu in the pile was a Chinese place. The blue paper was marked up with certain items starred or circled. Fine. He'd choose a couple of those and hope they were her favorites.

He was hanging up the phone as Michaela opened the bedroom door. She was in a salmon-colored satin pajama set.

"There's still lots of hot water if you want it, Granger." She walked into the kitchen, where Bobby met her with the bottle of champagne and both flutes. He topped hers off.

"I'll take you up on that, if you're sure."

"When I bought this place, I installed an extra-large-capacity hot water heater," Michaela explained. "I don't like running out in winter."

"In that case . . ." Bobby finished the last of his champagne and put the flute down on the counter. He headed into the bedroom, but stopped at the door. "I ordered Chinese food from the menu in the drawer. Figured it would be better than mediocre." He took the image of her smile with him into the shower.

By the time he came back out, Michaela was setting up plates on the coffee table so they could eat while looking out on the city. She looked up as he came into the room.

"You want to borrow a robe? You didn't have to get dressed again."

Bobby looked down at his fresh T-shirt and clean jeans, then to her satin ensemble. Somehow, he couldn't see himself in a matching robe. "These are fine."

"I think you'd be cute in salmon silk," she said, reading his mind.

"And I think I'll stick with this." Bobby sat down and draped an arm across the back of the sofa. Michaela snuggled in next to him.

"Oh, Granger, thank you for this." She rested her head on his arm and closed her eyes.

"You know, if I was at home," Bobby spoke, "I'd probably be reading one of your books."

"Really?" Michaela looked at him. "You reread?"

"You take too long between books not to," Bobby explained.

"What are you going to do when the Colonel's book comes out? You already know the story."

"I hadn't thought about it. Reread another one, I guess." Bobby grinned.

Before Michaela could respond, the intercom sounded.

"Dinner!" She jumped up and buzzed the delivery man into the building. "How much did you order?" she asked once he was gone. "It's so heavy."

Bobby shrugged. "Most everything that was marked on the menu, plus some of my favorites."

Carton after carton came out of the bag. Michaela was amazed but happy. He had, indeed, ordered all of her favorites. They could eat for a week. Plates loaded, they dug in. It was better than Chow's, he'd give her that. Much better, actually. Good enough that neither of them spoke much, but just smiled at each other, chopsticks clicking away.

She was relaxing, happy. He could see it. Home and this kind of comfort looked good on her. Real good.

"Why're you looking at me like that, Granger?" Michaela asked, finally putting her plate down, stuffed.

"Like how?" he asked, stacking his plate on top of hers.

"Like you'd rather have me for dessert than a fortune cookie."

"A smart woman like yourself can probably figure that one out," Bobby answered, his voice low.

"How do you feel about cleaning up in the morning?" she asked, her voice matching his.

"I think it's a fine idea."

They stood up. Bobby took her into his arms, kissing her deeply. She broke away and took his hand, leading him into the bedroom.

Their bodies found each other familiarly in spite of the new surroundings. Bobby's fingers remembered her most sensitive places. Michaela knew the pressure he preferred under her hands, her mouth. Under his touch, Michaela reacted the way she always did. Bobby let out a breathy sigh as Michaela's kisses made his body respond. When he lay her on her back and she opened her legs for him, they were both ready.

Bobby slid inside her, giving in to the welcoming embrace. Michaela slipped her legs around his hips, guiding him. Their pace was slow, almost sleepy, but the tickle in her stomach was building insistently.

"Oh yes, Granger," she whispered into his neck, "yes." The tickle was growing, spreading, in response to his long, slow movements.

Her heart rate was picking up under him. He could feel her breath coming faster, as his was getting more ragged. She was getting close. They moved together; they built together. And finally, when she started to spasm, pulling on him, tugging at him, they exploded together.

He wanted to snuggle her, share pillow talk, listen to her whispers in the dark. He wanted to do all of those things. If only he wasn't so full, so satisfied, so . . . happy.

"What's our schedule tomorrow?" he found the energy to ask.

"Mmmm . . . what was that, Granger?" She lifted

herself up and looked down at him. "I didn't quite hear you."

"What—" Bobby cleared his throat and found his voice again. "What's the schedule tomorrow?"

"Lunch with Justin at one and then Steven will pick us up at seven for the auction at eight." She snapped off the lamp next to the bed and stretched out next to Bobby. "You're not going to see much of New York, Granger."

Bobby placed a kiss on her temple. "I told you before, I'm seeing as much as I want to be seeing."

With a smile, Michaela fell asleep in her bed, in her city. Home again.

Chapter 8

"You must be Bobby Granger. I'm Justin Erixon." Justin stood up from the table, extending his hand. Bobby shook it and held one of the chairs for Michaela.

"Hello to you, too," Michaela teased Justin.

"Please." Justin rolled his eyes. "I know you. He's the new guy," Justin teased back, but he still embraced her warmly. "Seriously, though," he continued after they had all taken their seats, "it's nice to meet you."

"And it's nice to meet the man who forgot to tell us Howard Michaels was a woman," Bobby joked dryly.

Justin laughed. "Did I forget to mention that?"

"Justin has an unusual sense of humor," Michaela said with a roll of her eyes.

A server came by with menus and took their drink orders. By the time the waitress returned with three coffees, they were ready to order. The basics handled, Justin turned back to Bobby.

"How do you like the city?"

"We're not getting to see much of it, I'm afraid," Michaela answered for him. "I just wanted to stay home last night and today's all business."

"But we had great Chinese delivery, so it wasn't a complete loss," Bobby joked.

Justin stared at him for a moment before starting to laugh. "I like him, Mike. Tell me"—he turned his attention to her—"does Sean know you're in town?"

"No." Michaela spoke quickly, giving her agent a stern look. "Not this weekend. So, how's the baby?"

Justin grinned. Reaching for his wallet, he produced pictures of a beautiful woman and an even prettier baby girl. Bobby looked politely and made the appropriate noises. Still, he hadn't missed the hard look Michaela had given the other man when he had mentioned Sean—whoever that was. He'd let it go for now, but it was worth a conversation. He didn't want to be trespassing, so to speak.

"And how's the book coming?" Justin asked, putting away the pictures. "All issues with access resolved?"

"The access issues are handled, even if Betsy's still not happy." Michaela and Bobby exchanged amused smiles. "And the book is coming along well."

"Really?" Justin double-checked.

"Well, enough that I completely forgot about this weekend and didn't want to break away from it," Michaela explained.

"I see you were so unwilling that you brought your primary research source with you," Justin noted.

"Sure, Justin." Michaela matched his amused sarcasm. Bobby just sipped his coffee. "Moving on," Michaela continued, all business, "what was Teri telling me about PBS?"

Justin's enthusiasm was interrupted as the server brought their food. "Why, when we need some time to really talk, is this the one time the kitchen decides to break a speed record?" he muttered. "Anyway"—he

stressed the word as everyone settled into their meals—
"they want to make *The Motherland Wars* into a TV special."

"And what do you think about it?" Michaela asked
him.

"Mike," Justin sighed, "of course you should do it. I
wouldn't have brought it to you if I didn't think you
should do it."

"For what it's worth," Bobby spoke up, "that's probably my favorite of your books. I think it could be done
really well."

"See?" Justin lifted his hands, motioning to Bobby.

"However"—Bobby turned to Justin—"I think it could
be done really badly, too. How much say will Michaela
have over whether it's done well or not?"

Michaela lifted an eyebrow, waiting for Justin's response.

"It would be your first television program, Mike."
Justin directed his answer to Michaela, but included
Bobby in the conversation as well. "So you may not be
able to get as much input as you will eventually. At the
same time, I can get you enough that they won't be able
to make any major changes that you don't like."

"Teri mentioned the possibility of two?" Michaela
asked. She would decide once she had all the information, not before.

"I was thinking about pitching two, yeah. Either the
one you just finished up or"—he turned to Bobby—"we
could contract now for the rights to the current book."

Bobby stopped with his fork halfway to his mouth,
cleared his throat, then continued eating. Michaela was
looking at him, too.

"What do you think, Granger?"

He bought some time by chewing more than he really
needed to. A television program about his family, his

town . . . hand to God. "I'd have to think about it. Talk to the girls."

"Unfortunately, Bobby," Justin said, "you don't have a lot of time to think about it. I'm meeting with them Monday and really need to be able to pitch."

"Then the answer is no," Bobby answered plainly. He turned to Michaela. "I'm sorry."

"There are other books." Michaela reached out and touched his hand.

"Now don't answer so quickly." Justin started the sales pitch. "This could be a big deal for Lambert Falls. Think about it. The Colonel's story is completely intertwined with the town's. Your family could benefit, too. Plus," he continued, "since we're talking about PBS, the exposure would be nice, but probably wouldn't mean absolute craziness." He stopped to take a breath and Bobby took the opportunity to speak up.

"Even a little craziness is too much, Justin." His voice was soft, calm, determined. "Without any time to think about it, talk it over with my girls—" Bobby shrugged. "I know I don't really have a say in it, but you asked, so I'm answering."

"Michaela—" Justin turned to his client. "Talk to him."

Michaela shook her head. "I've written other books, Justin. You said so yourself."

Justin laughed with a bark. "My God. Okay. I'll pitch the UK book along with *The Motherland Wars.*" He tilted his head toward Bobby. "But if you change your mind by Monday—"

It was Bobby's turn to laugh. "You'll be the first person to know."

"So tell me about Lambert Falls." Justin changed the subject.

Michaela and Bobby kept him amused with stories of the town, filling in the details of people Michaela had been mentioning for the last several weeks. He was entertained by Betsy Abernathy's attempts to both attract Bobby for years, and run Michaela off since her arrival. By the end of the meal, he was convinced that the Falls was exactly where Michaela needed to be in order to write a good book. He paid the bill and the three of them headed out to the street.

"It was good to meet you, finally, Bobby." Justin clapped him on the shoulder. "Michaela—" He hugged her. "Knock 'em dead tonight. I know you will. And be sure to stay in touch."

"You know I will." She hugged him back. "Let me know how Monday goes. And give my love to Andrea and the baby."

"Absolutely," Justin agreed. Giving them a last wave, he headed down the street.

"We're this way," Michaela said, walking in the other direction.

"Thank you for not pushing about the TV show," Bobby said, falling into step next to her.

"It's one of the things that makes him such a great agent, actually," Michaela said. "He gets excited."

"And thinks very quickly," Bobby added.

Michaela laughed. "Justin does everything quickly."

"And this coming from another New Yorker." Bobby sighed. Now was probably the best time. Might as well get it out of the way. "Can I ask you a question?"

"Sure," Michaela answered. "Anything."

"You changed the subject awful quick when Justin mentioned someone named Sean."

"Ah yes." Michaela nodded. "Sean."

Bobby knew what he wanted to ask. He just didn't

know how to ask it. He wasn't a jealous man. It wasn't about that. He just didn't want . . . he wasn't sure what he didn't want. But he knew he needed to know. "Am I stepping on another man's toes?"

Michaela stopped mid-stride. "I beg your pardon?" She was trying not to laugh, but the phrase was so quaint.

"I know what you and I have—and what we don't have," Bobby added quickly. "I'm just not real comfortable with another man waiting on a phone call from you this weekend . . ." He trailed off, still not sure what he was saying.

"Granger." Michaela cupped his cheek. "There's no one but you right now. I promise. Sean is—" She thought for a moment. "A friend of mine who sometimes accompanies me to events like tonight's."

"And is he a friend friend," Bobby asked, "or is he a friend like I'm a friend?"

"Aren't you a friend friend, Granger?"

Bobby sighed in exasperation. "You know what I mean, Michaela."

"We've had a sexual relationship in the past, yes." It was the moment of truth. How would he react? She realized she was holding her breath.

"But not now?"

"Not now," Michaela assured him. "We had . . . an understanding. But he moved to Boston about a year ago. Justin always hopes he'll come in for events. Doesn't think it's good business for me to be going stag."

Bobby took her hands and lowered his forehead to hers. "I've had . . . understandings, too."

Michaela exhaled. The noise of the streets and the traffic came back. The city was alive and all around them.

"Thanks for being honest, though," he added.

Michaela kissed him quickly. "Thanks for asking instead of just assuming. Now—" She started walking again. "Let me show you just a little bit of my city on the way home."

The town car pulled up right at seven, just as Michaela and Bobby closed the building door behind them. Steven had the passenger door open by the time they had reached the curb.

"Good evening, Ms. Howard, Sheriff Granger," he said as Michaela slipped into the backseat. He shut the door behind Bobby and got in to drive them.

"Do you mind if we don't stay long?" Michaela asked Bobby.

"I wasn't expecting to be out late. Early is fine with me," Bobby assured her.

"Steven—" Michaela raised her voice so the driver could hear her. "This will be a short night. Just an hour or so." She sighed, thinking realistically. "Maybe two."

"Very well, Ms. Howard." Steven acknowledged her in the rearview mirror. "I'll simply park out front. You come out when you're ready."

Michaela turned to Bobby and reached up to straighten the knot in his tie. "I should've told you this inside, but"— she trailed her fingers down his tie—"you look really nice tonight."

Bobby clasped her fingers in his. She had such small hands. Perfectly painted nails. He studied them for a moment. She shouldn't have had to say it first. But when he'd come out of the bedroom and seen her there, looking out the window . . . Her legs had gone all the way up. He knew what was underneath the black silk dress, but it hadn't mattered. It was like he was fifteen again, and he hadn't even been able to tell her how beautiful she was that night or any other night.

"Okay, then." Michaela pulled her hand away and tried to look out the window.

Bobby stopped her with a touch to her cheek. "Michaela." He took her hand again.

When she looked back at him, she wasn't quite able to hide her hurt.

"Never mind saying it earlier." Bobby entwined his fingers with hers. "You shouldn't have had to say it first." Michaela's eyes softened as he continued. "You just took my breath away. You're beautiful."

"Oh." Michaela smiled at him almost shyly. "Thank you."

Steven looked back at the street with a smile. It was about time he'd seen someone treat her like a lady and not like a business associate back there. Shame the sheriff wasn't from the city. But maybe that's why he treated her so well. Glancing in the rearview mirror again, he watched as Bobby placed a kiss on Michaela's knuckles. Unless he was mistaken, she was blushing.

Focusing entirely on the traffic, Steven gave them as much privacy as possible. Nothing inappropriate would happen—had ever happened—in the backseat. Ms. Howard was too much of a lady. Still, they didn't need him watching them in the mirror.

Before Bobby realized it, Steven had pulled over, stopped, and was opening the door curbside. Maybe he'd get used to another man opening his door—but he doubted it. At least Steven had gotten used to him. The driver had stepped aside so Bobby could be the one to help Michaela out of the car.

"Thank you, Steven," he said as he stepped out and reached for Michaela's hand.

"We're in and out tonight, Steven," Michaela reiterated. "Hopefully, anyway," she added with a wry smile.

"I'll be here, Ms. Howard," Steven assured her.

Taking a deep breath, Bobby escorted Michaela into the building. A round, balding man in a black suit met them just inside the door.

"Michaela, thank you for joining us this evening!"

"Joseph." Michaela reached out for him. They clasped hands and air kissed, cheek to cheek.

"And it's so good to see you again, Mr. . . . ." The man turned to Bobby and clamped his mouth shut with a click of his teeth.

"Joseph"—Michaela stepped in quickly—"let me introduce my friend, Bobby Granger. He's helping me with my latest book."

"Ah, Robert." Joseph recovered quickly. "So good to meet you. Welcome."

"Thank you." Bobby shook the man's hand. "And call me Bobby."

"Bobby?" Joseph asked before correcting himself again. "Bobby it is." He included Michaela in the conversation. "Please, come in. Everyone is excited to have a chance to meet you in person." He turned and started walking them through a small lobby. Bobby took Michaela's arm as they followed him.

"I'm so sorry," Michaela whispered.

"Michaela"—Bobby patted her arm—"I came into the middle of this story. It's okay."

She rested her head on his shoulder momentarily. "Thanks, Granger."

He had a chance to drop a kiss into her hair before she straightened up. They reached the door to the large event room. With a nod and a smile, Joseph waved them into the room and let them be.

"Here we go," Michaela sighed. She slipped her arm out of Bobby's as they entered the room.

The lights were dimmed. The walls were lined with tables covered in auction items and their descriptions. About a hundred people mingled, chatted, and walked the tables, stopping occasionally to read a write-up or comment on an item.

"Want a glass of wine?" Bobby asked her. There was a small bar set up in a corner.

"No," Michaela declined. "I don't like to drink at these things." She turned to him. "Feel free to have a glass if you'd like, though."

Bobby shook his head. "No need."

An older woman approached and spoke to Bobby. "Are you Howard Michaels?"

"Oh, no." He motioned to Michaela.

"I'm Michaela Howard," she spoke up. "I write as Howard Michaels."

"Oh my," the woman gushed, "it's so nice to meet you. My husband is an even bigger fan. Would you come meet him? He'll be thrilled. Shocked, but thrilled."

"I'd be honored," Michaela answered. She turned to Bobby, who nodded and smiled. With a quick squeeze of his hand, Michaela followed the woman.

Bobby watched as she engaged the couple. Her appreciation of her fans was so obviously sincere. While he knew she was hoping to be in and out quickly, they would never guess it. Now that she was here, she was doing right by them.

As if she could feel him, Michaela looked over at Bobby. She returned his smile and raised her eyebrows to check in with him. He lifted his hand to assure her he was fine, then gave a jerk of his head to the closest table. Michaela nodded and gave her attention back to the couple.

He might as well look at what was being offered for auction. Negotiating the crowd was easy enough, as everyone was moving in a choreography that allowed the best possible opportunity to see all the items. The first item was an original piece of art by an artist he didn't know. The two-foot sculpture twisted around and folded back on itself in a Möbius strip of green metal. It was . . . different. The paper next to it had the minimum bid set at three hundred dollars. It had already doubled. Giving a low whistle, Bobby stuck his hands in his pockets. Six hundred bucks for a piece of painted metal was a bit out of his range.

Maybe he would have a glass of wine after all. He moved through the room again with a little more effort now that he was moving away from the tables, against the flow. Armed with a glass of wine, he looked over to the table next to the bar. This was apparently the gemstone table. Angie and Carter Anne might know what he was looking at, but, well, there were no diamonds or pearls, so the extent of his knowledge was useless here. A man dressed in Colonial American garb stepped up next to him with a cheese tray. With a grateful nod, Bobby speared a cube and accepted a napkin. Nibbling on the Gouda, he kept looking around.

Michaela was engrossed in a conversation with two older gentlemen now. Most of the people in the room were his and Michaela's age or even older. It seemed historical societies didn't draw many younger people. He certainly couldn't see Carter Anne spending an evening here willingly. Although she had been right about the suit. His Dockers wouldn't have worked here.

Another server, a woman dressed in an Elizabethan-era gown, stopped by. He put his empty wineglass on the tray she was carrying. Maybe some air would help.

He made his way through the room yet again, heading to the door. The temperature had dropped. There was, he thought, the smell of winter in the air—underneath all the other odors that, really, he didn't need to identify.

"Sheriff Granger?" A voice behind him asked the question.

Bobby turned. Steven had approached him from the car on the corner.

"Is everything all right?" Steven asked.

"Sure." Bobby nodded.

Steven waited, but Bobby didn't say anything else.

"Well," Steven continued, "if everything's okay . . ." He thumbed over his shoulder, back toward the car.

"So you have to stay out here through the whole event?" Bobby asked him.

Steven turned back with a shrug. "It's part of the job."

"Do you work for Michaela?"

"Oh, no." Steven shook his head. "Mr. Erixon keeps my company on retainer. I've driven for Ms. Howard, at her request, for a couple years now."

Bobby nodded his head. For the life of him, he couldn't come up with anything else to talk about, to keep him out here. He sighed. "I guess I have to get back in there."

"It's that much fun, huh?" Steven asked.

"Six hundred dollars for twisted green metal," Bobby answered.

Steven laughed. "I'll be out here if you need another break."

Bobby smiled at him. It was time to head back in.

Michaela waved to him as soon as he stepped into the door of the event room. If he felt a twinge of pride to be heading to the side of the most striking woman in the room, well, he was man enough to admit it. She reached for his hand as he took his place beside her.

"There you are." Michaela smiled. Who wouldn't smile when the best-looking man in the room was looking at her like that? "I'd like to introduce you to some friends." She turned to the couple standing with her. "Thom, Nita, this is Bobby Granger. One of the descendants of my Colonel and"—she squeezed Bobby's hand—"a good friend of mine."

Bobby shook their hands.

"These are two of the society's largest donors," Michaela continued.

"And two of Michaela's biggest fans," the man said.

"That we have in common," Bobby agreed. "I'd read everything she'd ever written, even before she came to the Falls."

"You must have been thrilled to have her interested in writing about your ancestor," the woman added.

"It was a pretty big deal, all right," Bobby conceded.

"But I think Grang—" Michaela caught herself. "Bobby was the only one who'd even heard of me, let alone read my stuff, before I got to town."

"And even I was surprised when a woman walked off the plane," Bobby added.

"Really?" Nita asked. "I guess I never thought about it. We only know her as a woman."

"I'd never thought about it, either." Bobby smiled. "I only ever knew her as a man."

The group laughed.

"So what do you think of the auction?" Thom asked.

"I'm not sure the artwork is quite my style," Bobby confessed, waving to the sculpture table.

Thom laughed. "Be sure to check out the books

table. It's less flamboyant, admittedly, but less ostentatious as well."

Nita elbowed him, but they all laughed again.

"Should we check them out?" Bobby asked Michaela.

"Love to," Michaela agreed. "I haven't gotten over there yet."

"It was good to meet you." Bobby shook hands with Thom and Nita again. Michaela gave them kisses on each cheek before taking Bobby's arm.

They hadn't taken four steps before another woman stepped up to Michaela, wanting to chat.

"Go on," Michaela whispered to Bobby. "I'll try to get to you." She turned her smile to the new woman as Bobby continued across the room. The table was devoted entirely to Michaela's collection. A large picture of the man Bobby recognized from the back of her books was framed next to hard copies of each of her books.

"Do you know Michaels's work?"

Bobby turned to the man next to him. "I do."

"By the look of the bid sheet, we're not alone. Technically, since I was here first, I should push in and get my bid down before you reach for your pen."

Bobby took a step back. "Be my guest. I'm not bidding."

"Not even for a complete set of first editions, personally inscribed to the winner?"

"I've got all her first editions. Bought 'em when they first came out," Bobby explained.

"Me, too," the man laughed. "I was just trying to get the price up for her and the society."

"You know Michaela?" Bobby asked.

"She and I go way back. You?"

"Not as long," Bobby conceded, extending his hand. "Bobby Granger."

"Kenneth Bateman." The men shook hands. "Last I heard, she was down in Podunk, Virginia, somewhere, tracking down an obscure general and his descendants."

Bobby coughed hard. "Yep, that's what I'd heard, too." The man might have been tall and had a full head of sandy blond hair, but his height had stooped his shoulders and the corners of his eyes were unnaturally smooth. Plus, he was an idiot. Surely, he didn't know Michaela well.

As if he'd spoken the thought aloud, Ken continued, "Michaela and I met ten years ago or so, and I've never known her to be away from home this long. She just barely got back from Europe when she left again."

Bobby nodded. Two could play this game. "She hasn't been away from home this long since her first couple of books. Decided then she didn't like it. Calls it her 'rookie mistake.'"

"Really?" They locked eyes. "And how do you know Michaela?"

"I'm the sheriff of Podunk, Virginia. Only it's actually called Lambert Falls, North Carolina."

At least the other man had the decency to look abashed, even if he didn't quite blush. "My apologies, Sheriff." The tension stretched. Ken looked away first. "Well, I should see what else is available. Maybe there's something I'm interested in bidding on."

"I'd suggest the table with all the statues. You'll probably like 'em."

The two men nodded at each other and Ken made his way through the crowd. Bobby turned to the table of Michaela's books, exhaling through gritted teeth. With an effort, he unclenched his fists. When was the last time someone had gotten to him like that? Hand to God, he couldn't remember. Two more deep breaths and he felt in control again.

Nearly an hour later by Bobby's watch—but who was counting—Michaela finally put her hand on his shoulder. "Want to get out of here?" she asked with a sympathetic smile.

"Don't you need to stay to the end of this thing?" Bobby asked, unwilling to get his hopes up.

"That's one of the joys of being the guest of honor." Michaela spoke in a conspiratorial whisper. "I get to skip out after making a legitimate appearance."

"And does"—he checked his watch—"two hours count as a legitimate appearance?"

"Tonight it does." Michaela took his hand. "Come on."

"Where to now?" he asked as they headed out of the room, through the lobby and onto the street.

"I'd like to take you to a club tonight, but the show starts at midnight, which gives us plenty of time." She gave a wave to Steven, who got into the car and pulled it forward. "How do you like Indian food?"

"Honestly, I've never had it," Bobby answered.

"Excellent." Michaela grinned at him, as Steven opened the door for them. "I know just where to take you."

The lights were already down by the time they got to The Divine Club. Colored spotlights blurred over the stage, around the room, across the tables, almost all of which were occupied. Michaela went directly to the man sitting behind the host's station. Without looking up, he started to speak in a bored French accent.

"Seating is closed now that the show is started." His boredom was palpable. "If you'd like to have a seat at the bar, we may be able to get you a table at intermission."

"What a shame," Michaela said with a smile.

The man looked up, eyes wide. "Michaela!" he exclaimed. He was around the host station faster than Bobby thought possible. "Chère, why didn't you tell us you were coming tonight?" He kissed the air next to both of Michaela's cheeks. "Does Matt know? He didn't say anything, so I'm thinking 'no.'"

"I wasn't one hundred percent sure we would make it, Jean Paul. I didn't want to disappoint him," Michaela explained.

"Come, chère, come. We will get you seated quickly." Jean Paul linked his arm with Michaela's, then turned to Bobby. He eyed him head to toe before making a low purring noise. "And at intermission, you can introduce me to your lovely new friend."

"Be nice to him, Jean Paul. It's his first time—"

"Even better." Jean Paul's purr became a growl.

"In New York," Michaela continued, as if Jean Paul hadn't spoken.

Jean Paul laughed at the look on Bobby's face. "Oh, poor man. I promise I don't bite unless you ask, and I never convert . . . unless you ask. You are safe with me." He dropped Bobby a playful wink. "Still"—he turned to Michaela to scold her—"you should have come early. Now I have to wait to hear the story of this man and how he is on your arm. So unfair."

"You'll live, Jean Paul." Michaela patted his cheek. "Now seat us before Miss Betty takes the stage or she'll have both our heads."

Jean Paul clucked and led them into the main room, weaving them through tables and crossed legs. They stopped at a table, lit by a low red candle, sprinkled with multicolored glitter. Bobby and Michaela slipped into two of the four chairs. Before he left, Jean Paul turned to the back of the room and waved to signal the cocktail waitress. The music swelled.

"We'll talk soon, chère," he whispered before scurrying away.

"Michaela . . ." Bobby whispered. His voice was low and hard. "Where the hell are we?"

Michaela turned to him and took his hand. Her voice was equally low and, if not hard, firm. "We are at my best friend's cabaret club. My best friend's." She stressed the last two words, making her point.

A muscular server in a tight black T-shirt and dress pants brought over two glasses of champagne. Bobby waited for him to leave, shook his head and sat back, arms crossed over his chest. Michaela opened her mouth to speak, but the curtains parted and a comfortably round woman with curly shoulder-length hair and glasses stepped out onto the stage. She looked more like everybody's favorite grandmother or elementary school teacher. Not at all what Bobby had expected at a club like this.

"Hello, hello, hello!" she announced. "I'm Betty Desire and you"—she spread her arms expansively—"are my guests!"

The crowd roared. Bobby looked and looked again. Betty Desire was a man. A man. In a dress. Hand to God . . .

"Michaela . . ." he whispered again. This time there was a hint of panic in his voice.

"Granger." Michaela reached out and took his hand again, squeezing gently. "Trust me. Please?"

The woman . . . man . . . person on stage was still talking. Bobby recognized the rhythm as an opening monologue. Around him, people were laughing at the patter. But he wasn't really listening. His eyes were locked with Michaela's. The look in her eyes was both guarded and hopeful. He could tell she wanted them to stay. And what was he supposed to do, anyway? Leave her here? Take a cab . . . to where? The house keys were in her purse. Make a scene and insist that they both leave? He snorted at the thought. First, he wasn't an asshole. Second, she wouldn't go if he tried that tactic anyway.

She could've at least warned him, dammit. He wasn't a complete country mouse. He knew clubs like this existed. He just . . . never thought he'd be in one, is all. Well, it'd make for one hell of a story to tell Jimmy—if he ever admitted it to anyone, ever. With a sigh, he sat back in his chair.

"Goodness," Betty continued, "I'm parched already. Brian, darling?" She looked offstage. "Could I bother you for a drink of water?"

A handsome younger man in a white dinner jacket and perfectly pressed black pants came out onstage, carrying a drink.

"Ah, Brian. You're a lifesaver." Betty took the glass from him. "My lovely prince, ladies and gentlemen, Brian Storm."

Brian turned and inclined his head to the audience in a slight, if gracious, bow. The crowd applauded loudly.

"Isn't he handsome?" Betty continued. She leaned forward to the audience and spoke into the microphone in an intimate whisper. "Plus, he's got a great butt. Check it out when he leaves. Just don't tell him I said to."

Brian laughed, along with the audience, and kissed Betty's hand gallantly before leaving to another round of applause.

"See why I keep him around?" Betty asked the crowd. "Cute butt. Old school chivalry. And he brings me my water." She took a deep swallow. "Unless it's my gin," she added mischievously, taking another deep drink. "Bet you're curious now, aren't you?"

The audience laughed.

"As much as I love being here with you, I know I'm not the real reason you're here tonight." Betty started to wrap up her opening spiel. "So, without further ado, welcome to The Divine Club, where the boys are divine, the girls are divine, and the audience is . . . divine!" She threw up her arms as the curtains rose behind her and eight dancers came on stage, lip-syncing to a Beyoncé song. Betty disappeared backstage with her water and the show had started.

Bobby was stunned. Never in a million years. The most amazing thing, though, was the performance. It was actually good. He knew they were lip-syncing. Hell, he knew they were men. But it looked more like a show he'd seen in Vegas at a police convention than a bunch of men in dresses.

Looking around, he watched the people. You learned more watching people than you learned looking in the same direction they were. Most everyone was having fun. Okay, it wasn't the kind of crowd that would gather at Sartini's on Saturday nights for Sinatra covers, but . . . this was New York City, not Lambert Falls, after all. And he and Michaela weren't even the only normal people in the place.

He could feel that most people were relaxed, happy, enjoying themselves. Except for . . . he identified the source of the problem. Something was happening in the corner. A younger man, college age maybe, wasn't happy about something. Bobby looked back to the stage. The performer was propped on a stool, mouthing the words to a slow Judy Garland tune. Michaela was swaying in time to the music.

Bobby tried to concentrate on the performance, but the incident in the corner was building.

"Granger?" Michaela whispered. "Do you want to leave?" Her voice was a resigned sigh.

"What?" Bobby responded as quietly as possible, before it registered what she thought. "No," he reassured her, "I'm fine." He was surprised to discover it was honestly true. Truly and really, as his girls would say. "But there's something going on in that corner."

Michaela looked to the table Bobby indicated. The couple seemed fine to her. "I don't think there's anything wrong."

Bobby frowned.

"They've got good security here," she assured him, a hand on his arm. "The bartenders are trained to spot trouble and handle it. And there's always Jean Paul. He's a black belt." He wasn't satisfied. Somewhere along the line, she'd learned to read him. Pushing the thought away for the time being, she gave in. "Do you want me to go get him?"

"No." Bobby shook his head. "This number's almost over. I'll go between songs."

Michaela rolled her eyes and looked back at the stage. This counted as a mistake. Granger was obviously looking for a reason to get away from the show, dammit. But better to learn it now before . . . well, not before anything. It was just good to know. Settling back, she decided to enjoy the show.

When the song ended, Michaela applauded, but Bobby slipped out as discretely as possible. He glanced into the corner. The young man's agitation was becoming more obvious. Bobby moved faster to the host station. Behind him, he heard Betty Desire return to the stage. It must be almost intermission.

"And what can I do for Michaela's new friend?" Jean Paul asked, as Bobby approached the station.

"There's a young man I think you might want to be aware of," Bobby explained quietly.

"Youngish? Hot college stud with issues about his masculinity?" Jean Paul asked.

"Um . . . I guess so," Bobby answered.

"Just the other side of this wall?" Jean Paul nodded to the wall behind him.

Bobby smiled with a nod. "You got him already?"

"I noticed him when he and his girlfriend came in. It was too obviously her idea." Jean Paul lifted an eyebrow at Bobby. "The boys behind the bar have been watching him all night. Is he acting up?"

"Michaela didn't notice anything." Bobby shrugged.

"But you did." It wasn't a question. Bobby nodded. "And you didn't think we would?" Jean Paul continued.

"I'm a sheriff back home," Bobby said simply. "I don't like assumptions."

Jean Paul thought a moment, then stuck out his hand. "Thank you, then."

Bobby shook it with a nod. "I'm Bobby Granger, by the way. Sorry to doubt your . . . boys."

Jean Paul laughed, trying not to be too loud. "We will not doubt each other again, I think, Bobby."

The song "Black Velvet" started in the other room. Jean Paul stepped out from behind the host stand. "This is her signature number. We're about to get busy with intermission. I will bring a drink to you and ma chère, though."

Bobby moved to the door of the seating area with the other man. Sure enough, he noticed one of the bartenders, a large one at that, keeping an eye on the kid in the corner.

"See?" Jean Paul whispered. "All is well."

Bobby nodded. "I'll wait until the song is over to rejoin Michaela. I can't imagine . . . she . . . would appreciate me walking in right now."

Jean Paul chuckled low. "Oh, you learn quickly, don't you, Monsieur Sheriff?"

The last few notes might have been popularized by Alannah Myles, but the performance was all Betty Desire. With a gracious bow, Miss Betty left the stage and the lights came up. Jean Paul clapped Bobby on the shoulder and headed to work the room. Bobby noticed the large bartender moving calmly to the corner. Smiling, he returned and sat down with Michaela. She raised an eyebrow at him, eyes questioning. Bobby shrugged.

"Jean Paul has everything under control. Already did. Look." He indicated the corner with a jerk of his chin. Michaela looked just in time to see the bartender escorting the couple, a strong if discreet grip on the man's arm, out of the room.

"Well done, Granger." Michaela turned back to Bobby. She felt . . . nice . . . at the thought he hadn't just been trying to get away from the show. Maybe she needed to give that some thought, but, right now, she'd just enjoy it.

He fiddled with a paper coaster. "I felt a little stupid actually."

Michaela reached out and took his hand. She was trying to think of something to say when Jean Paul arrived at the table, carrying two more glasses of champagne.

"Chère"—he spoke quickly—"a man who can see trouble, when even you cannot?" He winked at Bobby. "Well, that is a good man to have around. Enjoy the rest of the show. We will talk more when the show is done."

He cleared the table of the first glasses and was gone. Michaela raised her glass to Bobby. "You even impressed

Jean Paul, Granger. That's not easy. No need to feel even a little stupid."

"Apparently not." Bobby touched his glass to hers. He took a sip. Two nights in a row of champagne, with nothing to celebrate. He wasn't sure if it was unreasonably decadent or something he could easily get used to.

"Do I want to know what you're thinking?" Michaela asked.

"Just thinking about Carter Anne's reaction when she hears I had champagne two nights in a row," Bobby answered, looking through the golden liquid and twirling the stem between his fingers.

"She doesn't like Lambert Falls very much, does she?" Michaela took a sip of her own drink.

"It's not that she doesn't like it here . . . there," Bobby corrected himself. "It was a good place for her to grow up. She has friends there. It's her home."

"But . . . ?" Michaela encouraged.

"But . . ." Bobby thought a moment before continuing. "She wants more than the Falls. Someplace bigger. Louder," he added, grinning.

Michaela nodded. "Somehow, I gathered as much. What about Angie?"

"Angie?" Bobby laughed. "Angie is perfectly happy in the Falls. Made that decision around her relationship with Chris. Mind you, Chris is still working on getting her to do some traveling with him, but they'll never live anywhere else."

"And which one of them takes after their uncle?"

Bobby snorted. "I'm somewhere in the middle."

"How so?" Michaela pushed, in that way of hers.

"Isn't the show starting again soon?" Bobby answered, with a twinkle in his eyes.

Michaela made a face, but let it go. It didn't really

matter anyway. She took a sip of champagne. "We'll have to make sure Carter Anne has champagne a night or two for no reason. It's my favorite wine, so . . ." She shrugged and took another sip.

Bobby grinned at her, but the lights dimmed before he could say anything else. Betty appeared on Brian's arm and started the second act. Without the college kid in the corner distracting him, Bobby discovered he was actually enjoying the show. A couple of times, he wasn't even completely sure the . . . performers . . . were lip-syncing. Betty was funny and knew how to work the crowd. And the audience was warm and appreciative. Including him. Nope, Jimmy would never let him live this one down.

The finale had all eight performers joining Betty onstage. The colored spotlights were back, spinning and dancing around the house and across the stage. Bubbles came from hidden alcoves in the walls, making the audience gasp and cheer. Once again, Bobby was reminded of the Vegas show. It was every bit as good. Finally, the show ended and the crowd started to leave. Bobby went to stand, but Michaela stopped him with a hand on his arm.

"We'll hang out here," she explained. "The guys will join us soon."

The lights came up full as the last of the audience members left. The club staff started cleaning up, laughing and joking with each other, occasionally including Michaela. Closing-time routines were the same in New York as they were in Lambert Falls, apparently. By the time the floors were swept and the tables cleared, a door next to the stage was opening. Two men came out and beelined to Bobby and Michaela's table.

Michaela stood up and hugged the older man hard.

Finally she pulled away from him, keeping an arm around his waist. She turned him to Bobby, who stood.

"Granger, this is Matt Parker, my best friend. Matt, meet Sheriff Bobby Granger."

"So you're the descendant I've heard so much about," Matt said, extending his hand.

"Nice to meet you, Matt." Bobby shook his hand. "Nice place you've got here. As good as Las Vegas."

"Thank you," Matt responded.

"And this is Brian Spencer," Michaela continued, introducing the younger man.

"Pleasure." Bobby shook his hand as well.

The four of them sat. Bobby looked closer at Brian and Matt. He spoke to Brian. "You were Brian Storm."

"I am, indeed," Brian agreed.

Bobby cleared his throat hard and spoke to Matt. "And you were . . ." He waved in the direction of the stage.

"Hello, hello, hello!" Matt cried, falling back into character before slouching back into his chair. "She's fabulously over the top, isn't she?"

"But she's you," Bobby said.

"And fabulously over the top," Matt agreed.

Jean Paul came over to the table. "Everything's shut down out front. The boys are almost finished in back. What are we drinking tonight? More champagne?"

"Not for me," Michaela answered first. "Just bring me seltzer and lemon."

Jean Paul looked at Bobby.

"Is there bourbon by any chance?" he asked.

"There's everything," Matt assured him.

"Jim or Jack?" Jean Paul asked.

"Jim Beam, please," Bobby said. "Neat."

"Just water for me, Jean Paul," Brian spoke up.

"Don't open a new bottle of champagne just for me,"

Matt finally answered. "Vodka's fine." He turned to Bobby. "It really is water when I'm onstage."

Bobby laughed as Jean Paul headed back behind the bar. A steady stream of employees, barbacks and performers both, wandered through, heading out the door, calling good night to the table.

"So why didn't you tell me you were home?" Matt scolded Michaela gently.

"We just got in yesterday afternoon. We leave tomorrow. I wasn't sure we would make it in and I didn't want to disappoint you," Michaela explained.

He rubbed her cheek. "Thanks for finding the time."

Michaela blew him a kiss. Matt looked at Bobby. "So, how're you liking New York?"

"Y'all move mighty fast up here," Bobby joked. "'Side from that, it seems a nice enough place."

Matt and Brian laughed. "I'm not sure anyone's ever referred to it as 'nice' before," Matt said.

"Especially if you're used to Southern hospitality," Brian added. Michaela and Bobby exchanged a look and a smile. "What?" Brian asked. "Is that a myth? Isn't that rumor true?"

"Of course it is," Michaela assured him. "Especially when we're having the conversation in front of a Southerner who carries a gun."

Everyone laughed as Jean Paul returned with a tray of drinks. "Don't tell me I missed something good."

"A juicy exchange that can't possibly be recreated," Matt assured him.

"New rule." Jean Paul put the tray in the center of the table where everyone could reach their own drinks. "No one speaks unless I'm at the table."

"But then how can we talk about you behind your back?" Brian asked.

"Please." Matt rolled his eyes. "You'd just tell him everything we say once you got home anyway."

Jean Paul took a glass of water and a beer off the tray and took the water to Brian. "Good show tonight," he whispered. They touched foreheads, then Jean Paul pulled up a chair and sat down next to him.

Bobby looked over at Michaela. She gave him a slight nod. Bobby blinked hard and took a deep swallow of his bourbon. It sure as hell wasn't Lambert Falls.

"So . . ." Bobby had been wondering all night how to approach the topic. It was the elephant in the room, but that didn't make it any easier to ask about. He decided the best thing to do was to just take the bull by the horns and ask. "So, Brian and Jean Paul?" He adjusted the pillows under his head. The bed was comfortable, even if it wasn't his own.

"Aren't they a great couple?" Michaela asked. She was in her slip, but nothing else. Rubbing her earlobes, she took the large gold knots from her ears.

"So, they are together?" Bobby confirmed.

"Yes, Granger," Michaela said gently. "They are together. They met at the club, actually."

"And Matt?"

Michaela sat down on the bed next to Bobby, and rubbed his leg through the blankets. "Matt's gay, too."

Bobby nodded. "I figured as much." He coughed. "And he owns the club and dresses . . . like that?"

"He makes a lot of money dressing like that," Michaela said. "Sometimes he even gets stars to come sing for him."

"Really?" Bobby asked. "Like who?"

"Bette Midler stops by some. And Celine Dion showed up one night."

"I like Celine Dion." Bobby was surprised.

"Do you really?" It was Michaela's turn to be shocked. "Well, you can't be perfect, Granger."

He laughed, but it was short-lived. "They were really nice guys." His voice was low and he was staring over her shoulder.

"Were you surprised?" Michaela asked.

"I just didn't know." He looked at her. "That's the truth."

Michaela patted his knee. "Fair enough, Granger." She could live with that. She stood and went into the bathroom, leaving the door open.

"Meeting you was important to Matt, I could tell."

"What do you mean?" Bobby asked.

"I've never seen him as him at the club. He's always Betty."

"Isn't he always him?" How was it possible he was even having this conversation? Nope, he wasn't telling a soul back home.

"When he's at the club, he always stays dressed." She appeared in the door of the bathroom. "Always stays Betty Desire." She threw open her arms with a flamboyant wave. "So for him to come to drinks as himself . . . it means it was important."

"I'm glad he did, then." Bobby still didn't understand the details, but he sure understood the concept. "It was important to me to meet him, too."

"Wanted to make sure he really was a man under all that?" Michaela teased.

"No." Bobby chuckled with a shake of his head. "No, I knew that. But he's your best friend. Best friends are important."

"Oh," Michaela said quietly. "Oh. Well, thank you."

The two of them exchanged a long look before Michaela smiled and went back into the bathroom to finish her evening routine. Bobby stretched. There was a pop or two, reminding him he wasn't a kid any longer. As if he'd forgotten.

"How often do y'all do this?" Bobby asked.

"Do what?" Michaela called out. She stepped into the doorway, rubbing her hands and elbows with lotion.

"Stay up until"—Bobby looked at the clock on the bedside table—"almost four a.m."

"Ugh. Is it really that late?" Michaela turned off the bathroom light, pulled her slip over her head, and crawled into bed next to him. He turned off the lamp.

"It is," Bobby replied.

"Not often," she assured him. She sighed deeply, stretching in the cool sheets. "Bed feels good. I'm not nineteen anymore."

Bobby grunted in agreement.

"Saturdays are the only midnight show, and I don't usually go to them," she continued, answering the original question. "This is a particularly late night for me."

"Gotta say, I'm glad to hear it," Bobby admitted. "The Falls was gonna seem even smaller to you if this is what you were used to."

"I don't know." Michaela snuggled up, her head on his chest. He wrapped an arm around her. "I like the Falls."

"Do you?" Bobby asked.

"I do," Michaela answered. "It's small, but"—she shrugged—"it's like a cozy room. Small but comfortable."

Bobby smiled into the darkness. That was the perfect way to describe the Falls. She spoke as well as she wrote.

"It's like," Michaela continued, her voice beginning to fade, "it's like the place you want to go away from for a little while, but always look forward to getting back to, as well."

"That seems about right," Bobby agreed.

"I understand Carter Anne," she muttered, "but I understand Angie, too."

"Somewhere in the middle, huh, Michaela?" Bobby asked.

Michaela snored lightly in response.

Chapter 9

"Boss!" Jimmy looked up as Bobby walked into the station. "When'd you get in? I didn't expect to see you until tomorrow."

Bobby took the seat behind the desk that Jimmy had vacated as soon as he'd seen the sheriff.

"How was the trip?" the younger man continued before Bobby could answer the original question.

"It was good," Bobby finally got to answer.

"The city as big as it looks in movies?" Jimmy brought him a cup of coffee.

Bobby laughed. "Bigger." He sipped at the coffee. Yep, it was mud. He took another sip anyway. "You should see it sometime."

"I want to"—Jimmy nodded, taking the seat at the second desk—"eventually."

"So, what's been happening here?" Bobby changed the subject.

"Not much, honestly." Jimmy shrugged. "You could probably be okay going on home and spending one more easy afternoon. I've got it here."

Bobby thumbed through the papers on the desk. Sure

enough, it was a small pile. Might as well take his deputy up on his offer. Michaela had gone back to the library for a rest. It wasn't a horrible idea. They hadn't gotten much sleep last night and he, unlike Michaela, hadn't been able to sleep on the plane. And everyone was coming to dinner tonight. He stood and stretched. Not a bad idea at all.

"All right, Jimmy," Bobby conceded. "You convinced me. If something happens, give me a call. Otherwise, I'll see you tomorrow morning."

"No problem." Jimmy waved him off. "I look forward to hearing about the weekend. And, Bobby?"

Bobby turned, halfway to the door. "Yeah, Jimmy?"

"Glad to have you back. Welcome home."

"Thanks." Bobby smiled at him. "It's good to be home."

As Bobby walked out into his town he realized, while it was true, it wasn't a desperate relief to be home. Parts of the trip, including the city itself, had been a good time.

He headed down the street, automatically checking his usual spots. The streets were quiet, even for a Sunday. So different from where he'd woken up this morning. He thought about stopping at Michaela's rooms, but decided against it. Let her sleep. He'd see her tonight. Mechanically, he checked Jack Beddingham's gate and scratched Jack's dog, Daisy, through the fence slats. As quiet as it was, he could easily sleep for a couple of hours and still have time to shower and dress before the family arrived for dinner. And Michaela, he corrected himself. The family and Michaela. Apparently he was more tired than he realized. A nap was definitely a good idea.

"Back already?" Carter Anne called from the kitchen as he opened the front door.

"Jimmy's got it until tomorrow," Bobby called back. "I'm gonna go lie down for a bit before dinner."

Carter Anne appeared in the kitchen door. "You know you're killing me making me wait until everyone gets here to tell me about the weekend, right?"

Bobby patted her arm as he walked by. "I just don't want to make you listen to it all twice, honey."

"You're a real humanitarian, Bobby," Carter Anne replied.

"So I've been told," Bobby agreed. "See you in a bit." He climbed the stairs, oblivious to his niece.

Chris and Angie were already there when he came back down after his nap, showered and feeling better. They were all in the kitchen, Carter Anne and Angie poring over books of invitations. The smell of baking chicken permeated the room.

"Morning, sleepyhead." Angie lifted her cheek for a kiss as Bobby walked through the room.

"Coffee's fresh," Carter Anne added.

"Thank you both," Bobby said, moving straight for the coffee pot. "Can I pour anyone else a cup?"

"I'm fine," Angie said with a lift of her Diet Pepsi.

"I'll take a cup," Chris said, standing, "so long as it's not decaf."

"You should know me better than that," Bobby laughed. He pulled two cups from the cabinet.

"I'm glad you're up." Chris's voice was low. "I was feeling outnumbered. How much wedding talk needs to happen, anyway? Isn't it done yet?"

Bobby poured out the coffee, while Chris found the cream and sugar, as comfortable here as he was in his own kitchen.

"We can hear you, you know." Angie looked over her shoulder at the two men.

"Hi, babe." Chris smiled over at her.

She made a face at him.

"We'll just be in here." Bobby picked up the mugs and nodded toward the TV room. "Give a holler if you need us or when dinner's ready, whichever comes first." He moved out of the room. Chris hesitated, kissed Angie, shrugged at Carter Anne, and followed. Bobby was already settled in his chair by the time Chris made it into the room.

"You know"—Chris picked up his coffee off the low table and sat on the couch—"I've been in combat. I've shot men and been shot at." He sipped his coffee with a shake of his head. "None of it was as intimidating as your niece when she gets the wedding look in her eyes. Your extrication was impressive, though."

"Years of practice," Bobby sighed.

"So." Chris leaned back, arm extended on the back of the couch. "How was the trip?"

"Carter Anne would kill me if I told you before I told her."

Chris raised an eyebrow.

"I didn't tell her about it earlier because I said I only wanted to tell it once," Bobby explained. He leaned forward, elbows on his knees, coffee held between both hands. Chris took the same position, listening.

"She took me to a drag club," Bobby said, studying his coffee.

"A drag club?"

"Men in dresses . . . ?" Bobby explained, hoping Chris would understand.

The younger man bit the inside of his mouth. Hard.

"I know." Bobby chuckled.

Apparently Chris hadn't hidden his laughter well enough. "Any particular reason? Or"—the laughter finally broke through—"just to make you squirm?"

Bobby joined in the laughter while explaining about Matt, Brian, and Jean Paul. "But the truth is, Chris," he continued, "that wasn't the weirdest part."

Chris just stared at his friend over his coffee.

"Okay," Bobby allowed. "It was the weirdest part. But those guys were good guys once you got to talking to them. It was just the . . ." He searched for the right word but couldn't find it. He finally settled on, "The rest of the weekend was just tougher." It wasn't right, but it was close and it was Chris. He'd get it. "Her life is fast, demanding. Lots of people, all wanting a piece of her."

Chris nodded. "Sounds tough."

"Hell," Bobby admitted, "half the time, I felt like I was on a completely different planet."

"Definitely tough," Chris agreed.

"I'm just glad to be home, honestly." He remembered the moment earlier when he'd realized there was no desperation and dismissed it. Glad to be home didn't have to mean desperate, after all. He took a sip of his coffee. "Of course, at dinner tonight, for the girls, I'll just tell how great it was."

"For the girls—" Chris paused. "And for Michaela, too."

Bobby thought about it. His friend was right. For Michaela, too. "Yeah."

In the hall, Michaela looked at Angie, both wide-eyed. She'd had no idea he'd felt so out of place. He'd seemed so calm and together the whole time. Maybe a little bored, but that was to be expected.

"They didn't hear you get here," Angie whispered. Admittedly, she'd only heard Michaela's knock because she was going upstairs to get some magazines out of her old room, but still.

"We shouldn't be eavesdropping," Michaela whispered back.

"But . . ."

Michaela silenced Angie with a look.

"You're right," the younger woman sighed. Raising a finger, she opened the front door and spoke much louder than usual. "Hey, Michaela, come on in." She circled her hand in the air, encouraging Michaela to speak up.

"Hi, Angie. Where's everybody tonight?"

Angie dropped her a wink and led Michaela into the kitchen, hollering over her shoulder. "Bobby, Chris, Michaela's here!"

"Hi, guys!" Michaela called as well, as she followed Angie into the other room. She had meant what she had said to Angie. They shouldn't have been listening. In fairness, though, they hadn't meant to be listening. But what interesting things she'd learned.

"Michaela?" Bobby stood. He made it to the door of the den before looking back to see Chris still sitting on the couch, watching his friend with a slight smile. Neither man spoke. Chris simply nodded, stood, and clapped Bobby's shoulder as they went to join the women in the kitchen.

Dinner was relaxed and happy. Angie wanted details about Michaela's apartment, especially the bathroom. Carter Anne grilled them about the city itself. Chris sat listening, chuckling lightly but mostly just taking it all in. The writer in Michaela came out and she told the stories so well, Bobby hardly recognized events he'd been present for. By the time the chicken was down to the bones, everyone had laughed at Bobby's discomfort—at the auction, the metal sculpture, and meeting Michaela's friends—several times, causing him to blush good-naturedly.

Michaela tried to mask a yawn, but Carter Anne and Angie both caught her.

"You know," Angie teased gently, "you're allowed to go home when you're tired."

"Don't let her fool you," Bobby interjected. "She had me up until four a.m. last night."

"But apparently a night like that makes me useless the rest of the week," Michaela sighed.

"Bobby, take Michaela home," Carter Anne said. "We can handle this." She motioned to the mess on the table.

"No," Michaela insisted. "I want to help."

"Next time," Carter Anne assured her. "When you've had more sleep."

Michaela started to protest, but another yawn stopped her. "I'll take you up on that," she agreed.

"I'll be back in a bit," Bobby said, standing and holding Michaela's chair.

"Take your time." Carter Anne winked at him.

"Good night, y'all," Angie said as Chris waved to them.

"Good night." Michaela waved back.

She and Bobby headed out.

"It wasn't the company," Michaela promised.

"Hey," Bobby assured her, "this gets me out of kitchen duty, too."

They laughed together and started the walk to the library.

"Remember when being up until four in the morning was the normal start to a weekend?" Michaela asked.

"Vaguely," Bobby replied.

Without thinking about it, Michaela slipped her arm into his and he covered her hand. Walking with her like this felt right.

"It was a good weekend, though," Bobby added.

"Still, I bet it feels good to be home," Michaela noted as he glanced down a side street.

"Honestly"—Bobby nodded—"it does. Getting away isn't exactly my style." He shrugged.

"Well, then thank you even more for coming with me," Michaela said.

"It wasn't as bad as I'd expected, though. Just so you know."

Michaela squeezed his arm. Bobby just shrugged again, but smiled into the night. A comfortable silence fell between them as they walked the rest of the way.

When they got to Michaela's door, Bobby turned her toward him, took her face in his hands, and kissed her deeply. Michaela gave in to the kiss, savoring the feel and the taste of him. She slipped her arms around his waist and pulled him closer. He nipped at her lips and Michaela smiled against his mouth.

"This is nice," she whispered.

He nodded and wrapped her up tighter—and she yawned.

"You need to sleep," Bobby spoke over her head.

"Would you mind if I don't invite you in?" Michaela asked, still not moving out of his embrace. His laughter rumbled in his chest.

"You know the old saying, 'The spirit is willing but the flesh is weak'?"

Michaela chuckled with him. "Somehow I don't think this is quite the situation that's usually meant to describe."

"That doesn't make it any less accurate."

Bobby moved her away from him, his hands on her shoulders. "Anyway, I need to sleep, too, and I don't think either of us needs to be dealing with my snoring or you stealing the covers."

"Thank you." Michaela kissed him lightly. "I'm even too tired to argue over if I'm the one who steals the blankets or not."

"I owe Jimmy at least a full day, but I'd like to take you to dinner tomorrow night."

"How 'bout Chow's? Even mediocre Chinese is better than nothing."

"Actually—" Bobby cleared his throat. Was he really about to do this? "I was thinking I might make reservations at Sartini's."

"Really?" Michaela hoped she didn't sound as surprised as she felt. Reservations? Well . . . "Okay."

"Good," Bobby said before either one of them could back off from it. "I'll pick you up a little before eight."

"I'll see you then." Michaela opened the door to her suite and watched as he went down the stairs, back onto the street.

He stopped and looked back up at her, silhouetted in the doorway. It had been a long time, but, unless he was mistaken, he was falling in love.

"Sheriff Granger—" Sal Sartini himself met them at the door. "Miss Howard, your table is ready. Please follow me."

He led them through the main dining room, to a small table in the corner. Michaela's eyes widened at the single rose across one of the place settings, but she smiled at the bottle of champagne chilling next to the table. Mr. Sartini waited for Bobby to help Michaela with her chair before helping Bobby with his. Once they were seated with their menus, the man opened the champagne with a flourish. Only once he'd moved away did Michaela speak.

"Is there an occasion I missed, Granger?" She lifted the rose to her nose.

Bobby raised his glass and held it for her to join him in a toast. "Just a nice dinner."

Michaela clinked her glass to his with a raised eyebrow. All she got in return was his enigmatic smile.

"The braciole is real good," Bobby said, looking at his menu. "I also like the Italian steak. The veal parm is supposed to be good, but I can't vouch for it personally."

"Don't like veal?"

"Love it," Bobby said simply. "Don't like where it comes from."

"Really?" Michaela was surprised.

"Really," Bobby repeated.

"You're a complicated man, Granger."

"If you're in the mood for pasta . . ." Bobby had moved on.

"No, no pasta tonight." Michaela shook her head. "But I don't like to eat veal, either." She looked back at her menu, but not before she saw him bite back a smile. Feeling more than a little confused, she tried to study her menu but failed. "You're the second person to recommend the braciole, so I think I'll go with that."

"You won't be sorry," Bobby assured her. "Want to split an appetizer?"

"Do you know how long it's been since I've been on a run?" Michaela asked by way of an answer. "The braciole is dangerous enough."

Bobby closed his menu and Sal appeared at the table before either of them could even look for him. They placed their orders and Sartini backed away. Michaela picked the rose back up, fingering the petals.

"So Granger—" she started, but was interrupted.

"Good evening, Sheriff." Mary Jones was standing next to their table. "Michaela." Her eyes twinkled in unabashed pleasure at the sight of them. "Don't y'all look cozy."

"Evenin,' Mary." Bobby lifted himself slightly from his chair, but Mary touched him lightly on the shoulder, allowing him to stay seated.

"Hello, Mary," Michaela added. "Is your sister here, too?"

"Oh, we're over there." Mary pointed to her sister a few tables over. Margaret waved. "I won't interrupt you long. We just decided I should come over to say we're glad to have you home, Sheriff."

"I wasn't gone that long, now, Mary," Bobby said.

"Long enough," she insisted. Her hand fluttered in Michaela's direction. "You, too, dear. The library wasn't the same without you."

"Oh. Well." Michaela hadn't expected to be included in the conversation at all. She reached out and took the other woman's hand. "Thank you, Mary. To be honest, it's good to be . . . back."

Mary smiled, her eyes brightening even more. "That makes me very happy to hear."

"Thank you for stopping by, Mary," Bobby spoke. "You give your sister our best, too."

"I'll do that," Mary said. She looked from one to the other, practically glowing. "And the two of you have a good night."

Michaela watched as the woman returned to her sister. They began their trademark back and forth conversation before Mary had completely retaken her seat. Michaela didn't need to read lips to know what the topic of conversation was. When she looked back to Bobby, he was staring at her.

"What?" she asked.

"You've just been accepted by the Jones sisters," he stated.

"They've always been nice."

"Nice is their way," Bobby explained. "But acceptance is something else." This didn't make his decision for him, not by any stretch, but it certainly made it easier. Confirmed he wasn't being a silly romantic ass for even thinking it. He lifted his glass again. "Welcome to Lambert Falls."

Michaela shook her head, amused. "I may not ever understand, but . . . thanks."

"Guess we can't expect a Yankee to understand our ways," Bobby teased.

"You're just way too friendly down here," Michaela teased back. "Obviously none of you can be trusted."

Bobby laughed.

"Take tonight, for instance." Michaela's voice was still light, joking. "Here I thought we were going to grab Italian food, maybe split a pizza. But this"—she looked at Bobby and got a little more serious—"this is unexpected."

"And unexpected makes me untrustworthy?" asked Bobby, playing along.

"The jury's still out on if it's untrustworthy or just unexpected."

"Makes me wonder where the line between the two is," Bobby parried.

"As soon as I figure it out, I'll let you know." She watched him for something, anything, that would clue her in, but he simply sat there, holding her gaze, with that cool smile. Damn him, she felt anything but cool. She was, truth be told, decidedly warm.

"So it's back to work tomorrow, I assume." Bobby spoke as if nothing had just passed between them. He had to if he was going to be able to play this out the way he'd hoped. Otherwise, he was going to start babbling like a schoolboy.

"For both of us," Michaela agreed.

Sartini appeared with their meals and a basket of bread. "You will tell me if anything is less than perfect tonight," he said.

"I'm sure we'll have no complaints," Bobby said.

"I never have yet." Michaela turned her brightest smile on him.

"Not even compared to New York City?" Sartini probed.

"Not even," Michaela assured him.

The man beamed. "Then we will hope tonight will not be the first, and I will leave you to your dinner." With a gracious nod, he turned to check in with the rest of the diners.

"You made his night, you know," Bobby said, picking up his knife and fork.

"I told him the truth." Michaela took a bite of her braciole and made a noise deep in her throat. "Besides," she said around the bite, "he just made mine. You and Chris were right about this."

Bobby sighed dramatically. "And here I'd hoped it would be me who made your night."

"Well"—Michaela leaned forward—"you brought me here and recommended the dish, so I'll give you some of the credit."

"Don't forget the rose and the champagne," Bobby added.

"Speaking of—" Michaela chewed slowly. "What's up with those? Seriously."

Bobby took a deep breath. "I wanted to talk to you about something."

"I'm here." Michaela managed not to take an equally deep breath, but just barely. The trappings said one thing, but a man wanting to talk . . . that rarely boded well.

"Remember in New York, when I said I know what we are to each other and what we're not?" Bobby asked.

Michaela nodded. And waited.

She was just sitting there, eating her meal, and looking at him. So cool. This had been easier in front of his mirror while he was shaving. Now, looking at her instead of his own reflection, the words wouldn't come.

"Well, I do," Bobby continued.

"You do what?" Michaela asked.

"I do know what we have and what we don't have. What we agreed to," Bobby clarified.

"Okay." Michaela kept eating. "I'm with you now."

This was crazy. He'd always been straightforward before. He'd be straightforward now. "Michaela, I've come to want more than just a friendly, physical relationship with you. I know that's what we agreed to, and I don't want to screw up your book or your research. And I don't really know what I'm expecting when your writing's done. But I knew I needed to tell you." He tried to exhale. It just didn't work. Of course, inhaling wasn't working, either. Michaela was looking at her plate. If he could see her eyes, maybe he'd be able to breathe again. She reached for the flower and inhaled its delicate scent. She could breathe. Why couldn't he?

"Michaela?" he finally asked. In the mirror, he'd hoped she would smile and tell him she had been waiting for him to say it first. He'd been prepared for the "it's not you, it's me" speech. No scenario had involved total silence.

"Granger." She looked up. Finally.

Bobby smiled before biting it back. He knew that look. He'd seen it in a few women before, including his Abby. Had seen it in the mirror for a few days now. He exhaled.

"I guess this changes some things." Michaela grinned lopsidedly at him.

"I guess it does," Bobby agreed.

She reached for his hand. "And maybe not too much."

"This isn't just an understanding, Michaela." Bobby entwined his fingers with hers. "As I said, I'm not sure what exactly it is, but it's not an understanding."

"Not any more, Granger," she agreed with a squeeze of his hand. Then she giggled. His sophisticated, elegant Yankee giggled. "I'm so glad you said it first."

Bobby lifted her hand and kissed her fingers. "I almost didn't," he confessed. "It's no easier now than it was thirty-five years ago."

Michaela picked up her knife and fork to continue eating. "Was it the pushy agent, the stuffy auction, or the gay drag-queen friends who finally pushed you over the edge?"

Bobby laughed with a snort. "It was the woman who introduced me to all of it."

A jolt of electricity shot through her chest, her tummy, and settled in her core. No, this wasn't just an understanding any longer. Not at all.

"Southern gentlemen aren't a myth, are they?"

"We may be a dying breed, but you can still find us in the wild occasionally." Bobby smiled.

"Granger." Michaela put down her silverware. "Get the check."

Bobby didn't miss a beat. He would never wonder what she was thinking or where he stood with her, that was certain. He raised a finger and Sartini materialized.

"Sal, we need the check, please," Bobby said.

"Are your dinners unacceptable?" the man asked, concerned.

"They're delicious, Sal," Michaela reassured him. "We promise. We just need the check."

Sartini looked from Michaela to Bobby, then his expression switched to one of absolute discretion, except for a slight twinkle deep in his eyes. "Right away."

It was insane. She'd had sex with this man more times than she could count. He had been her nearly constant companion for weeks. And yet her whole body was tingling and alive as if she were on a first date. At age sixteen.

Bobby signed the tab, tipping Sartini particularly well, and stood to escort Michaela out. They waved to several diners before stopping by the Jones sisters' table.

"Have a good night, ladies," Bobby spoke first.

"Are the two of you leaving?" Mary started.

"Without even having dessert?" Margaret finished.

"Tonight we are, yes," Michaela answered vaguely.

"Was everything all right?" Margaret picked back up.

"Because our dinners were delicious," Mary contributed.

"As usual," Margaret summed up for both of them.

"Everything was excellent," Bobby assured them. "But we need an early night tonight."

"Remember"—Michaela leaned in, bringing them into her confidence—"we're coming off a busy weekend in New York."

The sisters smiled at them both. Suddenly Michaela wasn't sure who was playing who. It was very possible these ladies knew far more than anyone in town, including her, had ever guessed.

"Then you'd best get home." Mary twinkled.

"And get our sheriff rested up." Margaret matched her sister.

"After such a busy weekend," concluded Mary.

"Good night, ladies." Bobby touched his forehead and, with a hand on the small of Michaela's back, guided her out of the restaurant.

The night had gone cold, much colder than she'd expected, but it gave her still another reason to snuggle into Bobby on the way home. The drive from one end of town to the other had never felt so long. Michaela kept her nose in the petals of the rose throughout, partly to enjoy the smell, but partly to hide the silly grin she couldn't quite get off her face.

When they finally arrived at the library, Bobby walked her up the back stairs to her door. Taking the keys from her, he unlocked the door and handed the keys back. Michaela started to open the door, but Bobby stopped her by grabbing her hand. He pulled her into him and kissed her slowly, sweetly. Michaela felt her knees nearly buckle. She broke away from him and inclined her head toward the suite.

She grinned. "Come on."

Bobby shook his head slowly. "Not tonight, Michaela."

She turned back to him. "Is everything okay?"

"Everything's fine." Bobby rubbed her arms against the cold.

"Then why aren't you coming in?" Michaela was puzzled.

"Because everything's fine," Bobby answered. "Better'n fine if truth be told."

Michaela laughed nervously. "We've had plenty of sex, Granger."

"That was different," Bobby said.

"I'm lost here," Michaela admitted.

"That was sex." Bobby stepped away from her. "This is courtin'."

He leaned around her and opened the door to the suite. Michaela opened her mouth to speak, but Bobby continued before she could find her words.

"Go on in now, Michaela. I'll call on you tomorrow."

Whistling through his teeth, Bobby left her watching him with a stunned smile.

"Miss Howard?" Langdon Howard's voice was uncharacteristically hesitant. Usually she was obnoxiously smug.

"Yes, Langdon?" Michaela didn't even look up from her notes. Sure, she was intrigued, but any sign of interest would just encourage her.

"Um . . . the first lady is downstairs." Langdon's voice was breathy.

"What first lady, Langdon?" She really didn't have time for this.

"The first lady of North Carolina," Langdon answered, as if Michaela were a child. "The governor's wife?"

Michaela looked up. Okay, Langdon had her attention.

"She wants to meet you," Langdon finished up, eyes wide.

"Then I guess I should get downstairs." Michaela stood. Why couldn't it have been Kerri, or even one of the Jones sisters? She wanted a moment to be human before going down to be an author. Ah well. She took a moment to straighten her skirt and smooth her hair before putting on a smile.

As she was coming down the stairs, Angie threw open the door to the library and ran through the lobby. "Lydia!" she nearly squealed, hurrying to the woman.

They embraced. "I'm sorry I'm late," she spoke over Lydia's shoulder. "I made the mistake of answering one more call." She pulled back and saw the tall man at the first lady's side, as always. "Hi, Scott." She flashed him a smile.

"Miss Kane." The man's nod and words were formal, but the smile in his eyes was warm.

Michaela stepped down off the bottom stair, followed closely by Langdon. At the click of her high heel, the other three turned.

"Here she is," Angie announced, moving to Michaela and taking her hand. She led Michaela to the first lady. "Lydia Bain Carmichael, I'm pleased to introduce you to Michaela Howard, the author Howard Michaels. Michaela, this is our first lady, Lydia Carmichael."

The two women shook hands. "Ms. Carmichael, it's my pleasure," Michaela said.

"The pleasure's mine, Ms. Howard," Lydia assured her. "The governor is a huge fan of yours. And please, call me Lydia."

"If you call me Michaela." She returned the woman's smile.

"And that's Scott." Angie pointed to Lydia's security man. She lowered her voice in a fake whisper. "But you're supposed to pretend he's invisible."

Michaela nodded to him. "I promise not to see you after this moment, Scott."

"Scott Nessel, ma'am," he said with an amused nod.

"I'm Langdon Howard." She pushed through Angie and Michaela, hand extended.

"Oh." Lydia was startled, but regained composure quickly. She shook Langdon's hand. "Nice to meet you. Any . . . ?" She wagged her finger between Michaela and Langdon.

"Oh no," Michaela laughed.

"She's from New York," Langdon added.

Michaela lifted an eyebrow to Lydia while Angie tried to cover a smirk with her hand.

"So—" Lydia turned her attention back to Michaela. "I'm heading to Richmond. Virginia's first lady and I share an interest in adult literacy, so we help each other out with events and appearances. When I have to drive, as I did today, I like to detour through Lambert Falls to have lunch with Angie," she explained. "This time, I suggested you join us. Do you like Chinese food?"

"I do," Michaela accepted with a grin. "And thank you."

Lydia spoke to Langdon. "It was nice to meet you." She turned, allowing Scott to lead her out of the library.

Angie and Michaela fell in behind them. Michaela grabbed Angie's arm and leaned down, whispering hard. "You couldn't have called me?"

Angie just giggled. Please, it would work. Angie didn't know exactly what was happening between Michaela and her uncle. What she did know was that Bobby had never been so happy. He'd gone to New York City, for goodness sake. But there was no way Michaela wasn't homesick. No way she didn't miss, well, intellectual conversation. Her friends were probably smart and witty and knew about politics and stuff. Maybe a friend down here who knew a little more than just the Falls would make it easier for her to stay. Maybe, anyway.

At Chow's, the four of them were seated in a small, private room. They ordered off the menu, then Lydia poured tea for everyone.

"Angie tells me you're writing a book on Colonel Lambert," she said, pouring Michaela a cup.

"I am," Michaela confirmed. "He's a fascinating character." She smiled to Angie. "As are his descendants."

Angie smiled back before speaking to Lydia. "Michaela and my uncle are dating. She's real fond of the Colonel's descendants."

"Angie!" Michaela gasped, laughing. "That's not what I meant."

"So you are"—Lydia's eyes were merry—"enjoying our fine state."

"Yes"—Michaela chuckled, giving in—"I am. So how do you and Angie know each other?" she asked, changing the subject.

"Lydia and the governor were two of my first clients," Angie explained.

"She redesigned our house on the Outer Banks," Lydia added. "We hit it off when she turned our house from a stuffy, old-fashioned plantation into an open, airy beach home. Or at least that's what it will be when the construction is finished."

"We removed walls," Angie added. "It should be done relatively soon, though, right?"

"Hopefully," Scott answered, then blushed at speaking up.

Lydia patted his arm. "Right now, if we want to get out of Charlotte, even just for a night, we have to go to a hotel. It makes more work for Scott and the rest of security."

"Which we don't mind at all," Scott asserted.

"Of course not." Lydia winked at Angie. "Have you been to the Outer Banks yet, Michaela?"

"Not yet." Michaela shook her head. "I've been focused on research."

"And the one time she left the Falls, she went back to New York," Angie said.

"That was for work, though," Michaela demurred.

"I still don't blame you," Angie said.

Michaela was surprised. "You love it here, Angie."

"Sure," Angie agreed, "but you're not me. You're used to New York and we're hardly New York."

"But as wonderful a town as Lambert Falls is"—Lydia spoke up with a nod to Angie—"there's so much more to North Carolina than just here. Do try to see more of it before you have to leave. At least Greensboro, if you don't have time to get to the beaches or down to Raleigh or Charlotte."

"Greensboro?" Michaela hadn't thought much about Greensboro. "Really?"

They paused in conversation as their meals arrived. Lydia and Michaela broke open chopsticks before Lydia answered the other's question.

"So, Greensboro—there are museums, theatres, a symphony, several very nice spas . . ." Lydia shrugged. "I could give you a list, but you get the idea."

"Good to know." Michaela didn't think it showed when her tummy did a flip, but she couldn't deny it to herself. There was culture, life, energy, and it was as close as Greensboro.

"In case"—Lydia gave her a knowing look—"you decide you want to enjoy Lambert Falls a little longer."

"I'll keep that in mind," Michaela replied.

"And, of course," Lydia continued, "should you . . . not rush back to New York, Michael would love to meet you."

"Michael?" Michaela asked.

"I'm sorry," Lydia said. "My husband, the governor."

"I'd be honored."

"I think he'd be the honored one, honestly." Lydia laughed. "He was very disappointed when his schedule prevented him from joining us today."

"Maybe I can send him a signed book or something," Michaela offered.

"I have three of his copies in the car, if you'd sign those before we leave."

Angie watched the conversation between the two women. She still didn't quite understand how her life had turned out so that they were her friends; she was only happy and grateful they were. And she'd seen Michaela's eyes when Lydia talked about Greensboro.

She wouldn't get excited. But Greensboro was close. And Lydia and Michaela seemed to really be getting along. Still, that didn't necessarily mean there was anything to be excited about. Taking a bite of her sesame chicken, she watched as Michaela laughed over something Lydia had said. So, she wouldn't get excited. That didn't mean she couldn't call Carter Anne tonight.

"Any chance you could take a break?" Bobby was leaning up against the door.

Michaela jumped with a laugh. "Where'd you come from?"

"Sorry to startle you." He moved into the room and sat down next to her.

Michaela nodded. "A break would be nice, honestly. What did you have in mind?"

"I was just about to walk rounds. Wondered if you'd like to come."

If she kept giving in to every distraction, she'd never get the book researched. Teri and Justin were already on her about how much time this one was going to take if she didn't pick up her schedule.

She'd already been here two months. They'd only scheduled three and she was nowhere close to where she should've been. "I'd love to." His smile was all she needed.

Stopping only long enough to grab Michaela's coat from her rooms, they headed out into the late February afternoon.

"I like your definition of winter down here, Granger," Michaela said, tucking her arm into his.

"It was cold enough in New York when we were there." Bobby patted her hand but kept his eyes on the town. "I don't think I need to experience it any colder. We'll be getting warmer real soon."

"That's another difference down here." Michaela shook her head. "In New York we'll be in heavy coats for weeks yet."

"You miss it, though," Bobby noted.

She didn't bother to ask how he knew. But there was no denying it. "I always do when I'm away for any length of time."

Bobby waved to a group of teenagers, bundled up, heading to the diner. They passed Bobby and Michaela with a chorus of greetings to the sheriff and a few laughs about his girlfriend. "What's the longest you've ever been gone?"

"Early on, I researched two books right in a row. Kept me away for nine months." Michaela laughed dryly. "I've never made that mistake again. I stop being productive or effective after five or six months. Where I am makes a difference, though."

Bobby nodded. "I guess . . . well . . ." He cleared his throat. "Lambert Falls doesn't offer much."

Michaela put her head on his shoulder. "Lambert Falls offers plenty."

He chuckled and kissed her hair. "While I appreciate the statement, I don't believe you. We have some real good people, but we're a little short on things to do."

What could she say? She was already getting tired of

Chow's and Sartini's. "Okay, you got me. Aside from the people"—she squeezed his arm—"there isn't much to do. But I met Lydia Carmichael the other day."

Bobby nodded. "Heard she'd come through town. You like her?"

"I do," Michaela said.

Bobby nodded again. He bent to pick up an empty coffee cup that had missed the trash can on the street. "And what did the first lady have to say?"

"She was telling me about Greensboro," Michaela continued. "It sounds as if it's not a bad little city. And Carter Anne and Angie tell me it's close."

"It is," Bobby agreed. "We go there for dinner sometimes to celebrate big events in the girls' lives."

"So you get there some?" Michaela tried to keep the excitement out of her voice.

"Some . . ." Bobby hesitated. "For special events."

"Well, maybe one of your next days off could be a special event."

"What's so special about a day off?" Bobby asked, feigning ignorance.

"Keeping me from missing New . . ." She realized he was kidding and nudged him with her hip. "Funny, Granger. So can we check it out?"

"You really want to?" Bobby asked.

"Nothing major," Michaela assured him. "Just dinner or dancing or something like that."

Carter Anne's little red convertible slowed to a stop beside them. Even with the top up, there was no mistaking her for anyone else. Bobby leaned down as Carter Anne put the window down.

"You okay, Carter Anne?" Bobby asked.

"Sure am, Bobby," Carter Anne answered. "I wanted to talk to Michaela, actually."

"Oh." Bobby straightened and motioned Michaela to the window. Michaela leaned down, taking Bobby's place.

"What's up, Carter Anne?" What could the young woman want with her?

"Angie, Kerri, and I are getting together tomorrow night and want you to join us," Carter Anne explained. "I was gonna call you, but here you are."

"Um . . ." Michaela wasn't sure what to say. "Sure . . ." It was almost a question.

"Great!" Carter Anne smiled. "I'll call you tomorrow with the details." She looked over at her uncle. "You look a little busy right now."

Bobby lifted a hand as Carter Anne took off down the street. "See"—he put an arm around Michaela—"real good people."

"And Greensboro's close," Michaela added.

Bobby sighed. Life used to be easy. And now there was Michaela. He smiled. "Yep. Greensboro's close."

Michaela shut down her laptop with an unexpected twinge of excitement. How long had it been since she'd had a night with the girls? Long enough that when Angie had first mentioned her coming out with them, Michaela thought it would be fun. Fun enough that when the arrangements started to get complicated, she'd been happy to offer her room as the gathering place. When the three others had started offering to bring the refreshments, she had known it was a good idea. Regardless, it had obviously been too long when the thought of a simple night with girlfriends made her this pleased.

She headed from the research room to her suite.

Carter Anne was bringing a deli tray, Kerri was bringing cupcakes, and Angie was bringing the beer. All she had to do was make sure she hadn't left dirty clothes on the bathroom floor and freshen her makeup. For that much work, she was getting a night with friends—or at least women she thought might become friends.

The first knock came just as she capped her lipstick. With a smile at her reflection, Michaela moved to answer the door. Angie and Carter Anne were at the top of the stairs.

Kerri's voice came from the parking lot. "I'm here, too!"

Even as the three women made their way into her rooms, Michaela realized, with delight, that the warm chaos that always accompanied the family arriving at Bobby's or Angie's houses had come through her own door. Trays were juggled, coats were hung, questions were asked and left unanswered in a cloud of hugs and air kisses. By the time it was over, Angie and Kerri were setting up food in the sitting room while Carter Anne and Michaela got plates and napkins from the kitchen.

"It's really nice of you to have us over here, Michaela," Carter Anne said, pulling paper towels from the roll on the counter for them to use as napkins. "It's not quite what we had in mind when we invited you to join us."

"Truth is, Carter Anne," Michaela said as she retrieved plates from the cabinet, "I'm grateful to the three of you for including me. It's not often I get to make friends when I'm on the road."

"Well, of course you're included."

Michaela had to laugh at the expression on the younger woman's face. It was beyond her that some people might not welcome the author from out of town quite so warmly. "Thank you, anyway."

"Good!" Angie exclaimed as they entered the sitting room. "I'm starving."

"I kept her out of the cupcakes, though," Kerri added.

"Barely," Angie confirmed. She opened two beers and handed them over to Michaela and Carter Anne. "We got started on these, though."

Michaela passed around plates and watched as the three women built their sandwiches. "So what's the occasion tonight, anyway? I don't think I was ever told. Wedding stuff?"

"No occasion at all," Angie answered. "And that's the occasion." Kerri rubbed her shoulders affectionately as Angie continued. "All we ever do or talk about or think about these days is the wedding."

"And that's bad?" Michaela asked, creating her own sandwich.

Angie giggled with a blush. "Not usually, no," she admitted, "but it's getting a little overwhelming, so just getting together because we're friends seemed like a good idea. Besides"—she waved her sandwich at Michaela—"you might not have come along if it was a wedding planning night."

"Of course," Carter Anne added, "it would've been a better invitation for you if you didn't have to host."

"I don't know." Michaela took a bite of her sandwich. "You brought food and my favorite beer. This hardly counts as hosting."

"So . . ." Carter Anne leaned in.

Michaela braced herself. She had figured this was part of the reason she'd been invited this evening. But how did one dish with the girls about your guy when the girls were his nieces? She'd have to wing it.

"What's your favorite place of all the places you've traveled?" Carter Anne asked eagerly.

Michaela blinked and blinked again. Well, this was unexpected. "Honestly—" Michaela thought about it. "I really like New York. Not only is it a great city, but it's home. I know that might seem like a cheat, but"—she grinned almost sheepishly—"I like home."

"I can understand that one, even if Carter Anne can't," Angie spoke.

"Well, if 'home' meant New York City," Carter Anne said, defending herself, "I'd understand it, too." Angie rolled her eyes and opened her mouth to respond.

"I'd like to travel," Kerri pitched in, before the sisters could continue their usual debate. "And I guess I'd be willing to leave the Falls for the right reason. I just don't see it happening."

"You better not be going anywhere," Angie teased. "At least not anytime soon."

"She's not even thinking about it right now." Carter Anne's eyes twinkled as she nudged her friend.

"Carter Anne!" Kerri shushed her friend with a laugh.

"What do you mean?" Angie asked.

The young English teacher's blush made her even prettier, Michaela noted. And it spoke volumes, in spite of Angie's confusion.

"What's his name?" Michaela asked.

"What?!" Angie exclaimed as Carter Anne snorted. "What's whose name?"

"I told you it wasn't obvious," Carter Anne reassured Kerri with a gentle laugh.

"But since it's out . . ." Angie encouraged.

"I'm sorry." Michaela winced. "I didn't know it was a secret."

"You know, too?" Angie asked.

"No—" Michaela laughed. "But, well . . ." She motioned to Kerri. "It was a little obvious once Carter Anne spoke up. Maybe not the *who* but definitely the *what*."

Kerri bit back a smile. "Kirk Deal," she finally admitted before taking a deep swig of beer.

"Kirk Deal, the shop teacher at the high school?" Angie asked, amazed.

Kerri simply turned a deeper red, so Carter Anne answered for her.

"The very same."

Kerri spoke through the smile she could no longer hold back. "That's how we met."

"The shop teacher," Michaela confirmed.

"He works especially with engines," Kerri explained, still blushing. "If it has an engine or a motor, he can make it run or keep it running."

"What's the difference between a motor and an engine, anyway?" Angie asked.

"I have no idea." Kerri laughed. "But you should see him with the kids. They really like him and respect him. That's so hard to pull off with teenagers . . ." Her voice trailed off; embarrassed, she looked at her friends. All three of them were just staring at her with smiles on their faces.

Without taking her eyes off Kerri, Carter Anne leaned into Michaela. "He's also a stud."

Michaela nodded wisely. "That never hurts."

"Blond," Carter Anne continued, "and built like he lifts heavy metal things all day." She wiggled her eyebrows.

"Okay." Michaela grinned. "That definitely doesn't hurt." She turned to Kerri. "So . . ." she encouraged.

Kerri shrugged. "He doesn't know I exist."

"In this small a town?" Michaela was incredulous. "He knows you exist."

"Thank you!" Carter Anne clapped her hands.

"You work together, Kerri," Angie added. "He's gotta know you."

"See?" Carter Anne nudged her friend before turning to Michaela and Angie. "I keep telling her she just needs to kick her game up a bit."

"Of course, Carter Anne"—Kerri changed the subject with a wink to Michaela—"if it works, you'd be the only single one."

"Don't rub it in," Carter Anne sighed.

Kerri took the opportunity to keep the subject changed. "So is that what you did with the sheriff, Michaela?" she asked with a smirk. "Kick your game up a bit?"

"Oh." Michaela looked for a stall tactic, but her sandwich was done and her beer was empty. "I don't know about that . . ." She looked from one sister to the other. Both were sitting, looking back at her expectantly. Taking a deep breath, she let it out in a laugh. "Whatever I did, I'm not sure it's a step forward from where we were. No"—she shook her head—"that's not true. It's just a very frustrating step forward."

Kerri looked blankly at Michaela. It was the older woman's turn to blush. Carter Anne gasped.

"The two of you aren't . . . I mean . . ." She turned to her sister for help. "Bobby's been sleeping at home since they got back from New York," she explained.

"But I thought . . . Ohhh," Angie breathed as she realized what Carter Anne was intimating.

"Y'all are still together, though, right?" Kerri asked. "Everybody's pulling for you."

Michaela rolled her eyes. "I wouldn't quite say everybody."

"Well, fine," Kerri conceded. "Anybody who matters."

Michaela rubbed her eyes and groaned. This had to

be one of the more surreal conversations she'd ever had. "He says we're . . . courting."

Her friends laughed out loud.

"Oh, that's so Bobby," Angie said. She reached for a cupcake and peeled the wrapper. "So, you're not . . ." She knew the words, but she couldn't quite get them out. She took a bite of cupcake instead.

"At all?" Kerri gasped.

"At all," Michaela stated, reaching for a cupcake of her own. "I really liked Guyana while I was there," she joked.

Carter Anne laughed. "But how do you like Lambert Falls?" she asked, refusing to let Michaela off the hook completely.

Ah hell. So much for distraction. "You're not going to drop this, are you, Carter Anne?" Michaela asked, knowing the answer.

"She's not known for that," Angie whispered loudly.

"I like the Falls—" Michaela paused. How did she answer this question to anyone but herself, when she wasn't completely sure what the answer was? She went with honesty. "Quite a bit more than I'd expected to."

"Well, what is that supposed—" Carter Anne started, but Kerri swatted her arm.

"Enough interrogation for one night, Carter Anne," she said.

Michaela breathed deeply, as the other women laughed. She'd known the conversation was coming. Hell, another one was coming. But she'd made it through this one and that was enough for tonight.

Chapter 10

Michaela answered her phone. "Yep."

"Michaela, it's Bobby."

"Well, hi, Granger." She smiled into the phone. But why was he calling when he knew where she was? "What's up?"

"Are you at a point in your work where you could meet me in the lobby?"

"Of the library, right downstairs?" she asked. Now she was really confused.

"Right downstairs," Bobby answered.

"Sure—" Michaela hesitated. "Be right down." She closed her phone, curious, and headed down the stairs. She saw Kerri before she saw Granger. The young woman was watching Michaela come down the stairs with a huge smile on her face. What was going on? As she came around the curve of the stairs, she saw him. Bobby was standing there, hat under one arm, a dozen roses in hand. The sight stopped her on the last step. She couldn't quite bite back her smile. Another glance at Kerri behind the reception desk had her blushing. If possible, the young woman's smile was even bigger. Michaela crossed to Bobby.

"What are you doing?" she asked.

"Courtin'." Bobby grinned as he leaned down and kissed her cheek. "These are for you." He handed her the flowers and she buried her nose in them. "Would you do me the honor of having dinner with me this evening? I taught Carter Anne everything she knows."

"You're cooking?" Michaela tried to hide her shock.

"And not even on the grill." Bobby grinned at her.

"Then it would be my pleasure," she accepted.

"Does six-thirty work for you?" Bobby asked.

"Perfectly."

Bobby turned to Kerri and gave her a nod. "Kerri." He turned back to Michaela and nodded to her as well. "Michaela." Whistling through his teeth, he headed back out the door.

Michaela breathed in the aroma of the roses. Roses. When was the last time she'd gotten roses from a man, other than Matt or Justin at book launches? With a light step, she turned around, to find Kerri wiping her eyes.

"Is he always like this when he's . . . courting?" Michaela asked.

"I've never known him to date anybody, Michaela," Kerri answered.

"Really?" Michaela was shocked.

"Really," Kerri answered, grinning back at her. "Angie says he dated some a while back, but none of us ever knew."

"Oh." Michaela put her nose back in the petals. Shit. "Kerri, does the library have a vase or something? These deserve better than a water glass and that's all I have upstairs."

"Oh, sure." Kerri stood up. "Come on, we'll find something back here."

The two women moved into the private area of the

library. Kerri started looking through cabinets. Michaela went to open a pantry. "Oh, it won't be in there. That's Christmas decorations and stuff like that. Whatever we need will be"—she opened another door—"in here!" She pulled out a vase.

"That's lead crystal, isn't it?" Michaela confirmed what her eyes were telling her.

Kerri shrugged. "I guess."

"Are you sure it'll be okay for me to take it upstairs?"

"You mean, will Betsy throw a fit, right?"

Michaela laughed. "That's exactly what I mean."

"She won't throw nearly as big a fit if you take it upstairs as she will if you leave the flowers down here in it." Kerri's eyes twinkled.

"It's tempting, isn't it?" Michaela admitted. "Still, I won't ask for trouble."

"You sure?" Kerri double-checked mischievously.

Michaela sighed. It was tempting. And Kerri wasn't helping. She made a great conspirator, though. No, she would be a grown up. "Give me the vase before I change my mind," Michaela laughed.

Kerri handed her the vase. "You know, Michaela," she said, "I never have seen Sheriff Granger date anybody. And Betsy's been after him forever."

Michaela closed her hand around the vase carefully. Up close, it wasn't only crystal, it was old. Her flowers would look magnificent in it. Her flowers. "Thanks, Kerri."

The two of them headed out to the lobby. "I'll take the elevator with these." Michaela pushed the button and the doors opened.

"Michaela," Kerri called to her as she stepped into the elevator. "You'll tell us what you have for dinner?" Michaela's laughter was cut off by the doors closing.

* * *

In spite of the desire to sit and stare at the bouquet, she still had work to do. But surely she had time for a quick call. She hit her speed dial. Matt answered with a grunt just before it went to voice mail.

"I'm only answering because it's you, Michaela."

"Then thank God for caller ID," she replied. "I just got a dozen roses and asked out on a date."

Matt perked up. "I'm awake. And what does your sheriff think of this turn of events?"

"It *was* my sheriff," she said.

"But you're already sleeping together."

"That's what I love about you, Matt." She laughed. "You're so subtle."

"Only with a classy broad like you, Mike. So why did he bring you flowers?"

"He calls it 'courting,'" Michaela answered with a roll of her eyes.

"And you're loving every minute of it, aren't you?" he asked. Michaela giggled. "Oh my God," Matt teased, "you've become a girl."

"And he's making me dinner tonight," Michaela added.

"I envision meat. On a bone."

"He said no grill, but we'll see."

"A handsome, intelligent man who cooks without a grill, brings flowers, and calls it courting." Matt thought a moment. "Does he have a brother or would that be too much to hope for?"

"I think he may be too much to hope for, Matt, let alone there being two of them," Michaela sighed.

"Ah-ah-ah—" Matt stopped her. "Don't go back to being your cynical self."

"It's either that or be a girl, Matt," she teased.

Matt let out a martyred sigh. "Ah, the dilemma. I guess I can live with having an actual girl for a best friend."

"The flowers are really beautiful, Matt." Michaela's voice had gone dreamy.

"Enjoy it, honey."

"I have to get back to work now," she sighed.

"And stare at your flowers," Matt added.

"Yeah." Michaela giggled again. "I'll let you know what we have for dinner."

"I expect a full blow-by-blow—" Matt started, then said quickly, "No I don't. But I do want to know what he makes for dinner."

Michaela laughed, full and loud. "Always such class." The phone disconnected in her ear and she closed her cell. She had roses. And they were beautiful.

As tended to happen, in spite of her excitement and the scent of flowers wafting through the room, the work absorbed her. She fell into the demands and rigors of the antebellum South until the grumbling in her stomach couldn't be ignored. Looking at her watch, Michaela gasped. It was almost six. She saved her work, but didn't even bother to back it up. Tonight there wasn't time. Instead, she hurried to the suite and, stripping as she walked through her rooms, got straight into the shower.

He didn't have to be nervous. Crab cakes were his specialty. They were in the refrigerator, ready to be browned as soon Michaela got there. The wild rice was Carter Anne's own recipe, so he could vouch for its taste. All of it would go well with the wilted spinach and hot bacon dressing. And he'd even found New York–style cheesecake at the Food Lion bakery. She'd like that.

The table was set. He'd even polished the silver and pulled out Abby's china. It might be a bit much, but he wanted tonight to be special. First dates should be special.

Bobby took his time in the shower. He'd gotten in just before six, so he had plenty of time to shave and get ready. Standing in front of his closet, he pulled out his Dockers. Carter Anne's voice sounded in his head and Bobby sighed. He changed them out for his gray slacks. He didn't have to be nervous.

The doorbell rang shortly after six-thirty, just as Bobby was straightening the knot in his tie. It looked good enough in the mirror. It would have to do.

He answered the door and Michaela took his breath away. She was wearing a long, red, flared skirt, a white blouse with elegant frills along the low-cut neckline and matching cuffs. Her heels brought her to exactly his height.

"Bet you turned some heads on the way over here," he breathed.

"As a matter of fact, I did." Michaela smiled, moving into the house. "But I'd settle for turning one particular head."

"And did you manage that on the walk over?" Bobby teased.

"Sadly, no." Michaela played along. "Maybe on the way home." She turned and ran her hands along the lapel of his blazer. "If you walk me home, you'll be turning heads, too. You look good, Granger."

Bobby's hands went to her waist. "We better wait until late then, or we'll be causing car accidents."

Michaela nodded wisely. "And car accidents are definitely bad."

"Far too much paperwork," Bobby agreed. He pulled

her closer to him and kissed her. Her lips were soft, as delightful as the rest of her. He touched his tongue to them, tracing them, teasing her. With a slight whimper, Michaela opened her mouth to him. The tip of her tongue flicked over his, then back into her own mouth, luring him. Of their own accord, his hands moved from her hips to her bottom, pulling her closer as his tongue accepted her invitation, tasting her, drawing her into him as well. Michaela felt butterflies take flight in her stomach and leaned into Bobby. With a squeeze and a light nip on her lip, Bobby pulled back, smiling at her.

"You hungry?" he asked.

Michaela smiled back. "Maybe for more than just dinner, now."

"Let's start with dinner, at least." He took her hand and led her into the kitchen. Sitting her at the table, he poured her a seltzer with lemon.

"Can I help with anything?" she offered.

"You can sit there and keep me company," Bobby replied. He pulled out the crab cakes from the refrigerator.

"Oh, Granger." She looked over, impressed. "What are we having?"

He talked to her about dinner, leaving out the surprise dessert, as he prepared it. That was one of the reasons he'd chosen this dish. Aside from tasting good, it went from prepped to table-ready quickly. He was surprised to hear Michaela had never had crab cakes; she was surprised Granger could make them. Now he kinda wished he had waited to put them together until she had gotten here, so he could teach her how to make them. Well, there was always next time.

"And what are you smiling about, Granger?" Michaela asked.

"Just dinner being ready," he answered as he put the crab cakes on a platter.

"At least let me help with that," Michaela said, standing. She picked up the bowls of rice and salad.

Bobby followed with the crab cakes. "Now, you sit and I'll be back with drinks. Another seltzer or a beer?" He leaned forward and whispered, in spite of their privacy, "Beer goes with crab."

Michaela looked up from her seat, wide-eyed. "Beer, of course. Everyone knows you drink beer with crab, Granger."

Bobby winked at her and returned to the kitchen. She looked at the table. It was elegantly set. The food smelled delicious. Who would've known that Granger was a chef?

He returned with two full pilsner glasses and took a seat next to her. "You've gotten me hooked on these Natty Greene's," he said. "I hadn't tried them before you introduced me to them."

"Glad I could help," Michaela said, taking a sip of hers. "They are good, aren't they? I'll miss them when I go back to New York."

"Well—" Bobby served up the crab cakes, keeping his eyes on the meal. "Maybe you don't need to be going back."

Her silence caused him to look up. A slow smile was spreading across her face. "Maybe I don't," she agreed.

They smiled at each other until Michaela finally giggled and looked away. "So how was your day?"

"Pretty slow," Bobby admitted. "I was able to run errands and still turn the station over to Jimmy for the rest of the night." He chewed and swallowed. Oh yeah, he still had it. "He's on this evening and overnight. How about your day?"

Michaela swallowed. "My God, these are good, Granger."
He smiled his thanks but motioned for her to continue
talking. "Just lots of research. The flowers were definitely
the high point of my day. At least until tonight."

"You know," Bobby said, "I always thought writing was
more glamorous than it seems to be."

Michaela laughed. "Oh yeah." She nodded. "Teri and
me, in sweats, eating pizza as we go through research
notes is very glamorous. Although"—she thought about
it—"living in the emir's palace was pretty great."

"You lived in an emir's palace?" Bobby tried not to
sound impressed, but knew he failed. Michaela lifted a
shoulder. "*The Real World Leaders,*" Bobby said, quoting
the title of one of her books.

"You've read it?" Michaela was shocked.

"I told you, I've read 'em all."

"If you've read that one, you have read them all."
Michaela nodded in apology. "I shouldn't have doubted
you."

Bobby grinned. "I will give you, it's not your best."

"Everybody's a critic." Michaela rolled her eyes in jest.

"But you're still better than three-quarters of the other
authors out there," Bobby added.

"There goes that Southern charm again." Michaela
fanned herself.

"Hey." Bobby sat up and straightened his shoulders. "I
don't carry a glittery purple sign into an airport for just
any author."

Michaela laughed loudly. "Game, set, and match to
you, Granger." She'd almost forgotten that silly sign.
Knowing him now, knowing Angie, it was even sillier.

"Save room for dessert." Bobby pointed to her rapidly
emptying plate. "I found something special."

"Then I am done," Michaela announced. "Although you have to promise to make those again."

Bobby reached for her hand and rubbed her palm. "Whenever you'd like."

She bit her lower lip, smiling. "Granger . . ."

He picked up her hand and kissed where his thumb had just been. "Let me clear the table."

"Let me help," she countered.

"I'm gonna give in to you a lot, aren't I?" Bobby laughed.

They cleared the table, but Bobby made her go into the TV room and wait for dessert. When he came in, Michaela was looking at his bookshelf.

"You do have all of them." She still sounded amazed. "I could sign them for you, if you want. Really make the collection impressive."

"When I first heard you were coming, I was going to ask you to," Bobby admitted.

"What changed your mind?"

"Well"—Bobby explained—"if I've got the author herself, I don't really need her autograph, do I?"

"Then I guess you don't need them signed," Michaela said quietly, looking at the books so he wouldn't see how happy his statement made her.

"Guess not," Bobby said, grateful she was looking away, so she couldn't see the foolish grin he couldn't hold back.

She had to face him sooner or later. Turning, she saw Bobby with a tray. He placed it on the coffee table and she giggled. "What's that?"

"It's New York–style cheesecake," he answered.

Thank God she looked at his face before laughing. For a poker player, he seemed pretty transparent to her, and the expression currently on his face was a combination of hope and doubt. This dear sweet man. He was so proud of it. "I can't believe you found me this, Granger. Thank you."

The doubt was erased by pure pleasure and no little pride. "I knew you'd like it." He served up two slices and handed her a plate. "I rented a movie, too. Hope you like Hitchcock."

Michaela leaned back. The cheesecake was pretty good, actually. "So long as it's the original black and white, I adore Hitchcock."

"How 'bout the ones that were filmed in color?" Bobby asked

"Oh, those are fine, too," Michaela corrected herself. "Just so long as it's not that colorized crap."

Bobby sneered. "I have yet to see a colorized movie. Movies in color are great. But if they were filmed in black and white, they should be viewed in black and white."

"Then which one do we have?"

Grinning, Bobby loaded his favorite into the DVD player and settled in next to Michaela. By the time Cary Grant was mistaken for a spy, they had finished their cheesecake. By the time he was meeting Eva Marie Saint, Michaela was completely absorbed in the story. It didn't matter that she couldn't count the number of times she'd seen the movie. All that mattered was the question of if he would be able to clear his name and solve the mystery.

As the credits rolled, Michaela stood up, stretching. "God, I love that movie." She started to stack the dessert plates on the platter Granger had used to bring them out.

"Don't worry about it, Michaela." Bobby put his hand over hers. "It's bedtime. I have the morning shift."

He stood up. Michaela was pleased to see he was pulling on his coat from the rack by the door. Honestly, that worked for her. A little privacy this evening would be nice. It had been long enough that she didn't want to worry about if they made a little noise. Spending the night at her place ensured more privacy. There was no way Carter Anne could come home at an inopportune time. She joined him at the door.

It was colder on the walk than it had been coming over. Bobby took off his jacket and draped it over Michaela's shoulders. She slipped her arms in the sleeves and snuggled up even closer to him. Automatically, she paused while Bobby looked down the alley and pulled on the gate holding Daisy in her yard. Daisy herself lifted her nose from the door of her doghouse, but left them alone.

The two of them continued the short walk to the library, around the back and up the stairs. Michaela opened the door and Bobby raised an eyebrow at her.

"Already gotten used to our way of life and stopped locking your doors, Michaela?" Bobby teased her.

"I guess so," Michaela shrugged. She took a step inside, but turned when she realized Bobby wasn't following her in. "Granger?"

He reached out and pulled her into a deep, powerful kiss. She could feel his arousal, as real as her own. Her arms went around his shoulders and she tilted her head to accept his kiss more fully. With a noise down in his throat, Bobby broke the kiss. Michaela groaned.

"You're still not coming in?" Michaela sighed.

"Soon, Michaela," Bobby whispered. "This time, it's about wantin' to take our time and me havin' to be up at five. We can't really be up all night and me be worth anything tomorrow."

"This isn't courting, Granger," she teased.

"Michaela," Bobby assured her, "I'm a gentleman, not a fool."

She took pleasure in the fact that his voice was ragged, his breath uneven, his accent heavy. At least she wouldn't be the only one watching the clock tonight. She removed his jacket and handed it to him.

"Have sweet dreams, then, Granger." With a wicked smile, she closed the door. With a shake of his head, Bobby started down the stairs. It was going to be a long, long night.

"Hi, Ms. Howard." Jimmy waved to her from his desk as she came into the station.

Michaela waved back. "Hi, Jimmy." She walked around Bobby's desk and put her hands on his shoulders.

"Hi there, Michaela," Bobby spoke, looking up at her.

"Jimmy," Michaela continued, still not looking at Bobby, "who's on tonight?"

"I am, Ms. Howard."

"And what time does the sheriff get off duty tonight?"

"'Bout thirty minutes from now," Jimmy answered with a grin. He had no idea what was going on, but the expression on the boss's face was worth playing along a little longer.

Michaela continued the questions. "How'd you like to come to work about thirty minutes later tomorrow afternoon?"

Jimmy laughed. "I wouldn't mind that one bit, Ms. Howard."

"In that case"—Michaela spun Bobby's chair until he was facing her, took his hands and pulled him up—"the sheriff'll see you tomorrow. About thirty minutes late."

"Do I have a say in any of this?" Bobby spoke up.

Michaela laughed. "If what you have to say is anything other than ''night, Jimmy,' then I may have to rethink this whole relationship."

"Boss," Jimmy added, "I have to say, I agree with her."

Bobby put an arm around Michaela and pulled his jacket off the back of his chair. "'Night, Jimmy." He kissed Michaela and they headed out as Jimmy shook his head with a chuckle.

"To what do I owe the prison break?" Bobby asked once they were on the street.

"I figured if the problem the other night was timing," Michaela explained, "then we needed to change the timing."

"You figured, huh?"

"Would you prefer supposed? Thought? Believed? Decided?" Michaela teased.

"Figured works," Bobby announced, "but apparently *decided* would've been accurate, too."

"Okay," Michaela conceded, "I decided we should change the timing."

"And how are we doing that?" Bobby asked. "Aside from the obvious of getting me off work thirty minutes early?"

"The meatballs have been cooking in the sauce for most of the afternoon, so we can eat as soon as the spaghetti is ready." Michaela led him up the back stairs of the library. No reason to announce to the lobby that the sheriff was being seduced right above their heads. "And since the only way to eat spaghetti is al dente, it won't take long at all."

Bobby breathed deeply as they opened the door. Not even Carter Anne's spaghetti sauce smelled like this. Sartini's didn't smell like this.

"Open this." Michaela handed him a bottle of red wine. "Let it breathe while the pasta cooks. You like garlic bread?"

"So long as you do," he joked.

"Garlic bread for two, then." Michaela sliced a fresh loaf as the water for the pasta began to heat.

"I thought you were Irish," Bobby asked.

"I am," she answered, "but I used to live above this great Italian restaurant. Worked there while I was a starving writer. Did a little bit of everything, from waiting tables to prep cook."

"While you were writing books?"

Michaela nodded as she finished prepping their meal. "I actually worked there past the time I needed to because I enjoyed the job. Plus, I knew if I ever needed a fallback job again, the more experience I had, the better."

"I'm sure Sal Sartini would be happy to let you bus tables," Bobby said, laughing.

"Taste this." Michaela held a spoon of sauce out for him. "And tell me I'll be bussing tables for Sartini's."

Bobby touched his tongue to the spoon. "You won't be bussing tables, Michaela." Bobby closed his eyes in pleasure. "You won't be doing anything at Sartini's, though."

"And why is that?" Michaela put a hand on her hip.

"Because Sal will kill you for this recipe."

"Oh." Michaela wiggled her hjead happily.

"I will, of course," Bobby continued, "arrest him and bring him to justice."

Michaela kissed him before going back to their dinner.

"I'll have to," Bobby assured her. "He'll have the recipe."

"Gee, thanks, Granger."

When dinner was ready, she served it and brought

both plates to the table. "No china or crystal, I'm afraid," Michaela said as they sat down. "I don't think they expect the residents of the suite to be hosting dinner parties."

"It's fine, Michaela," Bobby said, pouring the wine. He picked up his fork and took his first bite. It was even better than one taste of sauce had made him believe. "The meatballs are what? Beef and saus . . ." He gasped suddenly speechless.

"What were you saying, Granger?" Michaela asked with a devilish smile, as she moved her hand even farther up his inner thigh.

"Beef and sausage," Bobby repeated. "The meatballs are both beef and sausage."

Michaela nodded. "They are. The key is two kinds of sausage and very few bread crumbs. Less filler means more flavor."

"Well, it sure is tasty," he said with another gasp.

Michaela brought her hand back to the table and continued to eat her dinner. "Feel free to eat as much as you'd like. I'm afraid there's not dessert tonight."

"Mmm"—Bobby shrugged—"better timing."

"I like the way you think, Granger." Michaela laughed.

"Then would it be too forward for me to point out that spaghetti and meatballs can sit for hours and still taste delicious?"

"I *really* like the way you think, Granger." But her laugh was a little nervous. "I just didn't want you to think—well, you know."

"We're both adults, Michaela," Bobby assured her, picking up their plates and clearing the table. "I won't ever think . . . you know."

She stood, but Bobby caught her hand and pulled her

to him. Kissing her, he backed her up until her thighs pushed up against the table.

"Granger?" Michaela broke the kiss.

Bobby found her mouth again, silencing her. Hands on her hips, Bobby lifted her onto the table. He put a finger under her chin and turned her face up to his. His tongue danced in over her lips, down her jaw. His teeth scraped along her neck until he reached her collarbone. Nibbling along her collar, he stretched her out on the table. The cut of her blouse gave him the perfect map to the curve of her breasts. Teasingly slowly, he released her buttons until her skin was exposed. His breath was warm on her flesh as he kissed his way down her body.

His touch felt so good, Michaela felt her back arch in response. Bobby took advantage of the motion by slipping his hands beneath her and unhooking her bra. Lifting her arms, he had her out of her shirt and her bra off before Michaela could even take another breath.

"Granger." Her voice was ragged.

His answer was a low chuckle, as his mouth locked onto a hardened nipple. He rolled it between his teeth while flicking at the nub with his tongue. Michaela gasped and fisted her hands into Bobby's hair.

Ignoring the insistence in her grip, Bobby took his time, his hands and mouth exploring her. He moved her skirt up her thighs, tracing the path with the barest touch of his fingertips. Their contrast to his teeth still on her breasts had her writhing underneath him.

Michaela didn't know if it had been minutes or hours since Bobby had started his slow torture of her body. She only knew every nerve ending was on fire—she was on fire. And the harder she pulled on his hands, his hair, his body, the slower he moved. While his mouth explored her breasts and tummy, his hands had discovered her legs and hips. They met, and her hips thrust up to meet him. He placed one hand flat on her hip, holding her down, while the other continued to rediscover the most private parts of her. His fingers dipped and circled inside of her, finding their rhythm. He kissed her, teeth treating this bud as he had treated her nipples. Bobby listened and felt, matching his pace to her breathing, bringing her up, then lowering her down—again and again, until finally he brought her to the edge and over. The moan came from deep inside of her. Her back bowed, braced on her shoulder and her hips, which Bobby still refused to release.

Collapsing back onto the table, Michaela tried to catch her breath. Bobby still leaned over her, smiling. Unable to stop it, Michaela started to laugh.

"Wow."

"I take it as a compliment that I have made a writer speechless." Bobby's smile grew bigger.

"As well you should," Michaela breathed. "Somehow, I'm not sure this is what Betsy Abernathy had in mind when she voted to make this area into a guest suite."

Bobby laughed and didn't quite notice when Michaela stood.

"Come on." She took his hand without bothering to straighten her clothes. "The night's still young and the table's hard." With a twinkle in her eye, she led him into the bedroom.

His clothing was definitely annoying. There was too much of it and it included far too many buttons. Still, she managed to get most of them off in spite of her rush, without fumbling too badly. All she knew was she wanted them both naked and wanted it now. Bobby seemed to share her eagerness because his hands were less nimble

than usual. When she finally got him undressed, she let
her hands roam over him, following them with her eyes.

She'd missed looking at him. Missed the scar on his
hip. Had even missed his little paunch, that went unno-
ticed under his uniform and broad shoulders—unless
he was naked. When she lifted her eyes to his, again, the
heat she saw in them matched her own. Hands on his
shoulders, Michaela kissed him, and pushed gently until
he was sitting on the edge of the bed, then lying on it.

Grinning, she straddled him, using her hands to guide
him into her. The sound that came from him was part
groan, part sigh, and all music to her ears. His hands
moved automatically to her hips, helping her move.
When she lifted herself high on him, Bobby sucked air
through his teeth. When she lowered herself back down
again, he couldn't help but gasp her name. Michaela
kept up her pace, watching his expression.

Bobby was about to lose himself. As much as he
wanted to, he wanted something else more. Leaving one
hand on her hip, he moved the other between her legs.
Michaela's eyes widened, then she grinned down at him.

They moved together, eyes locked. Bobby saw hers
begin to glaze over and knew what was about to happen.
He braced himself to hold on, make it last, but he hadn't
counted on her legs contracting or her hips thrusting,
taking him so deep inside of her. Her orgasm rocked
them both, causing her to cry out and him to grit his
teeth, biting out her name.

First, Michaela collapsed on his chest. Finally she man-
aged to find the strength to roll off to one side of him.
Barely. She was a puddle. Her entire body had dissolved.
It was great.

"Whatever are you laughing about?" Bobby asked. He
leaned on an elbow and looked down at her.

"I wasn't laughing, Granger," Michaela muttered, then thought about it. "Was I?"

"Maybe a little," Bobby said.

"I should be embarrassed," Michaela said, eyes still closed, "but I don't have the energy."

"It's okay." Bobby kissed her shoulder.

The bed moved and shook suspiciously. Michaela opened one eye and peered at the man. He was getting up. Michaela stretched. She should care. "Where are you going, Granger?" she finally managed.

"Ssh." Bobby leaned down and kissed her again, on the lips this time.

She didn't want him to leave. She drifted.

"Michaela?" Bobby whispered. "Honey? You want to wake up?"

She stretched and yawned. "You came back."

"I never went away," Bobby assured her.

Michaela sat up, rubbing her eyes, looked at Granger—and laughed. He was standing, stark naked, holding two plates of spaghetti.

Lifting them, he grinned. "Dinner in bed?"

Michaela moved over and took her plate from him. He settled in next to her and spun the pasta around his fork.

"You came back," she repeated, a little amazed.

"I came back," Bobby said firmly.

Courting had been nice, but this was better. Michaela dug into her pasta. He'd come back.

"But he's drunk and stubborn and insisting there are UFOs hovering up over the old falls," Bobby spoke, the memory making him laugh, but not as hard as Michaela was laughing. "So we're wandering around up there knowing we're not going to find anything when we hear—"

Michaela's phone rang. She waved it off. "Never mind that," Michaela urged. "What did you hear?" The phone rang again. "Dammit. Don't forget where you are." She picked up her cell off the table between them. "Yep."

Bobby watched her expression change. One moment she was drying tears of laughter from her eyes. Now she was rubbing them in tired disbelief.

"But it's done, Justin," Michaela breathed. "It was accepted. They released the monies, for God's sake." She listened, shaking her head. "How long do I have?" With a barking laugh, she asked, "Are you serious?"

Bobby decided she might like a little privacy. Crossing to the small window of the research room, he gave her what he could without walking out on her.

"Fine." She exhaled hard. "I said fine, Justin. E-mail them to me; be sure to cc Teri. And then make sure everyone leaves me the hell alone for the next three days." Michaela hung up the phone and turned to her current research. "Dammit," she spit, bookmarking her pages and slamming the books shut.

"Everything okay?" Bobby asked from the window.

Michaela spun. "Oh. Granger."

Bobby came back over to the table and sat down. "Sounds bad."

"Not bad, so much," Michaela muttered, "but not good, either. My editors have decided they don't like some of the UK book."

"How much of it don't they like?"

"The middle," Michaela answered. "They love the first fifty pages. They love the last fifty pages. 'It's just the middle,'" she quoted Justin sarcastically. "So I've got three days to gut and rewrite about two hundred fifty pages."

"Is that—"

"Even possible?" Michaela interrupted with a harsh

laugh. "I don't know." She went back to stacking her current work. "It's going to be a hard three days, I know that much."

"Then I had better be one of those people who leaves you the hell alone." Bobby reached for her hand, but she kept building her piles of books. "The end of the story will have to wait."

"What story?"

"Eddie?" Bobby nudged her memory. "The UFOs?"

"Oh, right." Michaela spared him a glance as she pulled her laptop closer to her. "So, were there UFOs?"

"There were. Sucked Jimmy up into the light. I had to grab him by his ankles to keep him earthbound." Bobby waited.

"Then it's a good thing you were there." Michaela scanned the e-mail from Justin.

"Michaela . . ." Bobby touched her hand.

Oh shit. Michaela bit her lower lip and shook her head. "I'm sorry, Granger. It's just . . ." She pointed to her computer.

He stood and leaned down to kiss her. "Will you still be eating?"

"Sure." Michaela gave him a quick peck before turning back to the computer.

"Then maybe dinner tonight," he suggested.

"Sounds good." Michaela picked up her phone and opened it. With a deep breath, she looked up at Bobby. "Thanks, Granger."

Bobby nodded. He wasn't even at the door when he heard her voice.

"Teri, did you get Justin's e-mail?"

Well . . . he'd see her for dinner.

* * *

"What's wrong with this section?" Michaela muttered. "What can be wrong with this section? It's how it happened."

"Michaela?" Bobby walked into the research room. "Have you moved at all today?"

"I had to pee. A couple of times." She spoke to her computer.

"I brought dinner." Bobby lifted the bag he was holding. "Carter Anne put up plates for both of us when I told her you what you were up against."

"Granger . . ." Michaela groaned. "This is so sweet. Thank you. And thank Carter Anne. I just . . ." Damn. "I can't take a break right now."

"Oh." Bobby shifted from one foot to the other. "I thought we were doing dinner."

"I'm sorry, Granger." Michaela reached for his hand. "I thought we were, too. I just can't."

"No, no, of course not." Bobby shook his head. "Should I leave this for you?"

"What is it?" Michaela tried to peek into the bag.

"Carter Anne's tuna casserole," Bobby answered.

"God"—Michaela laughed—"I haven't had tuna casserole in years."

"Then I'll leave it." Bobby started to reach into the bag.

"Granger." She put a hand on his, stopping him. "By the time I get to it"—she made a face—"I can't imagine it'll be up to Carter Anne's usual standards. Cold tuna casserole even sounds disgusting."

"You have to eat, Michaela," Bobby reminded her.

"I've got bread for toast and a couple apples in my rooms," she reassured him. "I promise I'll eat."

Bobby nodded. What else could he do? "Okay."

"Granger." She stood up and slipped her arms around his waist. "It's gotta be done in three days."

He kissed her. "Three days then."

She grinned at him. "You're the best, Granger."

Maybe Chris needed dinner. Angie was at the house with Carter Anne. He'd driven, since he had both dinners to carry, so getting up to the old Montgomery place was fast.

Chris answered the door, opening it slowly until he saw who it was. "Hey, Bobby."

"Want dinner?" Bobby asked, holding up the bag.

"Sure." Chris hesitated but stepped aside. "Come on in."

Bobby walked straight through into the kitchen and put the bag on the table. As he unpacked their dinners, Chris poured two coffees.

"Carter Anne's tuna casserole?" he asked, sitting down. Bobby nodded. Chris took a bite and gave a little moan. "Is there anything she can't cook?"

Bobby nodded. "Steaks."

"You never let her near the grill, right?"

"I taught her everything else. Figured I was allowed to keep some secrets." Bobby gave Chris a sly glance.

Chris laughed. "So," he said, taking a bite of tuna. "Why're you here, Bobby?"

Bobby took a bite of his dinner, stalling.

"Come on, Bobby." Chris raised a brow.

"Michaela didn't have time for dinner," Bobby explained.

Chris looked at his friend. There was more.

"Didn't want the casserole to go to waste."

"Why not just go home?" Chris asked. "Put the casserole in the refrigerator."

"You want me to take your dinner away?"

Chris wrapped an arm around his plate. "It's mine now, Bobby."

Bobby laughed then and, with a shake of his head, answered his friend's question. "I just needed . . . I don't know. Sometimes I still miss Abby."

"Okay," Chris said.

"I just don't think Angie or Carter Anne would understand that." Bobby stirred his food before taking another bite.

"I love them," Chris said, "but I think you're probably right."

"I'm not sure I understand it," Bobby admitted.

"Do you have to?" Chris asked.

Bobby kept eating his dinner. That was why he came here. Some questions answered themselves.

Michaela knocked on the door, all but bouncing on her toes. Please, let him be home. She'd called the station to make sure he wasn't there, and Jimmy had assured her Bobby had the night off. So, please, let him be home. Carter Anne answered the door. Michaela spoke before the other woman could even say hello.

"Is your uncle home?"

"Sure, Michaela." Carter Anne moved aside so Michaela could come in. "He's upstairs." She yelled over her shoulder for Bobby.

"I'm right here," he answered coming down the stairs. "No need to yell. Hey, Michaela." He smiled at her.

The smile she returned was the warmest she'd given him since Justin had called her three days ago. "You made the deadline?" he asked.

Michaela wrapped her arms around him and held on tight. "I did!" she exclaimed. "They had no business asking for that kind of turnaround. Justin had no business agreeing to it. And I had no business turning it over, but—" She pulled back and grinned at him, arms still around his neck. "I made it."

"Congratulations." Bobby pushed his lips against hers hard, with a loud smack.

"Let's celebrate," she said, looking between Bobby and Carter Anne.

"What'd you have in mind?" Carter Anne asked.

"Chocolate and champagne," Michaela announced.

"That sounds a little . . . private," Carter Anne said.

"Box brownies," Michaela assured her, "not that romantic. But baking in my oven right now."

"Then we should get moving," Carter Anne said, grinning at Bobby.

Bobby nodded. "I guess we should."

"I'll drive," Carter Anne volunteered, picking up her keys and purse.

"Why not," Bobby agreed, putting an arm around each of the women.

Out of respect for her uncle, Carter Anne drove the speed limit. "Are Angie and Chris coming, too?"

Michaela flipped open her phone. "I hadn't called them yet. Angie—" She broke off the conversation with Carter Anne as the call connected. With a brief explanation to Angie, she hung up again. "They'll meet us there. I cannot believe I made this deadline!" Michaela rested her hands on the top of her head, confined by the small space of the car.

They got to the library and Michaela hurried up the stairs to check on the brownies. The timer was just going off. As she pulled them out of the oven, Carter Anne and Bobby gathered in the kitchen around the table. "Bobby, would you handle the champagne?"

"You stocked up?" he asked, looking in the refrigerator.

Michaela nodded. "When I realized I was indeed going to make the impossible deadline. Same time I bought the brownie mix."

By the time everything was ready, Chris and Angie had arrived. The group moved into the sitting room.

"To making impossible deadlines," Carter Anne toasted, lifting her glass.

"To authors talented enough to make impossible deadlines." Chris lifted his glass.

"To the Colonel, who brought Howard Michaels to the Falls in the first place." Angie raised her glass, too.

Michaela joined them. "I can drink to all of that."

"So can I." Bobby picked up his glass. He looked at the smile on Michaela's face, at how relaxed she seemed. Yes, he could drink to all those things. He could also drink to having Michaela back. It had been a long three days. For both of them.

"What was Justin's reaction to your hard work?" Bobby wanted to know.

Michaela humphed and took a bite of brownie. "He says he never doubted me for a minute."

"Of course not," Bobby said.

It made her laugh. "Well, that made one of us."

"Two," Bobby defended himself.

"Oh sure." Michaela rubbed her leg against Bobby's. "Thanks. Sometimes," she continued, "I think Justin might have too much faith in me."

"How so?" Angie asked, nibbling a brownie.

Michaela rolled her eyes. "When I called him to tell him I was done, he was very excited to tell me about a new opportunity for another book."

"But that's good, right?" Angie followed up. She

looked at her uncle. "Right, Bobby? You always liked it when her books came out quickly."

"Used to, sure," Bobby confirmed.

Michaela snorted. "Usually, sure, I like staying busy. But this would've meant three to four months in Nepal.

"Nepal?" Carter Anne was shocked.

Chris glanced at Bobby, whose face was blank. He hadn't known until right now.

"Nepal," Michaela repeated.

"What'd you tell him?" Angie urged.

"Absolutely not." Michaela took another brownie. "Not right now. I just can't." Bobby draped an arm around Michaela's shoulders. "I haven't been home longer than a week and a half since I left for Europe before the last book. That's almost a year ago, now." She looked at Bobby. "It's like making that rookie mistake all over again." She rested her head on Bobby's arm. "I need some time off, some time at home. It's no easier to be away now than it was at twenty-seven." Lifting a tired hand, she motioned to her friends. "But never mind that. What'd I miss while I was under my rock?"

"Nothing as interesting as a trip to Nepal." Bobby's voice was flat.

"What?" Michaela sat up, looking at him.

"Or a week and a half in New York," he added.

The room was suddenly tense. His words hung in the air.

"Michaela"—Angie stood up—"thanks for letting us celebrate with you tonight, but we need to be gettin' on." Chris stood with her.

"Y'all want me to drive you home?" Carter Anne offered, standing as well.

"That'd be great, thanks," Angie agreed, before anyone could object.

Carter Anne kissed Michaela on the cheek. "Proud of you, honey." She just glared at her uncle. "I'll see you later."

The three of them left faster than Michaela would've thought possible. She turned to Bobby.

"What was that about, Granger?"

Bobby shook his head. What had that been about? He had no idea why he'd reacted that way, hand to God. "Why'd you turn down the Nepal book, Michaela?"

"I told you, I needed time to be at home. These two books are enough for this year." Michaela reached out to Bobby. "We've got something new, too. Maybe now isn't the best time to be running off to the other side of the world."

Bobby lifted her hand to his lips. "I'm sorry I over-reacted, Michaela. I don't know what's going on."

"Why don't we finish celebrating"—Michaela lifted his face to hers—"now that the rest of the family has left." Leaning in, she kissed him, her tongue nudging past his lips to begin its exploration of his mouth. He tasted of chocolate-tinted champagne. His cheeks were stubbly under her hands.

Bobby reached up and covered her hands with his. Tilting his head, he accepted her kiss, deepened it. When she led him to the bedroom, he followed.

Chapter 11

The number on her caller ID couldn't possibly be right. There was no reason for him to be calling. Unless he didn't realize she was out of town . . .

"Yep?"

The laugh that rumbled down the speaker made her smile instinctively. "You still answer the phone the exact same way."

"And you"—Michaela laughed along with him—"still have the richest laugh I've ever heard. How the hell are you, Ken?" She leaned back in her chair, one hand holding the phone, the other behind her head.

"I'm somewhere called Danville, Virginia," Ken answered.

Excited, Michaela sat up. "But I'm in Lambert Falls, North Carolina. I'm just across the state line."

That laugh rumbled again. "I know. I've been told. And Teri told me. That's why I called."

"Wait." Michaela held up her hand and shook her head, as if her friend could see her. "Back up. Why did you call Teri? And what are you doing down here?"

"Believe me, I wouldn't be making this drive if I didn't have to be," he sighed. "I'm en route to Florida."

"Ken!" Michaela exclaimed. "NASA." It wasn't a question.

"NASA," he confirmed with a barking laugh.

"It's about damn time they gave you the recognition you deserve." Michaela smiled into the phone.

"You always believed, Michaela," Ken said. "And that's why I called. I was hoping to catch up with you the weekend of the silent auction, but that didn't happen."

"No, I wasn't in town very long. I'm sorry."

"It's okay. Teri told me I could catch up with you as I went through North Carolina instead."

"She didn't mention anything to me, and we just spoke last night."

"I asked her not to," he confessed. "I wanted to surprise you."

"Well, you certainly did that." The warmth she had felt upon seeing his number settled in. "If you're just en route, do you have time for me to buy you dinner?"

"Nope," Ken replied plainly. Before Michaela's disappointment could solidify, he continued. "But I've got time to buy you dinner."

"Deal," Michaela agreed.

"Where should I meet you? What's good around here?"

Damn. She hadn't thought that far ahead. The thought of seeing someone from home had trumped the actual logistics of seeing him.

"This could be a problem," Michaela stated.

Ken laughed. "Surely there's something good."

Michaela joined him. "Good, yes. Transportation, no. I don't have a car."

"Why don't I just come to you?" he suggested. "Give me the address for my GPS and I'll be there."

Michaela did and hung up the phone with a smile. It had been too long since she'd seen him. They'd been friends so long, it was easy to simply assume there would always be time to catch up. She'd missed him. Admittedly, she hadn't thought much about anyone from home since . . . Granger. Shit. She had to call him and call him right now. Jimmy answered on the first ring.

"Jimmy, it's Michaela," she said.

"Hey, Miss Howard," the younger man answered.

"Jimmy," Michaela sighed, "when are you going to call me Michaela? I've asked you to half a dozen times. You know it's okay."

"Yes, ma'am," he said. Michaela rolled her eyes as he continued. "How can I help you? Are you looking for the sheriff?"

"I am. Is he around?" Michaela asked.

"Hate to tell you, but he's gone home," Jimmy said.

"But—" Michaela checked her watch. "I thought he was on this afternoon."

"He was, but he's agreed to split the shift," Jimmy explained. "Went home to get some sleep. He'll be back on at seven and work the graveyard. Want me to take a message?"

"No," Michaela sighed, "that's all right." She was about to hang up when she had a thought. "Jimmy, why'd he switch schedules?"

"Ummm . . ." Jimmy hesitated. "See . . . I, um, I have a date tonight and he agreed to take my shift."

"Jimmy!"

Jimmy winced. "Ma'am?"

Michaela was surprised, but pleasantly so. The researcher in her wanted to press, but she could practically hear him blush. She'd ask the girls later. One of them would know. "You have a good night, then."

"Thank you," he responded. "You sure you don't want to leave a message?"

"It's fine, Jimmy, but thank you." Michaela smiled into the phone before hanging up. She'd walk Ken down to the station and introduce them that way. For now, she had just enough time for a quick shower before he arrived.

By the time she was showered, dressed, and had just started to wonder if he was lost, her phone rang.

"How the hell do I get in there?" Ken spoke without preamble.

Michaela laughed. "The dragon at the gate has gone home for the night. Come around back; you'll see stairs up to the second floor. The door at the top is mine."

"Back around near the parking lot?" he clarified.

"Right there," she confirmed. "I'll open the door."

"I'm walking around now."

Michaela went to the back entrance and opened it. "You getting old and slow there, Ken?" she teased him.

"I'll show you old and slow," he laughed.

Michaela heard the sound through her phone, but also drifting up through the night air. Looking down, she watched him see the stairs, follow them with his eyes, and catch sight of her.

"Ms. Howard," his voice sounded in an offbeat stereo, "you are a sight for sore eyes."

"You don't look so bad yourself," she teased back. "At least from what I can see at this distance."

"I've always told you," Ken spoke as he climbed the stairs, "your glasses are sexy. You should wear them more often, not just when you read."

"When I start needing to see faces in the dark on a regular basis, I'll consider it," Michaela quipped.

Ken stepped up in front of her. "Hi."

"Hi," she answered, flipping her phone closed and hugging him. "It's good to see you."

"You, too, Michaela." Ken squeezed her hard before finally letting her go.

"Come on in." Michaela led him into the suite and sat them down under the watchful eye of the Colonel. "So, tell me everything."

"The paper I wrote for MIT caught someone's eye at NASA, and everything went from there."

"So, NASA finally figured out what MIT and I have known forever."

Ken laughed. "You've known it forever. MIT only realized it about a year ago, remember."

"They still figured it out before NASA did," Michaela noted. "At least they listened to me."

He nodded. "At least NASA was willing to listen to MIT, even if they weren't wise enough to listen to you."

"And here we thought they were smart," laughed Michaela. "When do you have to be there?"

"By tomorrow night, so I can report first thing Monday."

"That's one hell of a drive," Michaela breathed.

"I'll need an early start," he agreed, "so you should tell me about what you're up to so we don't pull another all-nighter."

"Oh, God." Michaela laughed, throwing her head back. "What a night that was." She sniffed as the memory of their last night came back to her. "I had no idea I wouldn't see you for so long."

Ken shook his head. "Who knew you'd be away for so long."

"I guess I didn't," Michaela conceded. "Anyway"—she waved it off—"before we get started, let's get dinner. We'll talk while we eat. Plus—" She hesitated, looking away before she spoke again. "There's someone I'd like you to meet."

"Michaela?" He couldn't believe what he was seeing. Not from her. "Are you blushing?"

"Of course not." Michaela looked him square in the eye and arched an eyebrow. "I never blush."

"Of course not." Ken gave her a sly, knowing smile. "So, who is this guy?"

"Come on." Michaela stood up. "I'll tell you about him after you've met him."

Even with his back to the entrance of the sheriff's office, Bobby knew the sound of the click of her heels. With a smile, he turned—and stopped. He'd met the man walking next to her before, but this time he had his hand on the small of Michaela's back, possessively. Michaela's smile was as bright and open as ever, but Bobby could see something in the man's eyes. And he wasn't real fond of the smug smile on the man's face, either.

"What're you doing here, Michaela?" he asked, crossing to her. And yes, he might have been a little pleased when the man's smug look faltered, but he was still gentleman enough not to smirk when Michaela moved into his arms. Still, if he kept his arm around her instead of letting her move away as he usually would, well, who could blame him?

"I wanted you to meet an old friend of mine," Michaela said. Granger's arm tightened on her waist. Oh God. Here came the pissing match. "We were hoping"—

she gave him a squeeze back, then stepped away gently but definitively—"you could come join us for dinner."

"We met in New York," Bobby said, but still stuck out his hand. "Bobby Granger, Ken. Welcome to Lambert Falls."

"Oh." Michaela took a deep breath and exhaled hard.

Ken spoke, shaking Bobby's hand, before Michaela could say anything else. "I remember, Bobby. Any friend of Michaela's."

The words seemed polite enough, but Michaela knew men, especially these men, better than that. How had they met when she hadn't even seen Ken while they were in town? Oh, this could get ugly. She stepped up to Bobby and laid a hand gently on his chest. "Ken just called this afternoon from Danville."

"Really?" Bobby looked at Michaela, eyes wide but hardening.

"Yes." Michaela stayed very calm. "He's passing through the area and stopped for dinner."

Bobby looked at Michaela a moment longer and she held his gaze, with a slight tilt of her head. He didn't like it, but damned if now was the time. Turning back to Ken, he spoke again. "As you say, any friend of Michaela's."

Michaela sighed. Crisis averted. For now. "So can you come to dinner with us?"

Bobby did a quick mental calculation. During the week, the answering service would be handling the calls already. All it would take would be a call on his part and they'd handle it tonight, too. But people expected him or Jimmy here on weekends unless there was an emergency or extenuating circumstances. Wanting to keep an eye on a man so obviously infatuated with Michaela hardly seemed like either. More's the pity. Any other night, he would give Jimmy a call, but he couldn't do it—not tonight, not for this reason. Dammit, anyway.

"I wish I could," he finally answered. "Surely do wish I could, but I'm working alone tonight."

"Well, I'm sure your town will rest well knowing you're here," Ken said.

Michaela heard the sneer, as subtle as it was, in Ken's voice and knew there was no way Granger would miss it, either. Sure enough, his jaw hardened imperceptibly. Almost.

She spoke quickly. "What time are you off, Granger?"

Bobby stared at the other man a moment longer before turning to her. "Not until the morning."

"Then come by before bed." She placed herself directly between the two men, close enough to Bobby to rest her hands on his chest. "I'll buy you your last cup of coffee."

Bobby smiled at her. How could he not? Rubbing her arms, he agreed. "I'll see you then."

Michaela kissed him lightly and stepped back.

"Bobby—" Ken nodded. "Good to see you again."

"Ken." Bobby responded with a tip of his own head and watched as Michaela led him out. Chris and Jimmy had been after him to hire at least one more deputy. Come morning, he was going to start the process. Damned if something like this would happen twice.

As they walked out, Ken fell into step beside Michaela. "The sheriff, Michaela? Seriously?"

She looked hard at her old friend. "Seriously, Ken."

"Well—" He shrugged. "I guess the pickings are probably slim down here."

"Ken," Michaela said sharply.

"So where are we going for dinner?" he asked innocently.

Biting her tongue, Michaela decided to let it go for now. "There's good Italian, okay Chinese, a diner they're proud of because they're not from New York, or a true Southern tradition, just on the edge of town."

"What's the Southern tradition?" Ken was intrigued.

"Oh no," Michaela laughed, "it's too good. And really"—she looked over at him—"it must be experienced."

"Okay." Ken draped an arm around her shoulders. "Now you've got me. This I have to try. Lead on."

"We have to drive," Michaela explained, leading them toward the library parking lot.

"How is it you've been there?"

Michaela swatted at him. "I've been here for months. I've made some friends."

"Obviously." Ken knocked his head back in the direction of the station.

"If I promise to tell you about him, will you drop it until after we've eaten?" Michaela asked hopefully.

Ken gave in. "All right. Where are we going?"

"Ever heard of the Waffle House?"

"Waffle House?" Ken asked in place of an answer.

Michaela grinned at him. "Trust me."

When Ken sat back two hours later, putting his hands behind his head with a slight groan, Michaela knew she was out of time. She had stalled with stories of mutual friends, her last book, her current book, and questions about both NASA and his new job. He had played along, listening, asking questions and answering them. But now, dammit, he was going to expect answers of his own.

"You want more coffee, hon?" The waitress appeared next to them with a fresh pot. "Or anything else?"

"I wish I had room for more," Ken answered, patting his stomach. "She told me it was good, but wow. Hope you didn't make that fresh coffee just for us."

"Oh no." The woman laughed. "We're open 'round the clock, every day. It may be slow now, but it'll pick up here 'fore long. It's Saturday night, after all."

"I'll take some more coffee." Michaela moved her thick ceramic mug closer to the edge of the table. With a shrug, Ken followed suit, in spite of his earlier protestations.

The woman filled both mugs. "Y'all need anything else, just give me a wave. I'll be right over."

Ken waited until she'd walked away. "They're not this nice back home."

Michaela grinned, sipping her coffee. "It took some getting used to."

"So." Ken gave her a crooked smile. "Tell me about the sheriff."

"Oh, Sheriff Robert Granger." Michaela sighed and rubbed her forehead, moving her hands over her face and through her hair. "He was . . ." She dropped her head onto the back of the booth. "Unexpected."

"You're not—" Ken started, then laughed out loud. "Oh, God, Michaela, you are. You're in love with this guy."

"Don't be absurd." Michaela dismissed it with a wave. "I'm not in love with him."

Ken looked at her, still with his crooked smile.

"I'm not," she insisted plainly.

"Fine. You're not in love." He lifted his hands in mock surrender. "But if you're not in love, what are you?"

"I am . . ." Michaela thought for an honest answer, but what the hell was the honest answer? "Surprised."

"I guess there's a first time for everything," Ken teased.

"Where are you staying tonight?" Michaela asked, grateful to be changing the subject.

"I figured I'd just get a room in your hotel, but that's not going to work since you're not exactly in a Marriott." He rolled his eyes.

"No"—Michaela shook her head—"but there's the sofa at my place."

"Are you sure?"

"It's late, and you've got a hell of a drive ahead of you tomorrow," she assured him. "I promise I'll have you on the road early."

When he'd started the trip, Ken had had visions of stopping off, finding Michaela, and finally seducing her. Meeting the sheriff in New York had convinced him now was his time. If a small town hick had gotten her attention, she would be lonely for someone more like her. But he'd underestimated the other man and the feelings she had for him. With a sigh and a final sip of his coffee, he released his dream once and for all. "How can I turn down such a generous offer?"

It had been a long night. Not the longest of his life, no, but long enough all the same. He'd started to call her a dozen times and gone to call Jimmy for relief another dozen. In the end, though, he'd let them both be. Instead, he'd drunk a lot of coffee, answered seven calls, according to the log, and played solitaire on Jimmy's computer. And he'd drafted the letter to the mayor asking for the monies to hire two more deputies. One night like this was more than enough, hand to God.

"Hey, boss," Jimmy spoke from the door as he came in.

Bobby stayed at the coffeemaker, his back to his deputy a moment longer than necessary to ensure he was composed, but, thank God, the night was over. Once he was sure his face would show nothing but tired, he turned, two coffees in hand.

"'Morning, Jimmy." He met the other man at the desk and handed him a coffee. "How was last night?"

Jimmy shrugged, accepting his coffee and taking a drink. "I don't understand women, boss."

Bobby choked on his coffee. "Any man tells you he does is lying."

"Anyway—" Jimmy sat at his desk and spun the chair around to face Bobby. "How'd it go here?"

"Slow," Bobby answered with a yawn. "Everything's in the log. Nothing outstanding. Except that we're hiring two more deputies."

Jimmy perked up. "Something happen, Sheriff? Did you need me last night? 'Cause you could've . . ."

Bobby interrupted with a wave of his hand. Standing up, he answered the question by pulling on his coat. "I'd've called if I'd needed you, Jimmy. Nothing was in trouble last night but my ego."

"Well"—Jimmy sipped his coffee—"I can't say I'll be sorry for the extra help, but I don't really understand."

"It's okay." Bobby clapped him on the shoulder. "I'm gonna go get some sleep. See you in a couple hours."

"'Night, boss." Jimmy turned to the desk and saved Bobby's solitaire game while the man himself left the station.

Luckily, he was tired. Tired meant he couldn't race over to Michaela's to alleviate the niggling in the back of his mind. Tired meant it was easier to take his last lap through town. Tired meant, if his luck held, he wouldn't make a total fool of himself. But tired also meant those back steps were mighty steep this morning.

Sighing, he climbed the stairs and knocked at the top.

The delay was long enough that he knocked again, louder. She'd invited him, after all. The door opened. Bobby felt his eyes harden and his jaw clench. Ken stood in Michaela's door, wearing nothing but blue jeans.

"Sheriff." At least he had the decency to look uncomfortable. "Michaela's in the shower. Come on in."

"I don't think that's necessary." Bobby's voice was cold and he knew it. Better cold than the alternative, though.

"Sheriff—" Ken started but stopped. "Bobby." He looked at his friend's friend. "Come in. It's not what you think."

Michaela appeared over Ken's shoulder farther in the back of the room, dressed in her robe, her hair in a towel.

"Granger—" She smiled at him—until she saw the expression on his face. Oh shit. "Granger."

Ken stepped out of the doorway, as Michaela stepped into it. "Nothing happened." Michaela kept her voice calm and low. "He slept on the couch. I slept in my room. He's practically a brother. Will you please come in?"

He looked over her shoulder to Ken, then looked back at her, grinding his teeth.

"Come in, Granger." Michaela's voice was softer and she placed a hand on his crossed arm.

He walked in and went straight into the sitting room, Michaela and Ken close behind him. Sure enough, a pillow and blanket were still out on the loveseat. A shirt Bobby recognized as Ken's from the night before was draped over the wing chair. His shoes were stuffed with socks and kicked under the same chair.

"Excuse me." Ken moved by him and reached for the shirt.

"Just let me get dressed," Michaela said from the door of the room before hurrying into the bedroom.

Bobby stood beneath the portrait of his ancestor,

studying the man. Behind him, Ken sat in the chair to put on his shoes.

"Bobby." The man's voice was flat.

Bobby turned slowly to face him. Damned if it could be said that he wouldn't even face the man.

"If I were you right now," Ken spoke simply, pulling on his socks and shoes while he did, "I'd be beyond angry. From how it looks, you've got a right to be." He shook his head with a low, wry chuckle. "But friend—" He tied the lace on his shoe and looked up at the sheriff. "If anyone should be pissed here, it's me. Because you are one lucky s.o.b. She doesn't even know. She thinks I consider her a sister."

Bobby took a deep breath and let it out toward the ceiling. When Michaela came back in the room, she found them there, Ken standing up and reaching for his blazer; Granger with his hands clasped behind his back, staring at the ceiling. Both men turned simultaneously.

Ken spoke first. "I should go." He turned back to Bobby and spoke under his breath. "You're a lucky man." He walked to Michaela's side and squeezed her arm.

"Ken . . ." Michaela started. How the hell was she supposed to pull this off?

"Michaela." Ken's voice was understanding yet insistent. "I'll tell NASA you said hi."

She gave him a wan smile as he dropped a kiss on her cheek. As he walked out, she turned back to the situation with Granger. He'd taken it all in through his hard eyes, she could tell.

Head high, she entered the room fully and sat on one end of the loveseat, simply pushing the bedding out of her way. She waited.

"He's like a brother," Bobby spoke.

Michaela nodded. "He is."

"He spent the night with you." It wasn't a question.

"He spent the night here," Michaela corrected.

"The man was half-naked when he opened the door." Bobby's temperature was beginning to rise.

"I assume he took off most of his clothes to sleep." Michaela stayed calm.

"Michaela." Bobby rubbed his face hard. "I'm trying here. And I'm being real patient."

"Come sit down, Granger." Michaela held out her hand.

He couldn't quite take it. But he could sit. Michaela waited until he was seated then reached out. If he wouldn't take her hand, she'd take his.

"Nothing happened here last night, Granger. I promise. I want you to believe that. I hope you believe that. I can't make you believe that."

"This isn't—" Bobby started, but stopped almost as quickly. He tried again. "We don't . . ." He realized he believed her. Not because of what Ken had said, although that didn't hurt, but because this was Michaela. They'd fought, argued, and disagreed, but she'd never lied to him. But believing her wasn't the problem. He sighed, searching for the words. "I'm just not used to finding other men with the woman I'm seeing. It's not something I can understand, Michaela."

"But you believe me, Granger?" she confirmed. If he didn't . . . She couldn't think of it. He had to.

"I do, Michaela." He entwined their fingers.

She took his hand in both of hers. "That's what matters, Granger. We'll figure out the rest." She touched his cheek softly. "We just will."

He gave in to her touch, closing his eyes in response to her soft caress. "When I'm not so tired."

"Do you want to sleep here?" Michaela asked. "In my bed?" she added with a careful smile.

"Thank you, no, honey," Bobby declined, "but I'll call you when I'm awake."

With only a slight groan, Bobby stood. He reached a hand out to her, but was shocked when tears came to her eyes. "Michaela?"

She took his hand and stood, facing him but keeping her eyes on their clasped hands. "I thought I'd blown this over a stupid misunderstanding."

"Michaela." Bobby's voice was low, his Southern drawl wrapping around her as much as his arms, as he pulled her close. "Don't cry. I believe you."

Sniffing, Michaela rested her forehead on his chest. His arms felt so good around her. And he believed her when so many men wouldn't have. He needed to go. He needed his rest. There would be time to deal with everything else.

Lifting her head, she looked into his eyes. "I love you, Granger."

"Oh, Michaela," Bobby breathed, pulling her close again. He wrapped her tight.

She smiled into his chest. "I figured it was my turn to make another first move."

Bobby laughed low. "If I wasn't so tired . . ."

"You can make it up to me later," Michaela said, giving him a soft kiss. "Come on." She moved out of his arms, still holding his hand. "Go rest so you can."

"You have a good morning, Michaela." He kissed her gently.

"You have a good night, Granger," she whispered.

The stairs were as long going down as they had been coming up. He was tired. That was all it was. A beautiful, sophisticated, and worldly woman was in love with him. And she hadn't lied to him. He should be walking on air. He should be, anyway.

Chapter 12

Jimmy passed his menu back to Sarah with a smile and snapped open his newspaper. The news that they were hiring two more deputies was really good. It was about time the boss listened to him and Chris.

The door opened behind him. Chris was always laughing at him for sitting with his back to doors, but it was only the Falls. Nobody was gonna bust in blazing during the dinner hour.

"Betsy's said from the beginning that having her here would be trouble."

Jimmy perked up. The voice belonged to Grace Mason. There was only one person she could be talking about, but who was she talking to? Fighting the urge to turn around and look, he hoped they would keep talking, that they didn't realize he was there. Now he'd have a response for Chris next time. Sometimes, having put your back to the door was a good thing. Tonight he got lucky. Grace and her dinner companion took the booth on the other side of the door. He closed his eyes in a grimace when he heard Langdon Howard respond.

"And she would certainly know. She's always looking out for Sheriff Granger."

What had happened that was trouble for the boss? If Grace Mason and Langdon Howard were this interested, it couldn't be good for him. He strained his ears, hoping to catch more of the conversation.

"Did she really have another man spend the night with her?" Langdon asked.

"Tried to sneak him in," Grace announced. "Brought him in after dark and took him all the way out to the Waffle House for dinner."

"Waffle House?" Langdon sneered. "For all her New York airs, she takes him to the Waffle House."

Grace sniffed. "Class is as class does, Langdon. You learn that young and you'll be fine."

"And the sheriff has been stepping out with her for so long now." Langdon's sympathy might have been more believable if her eagerness had been a little better hidden.

Grace stopped her friend. "Now, Langdon, Bobby Granger would never have acted in such a manner if it hadn't been for her."

"Well, of course not." Langdon fell in line with Grace.

"Even the strongest man can be led. That's why it's important for you to take good care of your husband, honey."

"I know," Langdon agreed again. "That's one reason I'm so lucky to have Clark. He'll never be led anywhere."

Jimmy snorted, but was able to turn it into a cough. They had moved on to the merits of Clark Howard. Langdon's new baby would be next. He could stop listening, but he'd heard enough.

Sarah appeared with his mac and cheese. "Here you go." She leaned down farther than necessary to put his plate in front of him. Once she was close, she spoke again, her voice a low whisper. "You looked like you were listening hard, so I didn't want to interrupt. Not that you heard anything worth hearing," she spat. Looking at the expression on Jimmy's face, she gasped low. "Jimmy, don't you dare tell me any of that was true."

"Of course not," Jimmy insisted. "Still, can I get this to go? I need to talk to the boss."

Sarah didn't say a word, just picked up his food and took it back to wrap it up. Jimmy found a ten in his wallet and dropped it on the table. It would be more than enough to cover his bill and a generous tip, but at least he wouldn't have to wait for change or to sign a slip. When she got back with his takeout, Jimmy was already standing, coat on and paper under his arm.

It didn't take long to get to the station. He pulled the door open and felt his stomach drop when he realized Ms. Howard was there with the boss. They looked up from their plates; Carter Anne must've brought over a plate for both of them. Michaela smiled widely and Bobby waved his deputy over.

"What brings you in, Jimmy?" Bobby asked. "You got a problem?"

"Or did you just want dinner company?" Michaela asked, motioning to the Styrofoam box in his hand.

"Well . . . um . . ." Jimmy stammered. What to do now? "I'd actually hoped to speak to you alone, boss, but not if I'm interrupting. It can wait."

"Don't be silly." Michaela wiped her mouth on her napkin. "I've eaten more than enough." She grinned at Jimmy. "Carter Anne brings me the same size portions as she brings Granger. I'm done."

"It's okay, Ms. Howard," Jimmy protested. "It can wait."

"You're right." Michaela stood. "It is okay."

Bobby helped her with her coat. She turned in his arms. "Call me later?" Bobby nodded. Michaela kissed him and left, with a wave for Jimmy.

The two men waited until the doors closed behind her before sitting down. Bobby cleared up Michaela's place and offered her chair to his deputy.

"Any reason we can't eat while we talk?"

"Not at all," Jimmy answered. He sat and opened his dinner. It was still a little warm.

"So what brought you in here on your night off, Jimmy?" Bobby asked around a bite of his own meal.

Jimmy stalled, stirring his mac and cheese. At the diner, this had seemed his only logical course of action. Here in the station, actually facing his friend, he wasn't so sure.

"Jim." Bobby lowered his fork. "What brought you here?"

"There's some talk, boss," Jimmy said with a sigh. He repeated everything he'd heard Grace Mason and Langdon Howard say. Bobby listened, eating methodically, until he had the full story.

"'Preciate you bringing this to me." Bobby put his fork down for the last time. "Don't worry about that part of it."

"I still hate having to do it," Jimmy spoke around his mac and cheese.

"Jimmy." Bobby's voice was calm. "You know as well as I do there was bound to be talk. Hell"—Bobby leaned back in his chair—"I'm surprised we made it this long before the heavy gossip started. Finish your dinner."

Jimmy started to speak, then took a bite instead.

"What're you wanting to say, Jimmy?" Bobby opened the door for the younger man to speak his mind.

"I don't want to . . . I don't believe any of it about Ms. Howard."

Bobby sighed. "Michaela had a friend in town, just passing through. It got late so he spent the night on her sofa. I even met him."

"You knew about it?" Jimmy asked.

Bobby didn't flinch, didn't hesitate. "I did."

For the first time since the door had opened behind him in the diner, Jimmy felt hungry. Bobby watched him eat. Carter Anne needed to stop bringing him so much food. The portions were making him nauseous.

It was 12:30 a.m. and she was tired. Bobby had said he'd call when he was off duty, so she'd been trying to wait up for him, but it wasn't working. Yawning, she reached for her cell phone and saw that she hadn't missed a call. Normally he would've called by now. What could Jimmy have said to keep him at the station this late? Making her decision, she picked up the phone and called him. He answered on the second ring.

"Sheriff Granger here," he mumbled.

"Granger?" Michaela asked.

"Michaela?" He cleared the sleep from his voice. "You okay? You sound like something's wrong."

"No, I'm fine." She was feeling a little foolish, but otherwise fine. "I was just concerned about you."

"Why would you be concerned about me?" he asked. "I'm fine."

Michaela sighed. Had she really become one of those women? "I just thought you were going to call when you got off duty tonight."

"I'm sorry, Michaela," he sighed, "I just wanted to come home and get some sleep."

"Oh." Definitely foolish. "Well . . . okay, then. But you're sure you're okay?" She couldn't help but double-check.

"I'm fine. Promise," Bobby repeated. "I'll catch up with you tomorrow, okay?"

"Okay," Michaela agreed. "You sleep well. Good night."

"Good night, Michaela."

She listened to him disconnect the call before hitting the off button herself. That had been unexpected. Surely she was being paranoid or insecure. Everything was fine. It had to be. The last couple weeks were just about working out the glitches in a new relationship between two people who had been single a long time. That was all. Trying not to cry, she snuggled down. The bed felt so big. Sleep was a long time coming.

The next morning when Michaela reached the bottom of the stairs, heading out on her run, Bobby was waiting for her. His night had been long and he was tired. Still, better to do this tired than keep coming up with excuses to put it off. No good ever came from delays.

"Good morning, Sheriff Granger," Michaela teased. She was ridiculously relieved to see him after last night.

"'Morning, Michaela," he replied. Even dressed for her run, she was beautiful. What was his problem?

"Somehow I don't think you're here to join me on my run," Michaela noted, pulling her Yankees cap firmly on her head. "Not dressed in uniform, anyway."

"And you'd be right," Bobby agreed. "I just wanted to come by and apologize for last night."

"Want to apologize over breakfast? I'll skip my run," she offered. "Coffee and toast are right up these stairs."

Bobby declined. "I'm not really hungry."

"Okay." Michaela crossed her arms over her chest. What was she doing, getting her defenses up? She uncrossed her arms and tried not to fidget. "What happened last night, Granger?"

"I got tired is all, Michaela," Bobby sighed. "It's no big deal."

"Then why are you here apologizing for it?" Michaela asked archly.

"Because it seemed like the right thing to do."

"So, it was something. At least something that requires an apology."

"Not requires, no," Bobby countered.

"Did you come to pick a fight, Granger?" Michaela asked. She was getting confused.

"I came to apologize." Bobby stressed the words.

"Well, thanks for clearing that up." Michaela's voice mirrored her rising anger. "What the hell's gotten into you, Granger?"

Bobby's voice kept getting colder. "You're the one doing the yelling."

"This isn't yelling, Granger. Trust me, if I was yelling, you'd know I was yelling."

"And thank you for clearing that up," Bobby sneered.

"I'm going for my run now, Granger," Michaela said, trying to keep her anger in check. "Whatever the hell has been going on with you for the last several days, I really hope it's over by the next time I see you."

"'Morning, Michaela." Bobby tipped his cap to her and turned, walking away. This was getting out of hand. So what if the town was talking? So what if she'd had a man spend the night on her sofa? So what was the problem?

By the time he reached the station, he was more

confused than ever and feeling like an ass. Worse, he knew he deserved it. Something had to give.

"Hey, Michaela." Carter Anne rapped once on the door to the research room before stepping on in. "How's the book?"

Michaela took off her glasses. "Hey, Carter Anne. What brings you here?"

"Wanted to ask a favor. It's about one of my classes," she explained, sitting in the chair next to her friend.

"What's up?"

"My professor's a hard ass. Always on my case." Carter Anne rolled her eyes. "We've got a research paper coming up and I'd love to kick ass on it. Give him no reason to ride me about it." Carter Anne grinned. "I'd like to bring in a ringer."

"What's the paper on?" Michaela checked.

Carter Anne's grin became an ear-to-ear smile. "Current cultural differences among the original thirteen states."

Michaela laughed. "And you need a Yankee."

"Well, it certainly wouldn't hurt." Carter Anne laughed along with her.

"I think this can be arranged." Michaela's laughter settled into a smile. "Figure out what you need from me and we'll find the time."

"You're the best, Michaela." Carter Anne went to stand, but Michaela spoke.

"Now can I ask you a question?"

"Sure. Anything." Carter Anne sat back down.

Now that she had someone to ask, Michaela wasn't sure wanted to do so. "I just . . . I guess I wondered . . ." She decided to just plunge in. "Is your uncle okay?" She felt herself blush at having to ask the question. What was it about love that made perfectly sane, grown women have to resort to the same tactics they'd—she'd—used in high school?

Carter Anne sighed. "I was hoping you'd know. He hasn't been himself."

"How so?" Michaela didn't want to be relieved that it wasn't just her but she couldn't quite prevent it.

"Just"—Carter Anne gestured with her hands, grasping for the idea—"not like Bobby. Quiet. Moody. You know . . . not himself," she finished.

"I do know." Michaela nodded. "He's been different for days now, but this morning"—she shrugged—"he showed up in a foul mood, to the point that he picked a fight."

Carter Anne was shocked. "Bobby?"

"Exactly."

"Angie says he hasn't been talking to Chris. He sure hasn't been talking to us." Carter Anne shrugged. "We were hoping he might've said something to you."

"Nothing," Michaela sighed.

"Whoever figures it out first, shares?" Carter Anne suggested. Michaela agreed, so Carter Anne continued. "Want to come to dinner tonight? Maybe a relaxing dinner at home with two of his three favorite girls will snap him out of it."

Michaela wanted to think it was a good idea, but there was a niggle in the back of her brain. "Carter Anne . . ."

"If it brings him out of it, it will be worth it." Carter Anne answered the unspoken concern. "And if it doesn't, at least I'll have had decent dinner company, so it'll've been worth it." She smiled her winningest smile.

Michaela laughed again, holding her hands up. "Okay, okay, I'll come to dinner. What can I bring?"

"How does apple crisp sound for dessert?"

"Oh, Carter Anne—" Michaela patted her tummy. "I don't need dessert."

"I don't either," Carter Anne agreed, "but Bobby does. If it's gonna work, anyway."

"Then apple crisp sounds delicious."

"In that case"—Carter Anne stood up—"bring ice cream to top it."

"What time?"

"Six-thirty?"

"I'll be there," Michaela assured her. "With ice cream."

She worked for the next hour and a half before wrapping up for the evening and heading into the shower.

After a stop at the ice cream parlor, Michaela rang the doorbell at Granger's right at six-thirty.

"Michaela," Carter Anne scolded as she opened the door, "you can just walk in." She gave Michaela's cheek a kiss.

"There's one of those cultural differences for you, Carter Anne," Michaela said with a smile. She was comfortable enough, though, to just hang up her coat on the rack and carry the brown bag of ice cream into the kitchen. Bobby wasn't there.

Michaela looked at Carter Anne, who pointed toward the TV room. Handing Carter Anne the ice cream without a word, she headed to find the man himself. He was sitting in his chair, the news on TV turned down low, and her first book in his hands.

"I hope I got better than that one as I wrote more," she said, laying a hand on his shoulder.

He looked up with a wan smile. "I picked it up to read while I would sit with Abby in the hospital. I've always thought it was good. 'Course, I thought it was written by a man."

"Which made all the difference in the world, of course," Michaela teased.

He nodded. "Yep. I doubt I'll like any of 'em anymore, now I know you're a woman."

Michaela breathed easier. Maybe she'd just been imagining things . . . as had Carter Anne and Angie . . . so no, she hadn't been imagining things. Maybe it was just over.

Bobby stood up, putting the book facedown on the arm of his chair, marking his place. "Dinner ready?"

"You know"—Michaela laughed at herself—"I honestly don't know. Carter Anne sent me in here as soon as she took the ice cream from me, but she didn't say anything about dinner."

"Ice cream?" Bobby asked.

Michaela simply smiled.

"Butter pecan?" he asked, hopefully.

"What else?" Michaela answered, her eyes softening.

Bobby smiled. He loved those eyes, and the way she looked at him. What had he been thinking recently? He realized he was just staring at her. "Guess we should go check, then."

Michaela turned. In spite of those eyes, though, he knew what he'd been thinking. He just had to figure out what he thought now. Which would mean more thinking. It was making his head hurt. His life had been easy not that long ago.

"Bobby?" Carter Anne called to him from the kitchen. "Where'd you go?"

He shook himself and walked through the hall into the kitchen. "I'm right here. No need to be yelling."

Michaela and Carter Anne exchanged a look as he passed them, heading to the refrigerator.

"Dinner is ready," Michaela said.

"Good to know." His head was in the refrigerator. "Can I get either of you something from out of here?"

"I'll take a Diet Pepsi," Carter Anne answered.

"Ummm . . ." Michaela wasn't even sure what was available.

"There's club soda," Carter Anne spoke quickly. Bobby had gone from weird to rude, which was even less like him. "But I'm not sure we've got lemons."

"Seltzer's fine," Michaela answered to Bobby's back, "even without the lemon."

Bobby stood with sodas for him and Carter Anne and a seltzer for Michaela. "Here we are, then."

Michaela took the cans from him. While Carter Anne got the casserole from the oven, Michaela poured the drinks. The table was already set, so Bobby just sat down. Silences between him and Michaela were usually comfortable. Silences between him and Carter Anne were hardly even noticeable. So why was silence among the three of them so awkward?

Carter Anne finally spoke. "Michaela's gonna help me with a research project for the class I was telling you about, Bobby." She put the casserole on the table while Michaela brought the drinks.

"Well, that's good," Bobby said, "and mighty nice of you, Michaela. Thanks for helping out my girl."

"It's the least I could do, Bobby," Michaela answered. "Besides, the project sounds interesting."

"Hope you like chicken casserole," Bobby said to her, passing her the serving spoon before turning his attention back to Carter Anne. "What's the project?"

As Carter Anne explained, Michaela watched and listened. He relaxed more with his niece than with her, but Carter Anne was right; he just wasn't his usual self. On the surface, he seemed attentive enough, but there was a restless distraction about him that was noticeably different from his typical calm. She took a sip of her seltzer and nearly choked as an idea hit her.

"You okay, Michaela?" Bobby asked. "Missing that lemon?" he teased lightly.

"No." She gave him a slight smile, grateful for his attempt at levity, even in her concern. "But I had a thought."

When she didn't say anything else, Carter Anne spoke, frustrated yet amused. "Are you going to share?"

Michaela stared at Bobby. Why couldn't she have had this thought in private? "Is Jimmy okay, Granger?"

"Jimmy?" Bobby asked quietly.

Carter Anne's exclamation was louder. "Jimmy? What's wrong with Jimmy?"

Michaela held Bobby's gaze. "Yes, Jimmy. Is he okay? No health issues?"

"What do you mean, Michaela?" he asked.

"Is Jimmy sick, Granger?" Michaela spelled it out. Was he doing this intentionally?

"Why do you ask?" he responded.

"Bobby!" Carter Anne spat through clenched teeth. "Hand to God, stop asking questions as answers. Is Jimmy sick?"

He shook his head. "Not that I know of. Not at all." Bobby's voice didn't betray any concern, but his eyes did. "That's why I wanted to know why Michaela thought he was."

"It's . . ." Michaela shook her head. "Nothing."

"Michaela!" Carter Anne nearly exploded. "You must've had a reason for asking."

"Carter Anne," Bobby sighed, "leave it be. If she'd wanted to share, she would've explained when I asked."

"It's okay, Carter Anne." Michaela shot Bobby a hard look. "It was just a passing thought. No basis for it. Call it a hunch that didn't pan out."

Carter Anne humphed, but knew she'd gotten everything out of Michaela she was going to. Bobby's plate was empty and she and Michaela had eaten as much as they ever did. "We got crisp and ice cream for dessert."

"As good as it sounds," Bobby sighed, "I'm gonna have to skip."

Carter Anne turned, openmouthed. Bobby never skipped dessert, especially not when butter pecan was involved.

Michaela lifted her hands. It was time to go. Whatever she and Carter Anne had hoped would happen tonight, hadn't. "Do you need help cleaning up?"

They'd gotten close enough that Carter Anne usually accepted the offer, but there was something about her expression that kept Carter Anne from saying yes. "It's okay, Michaela," she said, "but thanks. I'll be in touch in a couple of days about my project."

"That sounds great," Michaela said, standing.

Bobby stood with her. "I'll walk you home."

"Thanks, Granger."

At least he helped her with her coat; that was something. Or she could hope, anyway.

They were halfway to the library before Bobby reached for her. It was just an arm around her shoulders, but it felt comforting anyway. This morning had thrown her more than she'd realized. It was just so out of character for him to go looking for a fight.

"Granger?" Michaela whispered. "What did Jimmy say to you the other night? If he's not sick . . ." She had another thought. "Oh shit, Granger, you're not sick, are you?"

"No, Michaela." He shook his head in the dark. "I'm not sick. Jimmy's not sick. No one's sick."

She wanted to scream. Instead, they finished the rest of their walk in silence. At the top of the stairs, Michaela turned to him. "Will you come in?"

"Not tonight, Michaela." His voice was sad.

Michaela took a breath and let it out slowly. "Bobby?" He turned and met her eyes. "Please," she continued, "I need to know what's going on."

"You're right." He nodded at the door. "I'll come in."

Without another word, Michaela opened the door and led him in. She sat on the edge of the loveseat and cut her eyes to the portrait of her Colonel. His eyes were so like Granger's . . . She looked from the portrait to the living man and waited.

Bobby paced, looking at his hands. What the hell was he doing here? "Michaela," he started, "I don't . . . I don't know how to start or what to say."

"Stop." Michaela's voice was steel. "Are you breaking up with me?"

Bobby stammered, looking for words. It was time. If it was going to happen, it needed to happen now. "Yes, Michaela." His voice was flat. "I am."

She bit the inside of her lip and swallowed hard. "Why?"

"Michaela . . ."

"I deserve to know why, Granger." She was amazed. Her voice wasn't cracking. Her eyes weren't tearing. Of course, her heart wasn't beating and her lungs weren't working, either, so maybe everything had just stopped and it wasn't amazing at all.

He supposed she was right. She did deserve something. "It's no one thing, Michaela," he started.

"I'll take the list."

Bobby stopped pacing. "You're not going to make this easy, are you?"

"I should?" Michaela asked incredulously.

"That's part of it there, Michaela."

"What?" Michaela asked. "I call you on your shit?"

"No." Bobby took a deep breath. He would stay calm. Logical. And maybe, in explaining it to her, he'd understand it better himself. "We're very different, Michaela."

"You're just realizing this now?" she scoffed.

This wasn't working. "I should go."

"Wait." She stopped him with her tone. "You want to go, I'll let you go. But first tell me why. And then . . ." Apparently everything hadn't just stopped; apparently she was still able to feel extraordinary amounts of pain. Some part of her that was separate and apart from this nightmare made note of it, intrigued. But her voice still didn't crack. "And then you can go wherever and not even look back. In fact, I'd appreciate it if you wouldn't."

He sat in the chair, leaving the loveseat for her. She curled up in one of its corners and pulled her knees to her chest.

Bobby rubbed his eyes and forced himself to look at her. "It's about . . . finding Ken here the other morning." He raised a hand, silencing her before she could speak. "I know nothing happened. And I believe you. But you didn't even call me, Michaela. I found him half-naked and you in the shower. And Justin asking you about other men, right in front of me."

"You knew I wasn't a virgin . . ." Michaela started, but Bobby interrupted.

"And I wasn't either. I know . . ."

"So you were fine with my having a sex life before you, in theory." Michaela couldn't believe this.

"No. Yes. It's not just that." He leaned forward, elbows on his knees, hands dangling between his legs. "It's about trips to India and Nepal and places I've—" He laughed in disbelief. "Places I've never even heard of. And you think nothing of just going. Have you listened to your own stories, Michaela? You've lived in tents and in palaces. I've lived in my little yellow house."

"This is about where we'll live?" Michaela couldn't believe her ears.

"No." he shook his head. "No." He wasn't making himself clear. "I'm a simple man. I'm old-fashioned. My friends and my life are simple." He laughed mirthlessly. "You've met Jimmy. You—" Bobby looked up at her. "You are anything but simple or old-fashioned, Michaela. You are extraordinary. You live an extraordinary life. Your friends are men in dresses. Can you imagine that dinner party?"

She couldn't help it; she laughed. Just once, short and hard, but he was right.

"See?" He held out a hand to her. "That's what I mean."

"No." The laughter was done. "I don't see."

Bobby stood. "And that's what I mean, too. We see different things. We need different things." They locked eyes until Michaela looked away. "Is there anything you want to say?"

"What?"

"I don't want to just . . ." He motioned toward the back entry. "Without giving you a chance to say your piece."

"Always a gentleman," she scoffed. Bobby shrugged. "No." Michaela shook her head. "I don't have anything to say. Go on. Go home."

Bobby made it to the door of the room before pausing. "Remember to lock the door."

She stared at the portrait above her. It wasn't until she heard the door close that she started to cry.

"'Morning, Bobby," Carter Anne yawned as she came into the kitchen. He turned from the coffee pot and Carter Anne woke up immediately. Her uncle looked like hell.

"Bobby—" She hovered by the table, hoping he'd come sit. Sure enough, he did. She dropped into a chair next to him. "Bobby, please tell me what's wrong."

"I'm fine, honey." Bobby sipped his coffee.

"No, you're not." She took his hand. "You've been out of sorts for a while now, you haven't been eating, and now you look like you didn't sleep a wink all night. You're a lot of things. Fine isn't one of them."

Word would spread soon enough. Might as well make sure the original story was accurate. "Michaela and I have gone our separate ways."

"What?" Carter Anne nearly laughed. That made it sound like they'd broken up.

"Michaela and I—" He stopped. If the story was going to be accurate, it should be accurate from the beginning. With a sigh, he continued. "I decided that she and I would be better off not together."

She wasn't hearing this. Of everything he might've said, she wasn't hearing this. "You"—Carter Anne could hardly get the words out—"broke up with Michaela?"

Bobby looked his niece square in the eye. "I did."

"But, Bobby . . ." Carter Anne took her hand away. "Why?"

"It's best this way," he said simply.

It was sinking in. He'd done it. How dare he? "No," Carter Anne said, trying to keep her voice level. "It's not." She had to get to Michaela. Get through to Bobby. Do . . . something. She stood up, but turned back at the door. Uncle or no, she couldn't keep totally quiet. "It's not okay and you know it," she spat. That was enough. It wasn't all—but it was enough.

Once in her bedroom, she called Angie.

"Hello?" Angie answered.

"You need to meet me at the library, right now." Carter Anne pulled jeans and a sweater out of her dresser.

"Is Michaela okay?" Angie asked, her concern obvious.

"Physically, yes," Carter Anne answered, "but our uncle's an ass."

There was silence until Angie realized what her sister was saying. "Oh, Carter Anne, no. He didn't."

"Meet me at the library." She pulled off her pajama bottoms and pulled on her jeans.

"What about work?" Angie reminded her.

"I'll call them. Leave a message that I'll be in late, if at all."

"They've been real patient with you recently," Angie said, remembering the days Carter Anne had taken off from work to be with her when things were bad with Chris.

"I've earned it," Carter Anne said plainly. "I still have more time off saved up than anyone else on staff. Be there, okay?"

"I'm dressing now," Angie assured her.

Twenty minutes later, Carter Anne and Angie were walking up the back steps of the library. Angie knocked but there was no answer. The sisters looked at each other. Angie shrugged, but Carter Anne stepped up to the door and knocked harder.

"Michaela! It's us. Let us in."

When she opened the door, Michaela was in a robe and had her hair up in a towel. "Hi, girls." Maybe her smile looked more genuine than it felt. "What brings you here so early?"

"Bobby's an ass," Carter Anne said.

The tears sprang to Michaela's eyes against her will. "No . . . he's not."

"Oh, honey." Angie wrapped her arm around Michaela's shoulders and moved her inside. Carter Anne followed, closing the door behind them. The three settled in the sitting room.

"What happened, Michaela?" Angie asked.

"You know—" Michaela sniffed, running a finger under each eye and taking a deep breath to restore her composure. "The truth is, I really don't know. I've spent the whole night trying to figure that out." She shrugged and sniffed again. "I thought—I thought we were good. It was . . . tense . . . after my friend Ken was in town, but we got past it. Or I thought we did."

She looked away and exhaled hard, holding on. There were so many questions she wanted to ask: Had they noticed anything? Had he said anything to them? How did he look this morning? But she wouldn't ask them. Not as long as she could swallow them down.

"It just doesn't make sense," Carter Anne huffed. "What is he thinking?"

"He said"—Michaela could answer this one—"we were just too different. Our lives were too different. But I never asked him to be anything other than who he is. I love him"—her voice finally did crack, dammit—"just the way he is."

"What will you do?" Angie asked, her own tears in her eyes.

"Finish my research and go home," Michaela answered flatly.

Carter Anne was surprised. "You aren't going to fight for him?"

Michaela looked at her. "He made himself very clear. He doesn't want me. If there was something to fight for, I'd fight. But there's not." She squared her shoulders. "And I won't beg."

"And you shouldn't," Carter Anne agreed emphatically.

"No," Angie agreed, "you shouldn't. How long do you think you'll be here?"

The thought of leaving was almost more than she could take. The thought of staying, though, was worse. "I can be done here in a week."

"That soon?" Angie asked, her tears pricking again.

"It's been coming along really well," Michaela explained. The hitch in her voice was small this time. She took some pride in that. "And I won't be distracted anymore." Her laughter was bitter.

"Do you want us to stick around today, Michaela?" Angie asked. "We could watch movies and eat ice cream."

"Or go into Danville for a shopping spree," Carter Anne offered.

Michaela shook her head and, jaw clenched, stood up. "Thank you, girls, but no. What I really want to do is finish up and—" She swallowed hard. "Go home."

Carter Anne and Angie stood. They couldn't fix this one. As much as they hated it, there was nothing they could do.

"Will you at least come to dinner tonight?" Angie asked. "Just the three of us," she finished quickly.

"No, Angie." Michaela shook her head. "That's not such a good idea."

"You're still our friend, Michaela," Carter Anne insisted.

"And he's your uncle," Michaela stressed. "Now, I need to get to work. I still have a contract to complete." She walked them to the back door. "But girls—" She fought to keep steady. "Thank you for . . . everything." She had the door closed before they had reached the bottom of the stairs.

Now that the sun was finally up, she could call Justin. "It's me," Michaela said without preamble when he answered. "I'll be home within a week."

"We were taking bets on if you'd ever be back," Justin teased her, "or if you'd stay there and become Mrs. Small Town Sheriff."

She closed her eyes but the tears still leaked out. "He broke up with me last night. Who won that pool?" In spite of the tears, she kept her voice hard.

"Oh, Mike." Justin's teasing stopped. "Screw him and come home now."

"I have never been run out of town." Her voice wavered a bit but she held on.

"No, you haven't," Justin agreed definitively. "Get what you need—then get the hell home. And Mike? You call me if you need me. Any time."

"Would you call Teri for me?" Dammit, the waver was becoming stronger. "I don't think I can . . ." She stopped with a cough.

"I got it, Mike. We'll handle everything from here."

"Thanks, Justin. I'll see you in a week." She hung up the phone. It was time to show them just how hard and cold a Yankee really could be.

Everything seemed off balance now. Had ever since the boss and Miz Howard had broken up. Jimmy pulled his coat around him as he stepped out of the video store. Seemed like the whole town was holding its breath, waiting. Since Bobby wasn't talking, even to him, the only thing to do now was rent a movie and stay out of the way until the Falls finally exhaled.

"Jimmy!" A woman called to him. Turning, he found Miz Howard hurrying up the street to catch up with him.

"You know—" Michaela laughed sadly. "I don't know where you live."

"Oh." Jimmy was stunned. Why would someone like Miz Howard want to know where he lived?

"I'm leaving tomorrow," Michaela explained. "I was afraid I wouldn't get to say good-bye. I haven't wanted to . . . well, I'm just glad I ran into you."

"Oh."

Michaela chuckled thinly, amazingly enough. She knew there was a reason she'd always liked him. "Anyway"—she stuck out her hand—"I'm really glad I got to know you, Jimmy."

He shook her hand but didn't let it go. "You really leaving, Ms. Howard?"

"I really am, Jimmy. It's time." She crossed her arms.

"Where're you heading? Can I walk you?" Jimmy offered.

"I'm just . . . I'm heading . . ." Michaela thumbed over her shoulder toward the sheriff's house. "Not far enough to need an escort."

Jimmy nodded. "It was good to meet you, Ms. Howard."

"You never have called me Michaela."

Jimmy smiled. "No ma'am, I suppose not."

"I'm expected." She motioned to the house.

Jimmy leaned over and kissed her cheek. "You take care now, Ms. Howard. I'll buy your books."

"You take care, too, Jimmy."

She had taken a few steps when he called, "Ms. Howard?" She turned back around. "I live in the apartments over there by the pond, on the other side of the statue."

Michaela smiled again, still sadly, but a smile nonetheless. It almost felt normal. She lifted her hand. "Bye, Jimmy."

He hadn't seen her all week. That hadn't been part of the plan. Not that he'd had a plan, but he'd assumed, in a town the size of the Falls, he'd at least see her. Bobby kicked back from his desk to go refill his coffee. He crossed the room, but didn't want a refill. He'd already drunk too much and had the sour stomach to prove it.

The first resumes for the two new deputy positions had come in. Those needed his attention. Once he'd gone through them, he'd get Jimmy's opinion, too. But first he needed to filter through them.

He went back to his desk and pulled out the folder of resumes. Dammit. The folder, the resumes, all of it came about because of her. And him wanting some kind of schedule that allowed for a personal life. He slammed the folder closed. Maybe a walk would help. Jimmy came in, just as he was standing up.

"Hey . . . boss . . ." Jimmy sounded surprised to find him here. "I thought you were . . ." He turned, looked at the door and turned back.

"Why would you think I was anywhere but here?" Bobby sat back down.

"I just thought . . ." Jimmy walked the rest of the way into the station, stopping in front of the desk. "I just ran into Ms. Howard. She was heading to your place. I thought she was going to say good-bye to you."

"Good-bye?" Bobby opened the folder of resumes. She was leaving . . .

"Boss?"

"Yeah, Jimmy?" Bobby put on his reading glasses, but the print didn't clear up.

"I can watch the station if you want to run home real quick."

"Thanks, but that's not necessary. Today's your day off. You'll have the whole place to yourself tomorrow." Bobby studied the resume on top of the pile.

"Boss." Jimmy's voice was firm.

"Yeah, Jimmy?" This applicant was a woman. That might be a good idea.

Jimmy waited. And waited. It was too important. Finally, the boss looked up.

"Yes?"

"Go see her."

Bobby sighed. "Why?" The question was sincere.

"Because you shouldn't be letting her go in the first place," Jimmy sighed back at him. "But if you're gonna, you should at least say good-bye."

This was Jimmy. If anyone outside of his family had earned his trust and respect, it was this man. "Michaela didn't even tell me she was leaving, Jim. This is the first I've heard of it." He took his glasses off long enough to rub his hands over his face. "It's better this way."

Jimmy sighed again. "Okay, boss." He wanted to say more. There was more to say. But Bobby was Bobby. He lifted his video-store bag. "If you want company tonight, I'm just watching movies."

"Thank you, Jimmy." Bobby gave his deputy a tight-lipped

smile. Putting his glasses back on, he went back to his pile of papers, trying to focus and almost making it.

Carter Anne opened the door. "Michaela!" she exclaimed. "Where have you been all week? Come in, come in." She wrapped her arms around her friend and didn't completely let go as she moved so Michaela could come in. "You aren't answering your phone. Kerri says the volunteers haven't heard hide nor hair from you. Angie and I were going to come over this weekend and make a scene until you opened up, if we hadn't heard from you by then." As she spoke, she guided her friend into the kitchen. "You can't hide yourself forever. The town's too small."

"Carter Anne." Michaela was half laughing, half crying. Carter Anne sat her down. "I know, Michaela."

"No, Carter Anne." Michaela was sharp, but it stopped Carter Anne's flow of words. She dried her eyes and cleared her throat. It was almost time to let down. But not quite. "I only came to drop these off." She handed the younger woman a folder.

"What's this?" Carter Anne opened it.

"Information on the differences between the cultures of the northern states and the southern states."

"You still did this for me?" Carter Anne was amazed.

"My family's mostly from the Boston area, too, so"— she reached over and flipped a few pages—"I've discussed the differences between the general northeast and New England."

"There's a difference?" Carter Anne asked, getting absorbed by the information.

"North Carolina and Florida are both southern states," Michaela pointed out.

Carter Anne laughed. "Got it."

"I've also," Michaela continued, "given you some good quotes from Howard Michaels you can use directly."

"Michaela, I can't believe—" Carter Anne started.

"And I'm leaving tomorrow."

Tears sprang into Carter Anne's eyes. "You can't."

Michaela swallowed until she could trust her voice. "I've gotten all the information I need to write the book. I've managed to avoid . . . your uncle . . . for a week in a town the size of a thumbtack. Not only is there no reason for me to stay, it's time for me to go before my luck runs out. And anyway"—Michaela swallowed again—"I really want to go home."

"Have you seen Angie and Chris yet?" Carter Anne asked.

Michaela nodded. "I just came from there." She patted Carter Anne's arm. "I'm sorry. Someone had to come first."

"It's okay, Michaela. But you won't even stay for the wedding? Or at least come back?"

"No." Michaela shook her head sadly. "They wanted me to, but no."

"Will we ever see you again?" Carter Anne was fighting for control herself now.

"Oh, Carter Anne." Michaela's tears threatened again. She blinked hard and forced a smile. "Come to New York. You'll love my city." She stood up. It was time. "And will you tell Kerri I'm sorry to have missed saying good-bye to her?"

"Of course. Will you say good-bye to . . . anybody else?" Carter Anne asked.

"He was—" She was almost home. "Very clear. I've said my good-byes."

They moved to the front door.

"Can I at least give him a message?" Carter Anne was practically pleading. "You know he loves you, Michaela."

Yes, she could still feel extraordinary pain. "No, Carter Anne." She turned and her eye caught the TV room, where he spent so much of his time. His chair . . . his books . . . her books. She looked back to Carter Anne. "Do you have a pen?"

Chapter 13

Chris knew what was going on, of course. There had, quite frankly, been no way to avoid it. Bobby and Michaela's split had been the most common topic of conversation throughout town. In his own house, it had supplanted even wedding planning. However, while he'd known what was happening, he'd also been trying to stay out of it. Last night, when Carter Anne had shown up furious with both Bobby and Michaela, had been the hardest.

"She's leaving!" Carter Anne announced as she came through the door.

"Hello to you, too." Chris made the mistake of attempting levity.

"How can you just . . . ugh!" She threw up her hands. "Where's Angie?"

"In here!" Angie called from the kitchen.

Carter Anne stormed down the hall, Chris behind her, shaking his head. He should go . . . somewhere else. Angie was sitting at the kitchen table, eyes red.

"Can you believe this?" Angie sniffed, as Carter Anne appeared in the doorway.

"I can't believe them," Carter Anne spat.

"What do you mean, them?" Angie asked. "Bobby's the one who broke up with her."

"Yeah"—Carter Anne dropped into a chair—"but they're both being stubborn. I can't believe she's sneaking out of town like this!"

"What?" Angie came to Michaela's defense. "She's hardly sneaking."

"She's hidden away all week and she's leaving without saying good-bye," Carter Anne countered.

"Would you want to face this town—Bobby's town—after all this? Why should she put herself through that if she didn't have to?"

Carter Anne pouted, lips pursed.

"And," Angie continued, "she did say good-bye. To her friends."

"But she's not even making him face her," Carter Anne responded. "Or fighting for him or anything."

"She said it herself—she wouldn't beg," Angie said. "You even agreed with her."

"There's a difference between begging and sneaking out of town."

"Chris—" Angie started the question he'd been dreading. "What do you think?"

Yep, he should've gone . . . somewhere else. "I think it's nobody's business but theirs," Chris replied.

Angie shook her head, eyes closed. "Not tonight, Chris, please?"

Carter Anne glared at him through slitted eyes.

"Did you discuss me like this last summer when Angie and I were having a hard time?" he asked, but lifted his hand quickly. "Never mind, I don't want to know."

"I'll tell you exactly what Bobby and I said if you don't chime in here, Chris," Carter Anne said. Her words were harsh, but there was a twinkle deep in her eyes.

"All right," Chris conceded. "I admit, I don't understand the choice Bobby's making. But I don't have to understand it. I don't have to live with it."

"But Michaela does," Carter Anne reminded him, "and she's not saying anything either."

"Maybe she doesn't want to fight for him," Chris suggested.

"Chris Montgomery!" Angie gasped.

"You don't even believe that for a minute," Carter Anne insisted simultaneously.

"You're right," Chris conceded, "I don't."

"And they say girls stick together," Carter Anne muttered good-naturedly to Angie.

"Anyway," Chris said with a mock stern look for Carter Anne, "I think we've all lost sight of the fact that Michaela is actually here to do a job. If, considering what this week must've felt like for her, she needed to keep her head down in order to get that job done, who are we to judge?"

Carter Anne stared at her hands. "I hadn't thought of it that way."

"I could barely get up every morning, just thinking about losing Chris," Angie reminded her.

She and Chris looked at each other. He reached for her hand and squeezed. He didn't like to think about how close he'd come to losing Angie. What would he have done if it hadn't been for Champ stepping up, giving him the kick in the ass he needed? It wasn't worth thinking about.

Angie looked at her sister. "None of us want it to end

like this, honey." She turned to Chris. "Can't you say something to him, Chris? Talk some sense into him?"

"Babe"—Chris lowered his voice gently—"we've had this conversation. It's Bobby's decision and none of our business."

"Well, it may be his decision," Angie allowed, "but as family, it is our business."

Chris chuckled low. They'd had this debate every night for a week. Standing, he put a kiss on each woman's head. "I'm gonna go watch some TV."

He'd left them there to dissect their uncle's decision. And he'd meant every word he'd said last night and every other night he'd said it. Only, once he'd been reminded of what Angie had gone through, of how close he'd come to losing her, and how necessary Champ's words had been—he couldn't quite forget it again. And Michaela was leaving today. To his knowledge, Bobby was sitting at home, just letting her leave.

Angie was meeting with a client, so he didn't even have to make up an excuse, he could just leave. Walking through town, he was still pleasantly surprised at how many people waved to him or stopped to ask after Angie or the wedding or even Bobby and Michaela. In less than a year, Lambert Falls had become home. Not everyone had accepted him. Not by any stretch. But many had. Of course, he'd been able to ride his grandparents' coattails, and their connection to the Falls, to be accepted. How much harder would it have been for Michaela? No wonder she'd hidden all week.

"Bobby!" He knocked on the front door. It took long enough that he was raising his fist to knock again when the door opened.

"Chris." Bobby nodded. His voice was flat, as were his eyes. Turning, knowing Chris would follow, Bobby headed into the TV room. Bobby took his chair, while Chris perched on the edge of the sofa.

"What're those?" Chris motioned to a stack of books out of the bookshelf, piled next to Bobby's chair.

Bobby didn't answer, just handed his friend the book on the top. Inside the front cover was the scratchy signature of Howard Michaels. "She did them all for me," Bobby spoke without looking at Chris.

"Well . . ." Chris was confused. "That's nice, isn't it?"

Bobby thought about explaining, but couldn't. It was too personal and too soon. Maybe one day, he'd explain. For now, he just accepted the book back from Chris and put it back on the stack.

"Too much wedding over at the old Montgomery place?" Bobby asked.

"No, actually. Angie's working with a new client," Chris explained. "It's pretty quiet."

The lull in the conversation stretched out to a silence. Under normal circumstances, it wouldn't have bothered Chris, but today he knew what was coming next.

"Michaela's leaving today," he finally said.

"Yep." Bobby nodded.

Chris crossed an ankle over the opposite knee. And uncrossed it. "Did you see her before she left for the airport?"

Bobby shook his head but didn't speak.

"Bobby—" Chris leaned forward. "It's time for us to have that talk."

"What talk?" Bobby asked.

"The one where I tell you you're making a mistake."

Bobby looked over at the younger man. "Chris—" he sighed.

"Bobby—" Chris stopped him. "I have to say it and you know it." Chris waited, but Bobby didn't speak so Chris continued. "I've never seen you like that before, Bobby. Not the way you were with Michaela. And before you remind me of how short a time we've known each other"—he risked a smile—"know that Jimmy's never seen you like that either."

"You've talked to Jimmy?" Bobby asked.

"It's the Falls. Everybody's talked to everybody."

Bobby acknowledged that truth with a dip of his head and a wry smile.

This was going nowhere. Chris could tell it already. He should go home. Leave Bobby alone.

"What the hell are you doing, Bobby?"

"What?" Bobby snapped his head around.

"You heard me," Chris replied. "What the hell are you thinking, letting her go?"

"I was thinking that we're better off going our separate ways."

"She may be," Chris said.

"I beg your pardon?" Bobby challenged.

"I've stayed out of this until now, Bobby." Chris calmed down. "Partly because I can only imagine what the girls have been putting you through." The two men exchanged slight, knowing smiles. "And partly because we both know it's none of my business. Not really," Chris conceded. "But mostly because I didn't think you'd actually do this."

"Do what, Chris?" Bobby sighed, turning back to his book.

"Let her go for no good reason." Chris stayed calm in spite of the ticking clock. Getting frantic or emotional wouldn't help. It never did. Of course, Bobby's silence didn't make staying cool any easier. "But I also know,"

Chris continued, "how important it is to have the right person speak up when you're about to screw up the rest of your life."

"As if I was about to screw up the rest of—"

"You are," Chris interrupted.

Bobby looked at him, a warning in his eyes.

"You've spoken really plainly to me in the past because you like and respect me and I've appreciated your honesty, even when I didn't like it. Well"—Chris leaned forward, elbows on his knees, eyes locked with the other man's—"I love you as much as I've ever loved anyone, and respect you more than most." He took a deep breath and committed, keeping his voice low, almost soothing, in spite of the words coming out of his mouth. "You're about to fuck it up. And if you let her leave now, you'll never get her back. Not a woman like Michaela."

Bobby closed his eyes and exhaled hard. What was he supposed to say to that? What could he say to that? "I don't know . . . I don't know how to live her life."

Chris waited. Now that he was talking, there'd be more. He knew Bobby.

"She's so busy, so blunt, so vivacious. A slow night in her world is a big night in mine. She has an opinion about everything." He was picking up speed. "She talks faster than anyone I've ever met and thinks faster than that. Her whole life is set and in motion. She's at the top of her game. She doesn't need anyone or anything, let alone a life in a small town or its sheriff . . ." Bobby froze.

Chris let the silence grow. Bobby looked at him, stunned.

"In spite of all that," Chris spoke slowly, "she appears to want a small town and its sheriff."

"She's so alive, Chris," Bobby nearly whispered. He studied the carpet between his shoes.

"And there's no guarantee she'll stay that way." Chris's voice was low.

"No"—Bobby shook his head—"there's not."

"That's a risk we all take with love, Bobby. None of us can see the future. Obviously." Chris was taking a risk here. Hopefully, it would be worth it. "Or else you wouldn't have married Abby."

"You need to watch yourself, Chris," Bobby warned.

"So you would've married Abby? Knowing what you know now?" Chris pushed.

"Chris. Don't."

"But you won't even risk it with Michaela?" Chris kept on.

"You know nothing about it." Bobby's voice was ominously low.

"Who're you talking to?" Chris spat out through clenched teeth. "You're not the only one who's watched people they care about die, Bobby."

"It's different," Bobby shot back.

"You're right. It is," Chris agreed. "You didn't lead Abby to her death the way I led my men to theirs."

Bobby rubbed his hands over his face, hard. This was out of control, hand to God. Sitting in his den, fighting with his best friend, practically his own son. "Chris, I'm sorry."

Chris waved off the apology as unnecessary. "She doesn't need you, Bobby. Not the way you're used to women needing their men. She will be a challenge; you won't often be bored. And yeah," he sighed, "she might die first. But she loves you. And you love her."

Bobby stood up, the movement interrupting Chris.

"Where are you going?" Chris asked, brow furrowed. Maybe he had pushed too hard.

"To Greensboro," Bobby answered. "To see if I can get her back."

Forty-five minutes. According to what Carter Anne had told him, he had forty-five minutes. He was already going five miles over the speed limit. Even the traffic was against him. No, it wasn't heavy compared to some places, but it surely wasn't the empty road he was used to. That he needed.

Bobby came around a corner and put on the brake behind a slow-moving truck. Who was he kidding? Michaela's flight left in forty-five minutes. There was no way to make it. Not this far out. He should just turn around, head home. Tomorrow, once she'd had a chance to get home and settle in, he'd call her. She might even take his call.

He sighed. There was really only one thing to do.

Had she made the right choice, leaving the Falls so fast? Maybe Carter Anne was right; maybe she should've fought harder. Her head sneered at the idea. Her heart screamed for her to go back, convince Granger what a mistake he was making. For now, she'd just sit here, let the passage of time make her decision for her.

For the last week, Michaela had worked whenever her eyes were open. She had more information, not only on the Colonel and his family, but the town, the area, and North Carolina's role in the Civil War, than she would ever need for this book. But it had kept her focused, given her something to think about during the hours she was trying to sleep.

Soon enough, she'd be landing in New York. Matt

would be meeting her plane and she could stop. Stop trying to be strong. Stop trying to not feel. Just stop. Until then, she still had to get through the wait here at the airport and then the flight. The book would have to keep doing its job. Ignoring the burn behind her eyes, she reached for her notes.

Bobby turned the blue light on his dashboard off as he pulled into the airport. While it had cleared traffic and allowed him to make the time he'd needed, he couldn't justify scaring the travelers by blazing in with full lights and sirens. It was bad enough he'd used them to get through town. He just—wouldn't tell. Anyone. About it . . . or about leaving the blue light on his dashboard so he wouldn't even have to take the time to feed the meter. Nope. No one really needed to know. And he didn't run into the airport. He moved expeditiously.

Once inside, he looked for the information screens. Michaela's plane was boarding. In spite of the urgency, he managed not to run to security. A uniformed police officer running through an airport was never a good sign.

He stopped and shook his head when he got to the security checkpoint. Well, at least now he knew where everyone on the road had been heading. They had gone from being ahead of him in traffic to being ahead of him at airport security. Hand to God, he couldn't catch a break.

She could've been one of the first on the plane. Could be sitting in an extra-wide leather seat, sipping a drink provided by a very polite flight attendant. Once she got on the plane, she could put Lambert Falls behind her, cash her royalty checks, and move on. Which is why she was sitting in the terminal with her notes strewn around her. It would be over once she got on the plane. And in another ten years or so, she and Bobby would hardly even remember each other. She wasn't ready for that.

The line for boarding was still long, but all rows had been called up and the airline was efficient. Ready or not, eventually they'd call final boarding and she'd have to get on the plane. Because no matter how much her heart wanted her to run back to the Falls, no matter how much she secretly hoped for one last romantic gesture from Granger, neither of those things were going to happen. She wasn't going to march into the station to-morrow and have him grin up at her, happy she came back. He wasn't going to drive onto the tarmac, storm the plane, and sweep her off her feet.

Michaela crossed to the wall of windows and looked out at the plane. She was being foolish. It wasn't something she was used to and she didn't much care for it. Really, there was no reason to not get on the plane. It was time to pack up.

He couldn't believe he was doing this. He shouldn't be doing it. He didn't even hesitate. Bobby made his way to the front of the security line and called over a TSA supervisor with the crook of his finger. Opening his wallet, he showed the man his ID.

"Sir, I need to get through here and I need to do it now. I have a weapon on me and need to skip the metal detector," he explained in his most official tone.

"Well—" The supervisor studied Bobby's ID. "Sheriff

Granger, I would've expected to get an official heads-up about something like this."

"I understand this is unusual, but it's urgent," Bobby stated.

The other man made his decision. "Right this way, Sheriff." He opened the barrier and allowed Bobby to move through. The gate was close by—still, he was running out of time.

Michaela was handing her boarding pass to the gate agent. "Michaela." Bobby was surprised to be panting. And here he thought he'd been so cool.

No. The grand gesture wasn't real. The fairy tale wasn't real. That was why she wrote nonfiction. Michaela whipped her head around. Granger was standing there, breathing like he'd been sprinting.

"Michaela," he said again, quieter this time.

The smile that split her face was automatic—and then she remembered. Her stomach clenched and tears filled her eyes.

"Ma'am?" The gate agent gave a slight tug on her boarding pass.

"Michaela." Bobby was all but whispering now. He'd come this far and now his feet wouldn't cross the last ten feet to reach her.

"Just a minute," Michaela said to the airline agent, taking her boarding pass back. She moved to him. Why was he here? What was going on? She placed herself directly in front of him. "Granger?"

"Michaela." He reached for her but she took a step back.

"What do you want, Granger?"

"I want you . . . to come home," Bobby said plainly.

"I'm going home," Michaela stated.

He rephrased the statement. "Then I want you to come back to the Falls."

"Are you kidding me?" Michaela stated loudly, then, with a look to the dwindling line at the gate, lowered her voice to a harsh whisper. "Do you know the week I've had? The week you caused?"

Bobby sighed deeply. "I do."

Michaela waited, but Bobby said nothing else. "That's it? You want me to come back to the Falls after all that because you know? Just like that?"

"No, not just like that," Bobby said. "Not until you understand I'm sorry. That I should never have broken up with you. That I need you, Michaela. It doesn't make any sense to me, but I know it's true anyway. And the only mistake worse than asking you to leave would be actually letting you leave without trying to get you back."

The tears she'd been holding back came, and damn him for them. "My life is exactly what it was last week, Granger. My friends, my schedule, my past, me. Nothing's changed."

"I know." Bobby nodded. "And Michaela, I still don't understand it all or know how we'll juggle it all or anything like that, and that scares the hell out of me because I'm supposed to know all those things. But I'm here because I was an ass to think any of those things were more important than you."

"Ms. Howard?" The gate agent called to her before lifting the microphone and announcing the final boarding call for the flight.

"I love you, Michaela, and I don't want to lose you. I will never hurt you like this again," Bobby swore.

"Ms. Howard." The agent's voice was urgent.

"I don't believe this." Michaela shook her head. This

wasn't happening. Without another word, she turned on her heel and walked away.

Bobby watched her go. Time slowed and he was grateful for it. It gave him the chance to study her, try to memorize the way she moved, the curve of her hip, the tilt of her head as she stopped in front of the gate agent. Memorize it for the long nights ahead of him when he had nothing to do but to remember and curse himself for a fool.

The gate agent and Michaela spoke. Then, with a look to Bobby, the agent smiled and moved to the gate, closing the door. Michaela was walking back. She was coming back to him. He thought the sound in his ears might be his heart beating.

Michaela stopped immediately in front of him. "You love me, Granger?"

"I do," Bobby said simply.

"Then kiss me, Granger. We'll figure out the rest later."

She moved into his arms. As he lowered his mouth to hers, Bobby knew—he was home.